Fearless in Love

~ The Maverick Billionaires ~

Book 3

Bella Andre & Jennifer Skully

FEARLESS IN LOVE

~ The Maverick Billionaires, Book 3 ~

Meet the Maverick Billionaires—sexy, self-made men from the wrong side of town who survived hell together and now have everything they ever wanted. But when each Maverick falls head over heels for an incredible woman he never saw coming, he will soon find that true love is the only thing he ever really needed...

After growing up dirt poor in a seedy Chicago neighborhood, Matt Tremont seemingly has it all now—brains, brawn, and billions. And most important, Noah, his five-year-old son, the one good outcome of a disastrous relationship that destroyed his last ounce of trust. The only thing he's lacking is the perfect nanny for his son. And Ariana Jones is absolute perfection. Utterly enchanting. Completely fascinating. And totally off-limits.

Like a match made in heaven, this is Ari's dream job. Swallowed up in the foster care system after losing her brother and mother, Ari has always dreamed of family. She showers five-year-old Noah with all the love she's kept bottled up inside. Love she could also offer to her gorgeous billionaire boss—if only he weren't the very last man she could ever hope to have.

But when sizzling sparks of attraction turn into a forbidden, sinfully hot night of pleasure, will Ari's love be enough to make Matt forget the past and love fearlessly?

A note from Bella & Jennifer

Few things in life are more fun than writing about sexy billionaires and the women who unexpectedly bring them to their knees! We want to say thank you a million times over to everyone who has fallen in love with the Mavericks. Because of you, we have the best job in the world—and we can't wait to write more delicious romances for you to read in the future.

We hope you love reading Matt and Ari's story as much as we loved writing it!

Happy reading,
Bella Andre & Jennifer Skully

P.S. Each book in the Maverick Billionaires series can be read as a stand-alone novel. However, if you would like to find out how it all began, please check out *Breathless in Love*, Will and Harper's love story, and *Reckless in Love*, Sebastian and Charlie's story. And watch for Evan's story, *Irresistible in Love*, coming soon!

Chapter One

Matt Tremont's home was amazing. Ten thousand square feet, maybe fifteen thousand—though it was hard to judge something that massive when Ari was used to living in three hundred square feet.

The man himself left her awestruck. As gorgeous as a movie star, with rangy muscles that made her mouth water, just looking at him was enough to make her lose her words right in the middle of a sentence. He was thirty-four—ten years older than she was—and he made guys her own age seem like boys.

When he'd approached her at the grand opening of Sebastian Montgomery's media headquarters in San Francisco, she'd actually started to tremble. It had seemed like a pivotal moment that would change her life forever, when a gorgeous, charming billionaire wanted to talk to *her*. She'd fantasized that the sparks flying everywhere weren't just in her imagination. *"Ariana,"* she could almost hear him saying in his deep, sexy voice, *"let me whisk you away to my private lair for champagne and caviar."*

Only to have her fantasies blown sky-high when

he'd asked her to interview as a nanny for his five-year-old son.

Ari was still laughing at herself; obviously, she'd been the only one feeling any sparks. But that didn't make him any less mouthwatering, even in jeans. Especially in jeans.

Her stomach did backflips as she sat across from him in his living room, but she had her crazy attraction under control.

Sort of.

"Ariana," Matt said.

Oh, that voice... It was enough to make a girl spin out into fantasy again.

"Please, call me Ari."

Only Daniel Spencer called her Ariana. Daniel and Matt were two of the Mavericks, five billionaires who had taken the world by storm with their business prowess in many different fields. She knew a little about Matt's past. Like Daniel and the other Mavericks, he hadn't been born into money. She knew what it was to be poor, and she admired them all for what they'd accomplished.

Daniel had given a glowing recommendation to Matt. Though technically he wasn't her boss, since he owned the whole company, Daniel had been really sweet to her since she'd landed the job at Top-Notch DIY when she was eighteen. She'd worked there part time ever since she'd aged out of foster care, scraping together every dime to go to college. Daniel had helped there too, with company-sponsored scholarships, something for which she could never thank him enough. He said she reminded him of his kid sister, Lyssa, who was close to Ari's age.

Not that she wanted Matt to think of her as a little sister. She already had a big brother, even if she hadn't seen him in years. Thinking of Gideon made her chest hurt, so she pushed away the memories as she focused on what Matt was saying.

"Daniel told me that in addition to working at his San Jose store, you also take care of kids."

Nodding, she said, "I graduated from San Jose State last May with a degree in child development. I'd like to be a teacher someday, but right now, I want the one-on-one, full-time experience." She didn't add that she also needed to beef up her cash reserves after using everything for college, even with the scholarships.

He looked at her with a penetrating gaze, seeming to weigh her every word, figuring out how it fit into the whole picture. She wondered if that was part of the reason he was hugely rich and successful—because he took note of everything.

Sitting in a big leather chair next to her, Matt shifted his legs a little wider. "That's very commendable, getting your education while you're working. So tell me more about how you envision teaching my son."

Swallowing hard at the ridiculously sexy picture he made, Ari settled into the buttery smooth leather of the sofa. With an intricate pattern of vibrant colors, the carpet was so thick it tempted her to take off her shoes and sink her toes into the plush pile. She couldn't imagine living in a place like this. Just walking from the front door to the living room had seemed like a mile across polished hardwood floors, past paintings and artwork that probably cost a fortune. But live here she would, *if* she got the job taking care of Noah.

Her smile grew bigger with the memory of the day she'd played with Matt's son at the youth center Daniel was building in San Jose. "I like to play in the sandbox rather than sticking kids in front of the TV to let their little minds get warped by cartoons. Not that there's anything *wrong* with cartoons," she clarified. "As long as they're the cherry on top of the sundae, rather than the entire meal."

"I agree," Matt said with a nod. "Children should be outdoors, enjoying nature, playing with insects, and chasing frogs."

As a kid, she'd lived in an apartment—lots of different apartments—and the only insects she could have played with were cockroaches. The only frogs she'd seen were in stagnant pools of water left behind in abandoned lots. When she wasn't in school, she'd spent her time buried in the pages of books.

"I like the zoo," she continued, hoping she was saying the right things. The problem was that he smelled so good, like clean, hot male. It was messing big-time with her concentration. "And you've got Henry Coe State Park almost in your backyard." His huge home was nestled in the trees overlooking Anderson Lake. Footpaths probably led up into the hills right from the back door. "Is that why you chose to live in Morgan Hill—because it's so much prettier than San Jose?"

"After I had my new factory located here, I figured it was easier to build our home nearby."

He was so matter-of-fact. Did he ever chase butterflies with his son? She hoped he did.

To prep her for this interview, Daniel had told her that Matt was a brilliant high-tech robotics manufacturer—and a bookworm. Crossing the mile-long foyer, she'd caught a brief glimpse of a library jammed with books. If she got the job, she'd love to spend as much of her free time there as possible. Evidently, Matt had put himself through college with scholarships and hard work, blowing through in three years instead of four. His ideas and inventions were so groundbreaking that his professors had told him to forget earning a PhD and move right into industry instead, so he'd started his company, Trebotics International, when he was about her age.

Though she admired him for his smarts and his success, she didn't know anything about him as a father. Or as a man. But Daniel had said he was the best dad any kid could ever have. He'd also mentioned that Noah's mom had dropped out of the picture early and rarely saw her son.

How had that affected Matt and Noah?

"One of Noah's previous nannies had a boyfriend

she constantly talked with on the phone when she should have been paying attention to my son. Will that be a problem for you?"

"I don't have a boyfriend, or unlimited texting and minutes on my cell phone." She couldn't afford a smartphone, and she'd signed up for the cheapest service plan she could get. "So you definitely won't find me distracted by my phone."

"I'm glad to hear that. How many children do you currently babysit?"

Interesting that he wanted to know more about her actual experience with children rather than what she'd taken in school, but she knew that book smarts weren't always the same as hands-on learning. "Six, but only part time for each. One is my best friend's little boy. She's a single mom, and I help out with Jorge." Ari gave it the Spanish pronunciation: *Hor-hay*. She loved Jorge and didn't charge Rosie. "I also work for four women in the South Bay who aren't working moms, taking care of their kids when they've got errands or appointments. I wouldn't be leaving them in the lurch if I came to work for you." She didn't want him to think she'd dump him if a better opportunity came along. "I've got friends who would love to work for them. I'd just have to make arrangements." It would be difficult leaving the kids, but she needed the full-time job. Both Daniel and the moms understood that, though it was harder for the kids to accept. "They all said they'd give you references."

"I'd like to speak with them."

She fished in her bag for the list. "Here you go." Their hands brushed, and she went warm all over.

As he looked over the names, numbers, and addresses, she noted that he had sun lines at his eyes, and she wondered if he swam with Noah in the huge kidney-shaped pool she'd seen through the French doors. Or maybe they spent time in the playground out back, with its swings, slides, monkey bars, and huge sandbox.

He was rich. He could give his son anything that was for sale. But she hoped he gave his son time too.

Looking back up at her, he asked, "How long have you been babysitting?"

"Since I was sixteen." Not counting the foster homes where she'd taken care of the younger kids.

"And you're twenty-four now?" He frowned slightly as he said her age, but before she became worried, he said, "Eight years is good experience."

She smiled, then dove in with her own question. "What would my duties be?"

"You would get Noah up in the morning, take him to school. He started kindergarten this year, and he's attending a private school in Almaden Valley."

That was twenty-five minutes away. She thought about the morning commute traffic and how brutal it was as more companies moved into Silicon Valley.

As if he could see the thought bubble over her head, he said, "My driver Doreen would drive you when you take Noah out." Matt Tremont and his son lived a life she'd seen only on TV, with private drivers and mansions. "You would also be responsible for his nutrition. I have a cook, but I'd want you to make sure he's eating healthy."

Nutrition had been part of her education. "No treats?"

He smiled for the first time. And she stopped breathing.

Literally *stopped.*

No one should be allowed that much gorgeousness. She would see that smile in her dreams.

"Treats were my favorite thing as a kid. Probably because I didn't get many." He said it with a laugh, but she wasn't sure she bought the way he tried to play off his difficult childhood with a smile. Ari hadn't grown up with much either—and she'd also learned how to smile through it. "In any case," he continued, "treats are fine every now and then, but I don't want him gorging on candy and soda." With that, he went on with her duties. "He's only in school in the morning, so I would want you to devise lesson plans for the afternoon. Trips to the zoo and other activities that teach him would be great. He's learning to swim, and I'd want you to continue, as long as he's got his water wings on."

A commotion in the hall drowned out the rest of Matt's list—a young voice, the stomp of running feet. For a little boy, Noah Tremont made big noise, which she loved.

He flew around the corner, sliding on the hardwood floor until his toes hit the rug. "Daddy, Daddy, you gotta see!" A moment later, he saw Ari. "I know you."

"We met a month ago at the house your daddy was building with his friends."

Noah had a mop of hair as dark as his father's and cheeks that hadn't lost their baby roundness yet. He ran around the coffee table and flung himself at her on the sofa, grabbing her hand. "You gotta see too."

"Noah," Matt interrupted. "We're in a meeting."

A harried older woman appeared in the doorway, wisps of hair flying out of a bun that had probably been neat that morning. This must be the temp Matt said he'd brought in while he was searching for a full-time nanny. "Mr. Tremont, I'm sorry. Noah, come here." Her voice was more tired than annoyed.

But Noah was too excited to listen. Ari plucked him up and set him on her lap, a wriggling bundle of boundless energy. He was adorable. She wanted to spend her days with someone so happy and sweet, take him to the zoo, chase butterflies, teach him the names of birds.

"You know"—she gave Noah the biggest smile—"it's nice to let people finish what they're saying. So as soon as your dad's done talking, then you can show us whatever you want."

"It's my new Lego set Jeremy gave me!" He

couldn't stop bouncing. Ari remembered Jeremy from the day at the youth home, a sweet young man—a brother of one of the other Mavericks, maybe?

"All righty then. We'll finish up, then you can show us your Lego." She gave Noah a solemn look. "I'm a Lego master, by the way."

"Cool, me too!" He nodded vigorously, his curls bouncing. Then he stopped and bit his lip, and she was struck by how much of a mini-Matt he was. "I forgot your name."

"It's Ari."

He beamed at her. Yup, the kid version of his dad's smile. "I like your name." With that, he hopped off her lap.

When Ari turned back to Matt, he was staring at her with his head cocked slightly. "A Lego master?" He shook his head. "Even I have a hard time putting some of them together."

"I doubt that," she said, which made him smile again. *Oh, that smile.* It got under her skin, made her hum inside. *Everywhere* inside. "You were saying? About my duties?"

"We've pretty much covered it." He began to list the things she'd get out of the deal. "You'd have your own suite next to Noah's. You could eat meals with us, but you'd be free to raid the kitchen. Sunday would be your day off. If you wanted to make prior arrangements to go out in the evening for a date or whatever, that would be fine. I try to be home in the evenings and on weekends for Noah."

"Like I said, I don't have a boyfriend, but I get together with my girlfriends sometimes in the evenings."

He nodded, then said, "The salary is twelve hundred a week, plus medical insurance."

She barely managed to keep her chin from hitting her knees. "A week?" She couldn't believe it. It rivaled what she made in a month. *Plus* benefits.

"Considering that you would be on duty almost twenty-four hours a day, six days a week, it's reasonable."

"Reasonable?" She was afraid she sounded like an airhead repeating everything he said, but his offer was beyond anything she'd dreamed of. "I mean, yes, it's totally reasonable."

Especially considering all she had to do was look after an adorable little boy and live in a fabulous mansion with her own *suite*. And she could have all the sizzling-hot fantasies she wanted about Matt, whose bedroom would undoubtedly be just down the hall. Completely secret fantasies, locked in a compartment inside her brain that she'd wait to open until she was alone.

If there was one thing she knew how to do, it was compartmentalize. She'd spent six years in the foster care system after her mom died, so Ari was a master at living a rich fantasy life without confusing it with reality. Everyone deserved a dream world. In fact, it was healthy—as long as you knew the difference between fantasy and reality, and Ari always had.

She knew what it was like to have things ripped away from you at a moment's notice, when you thought a foster family cared about you only to realize it was the money they received that meant the most, or their real daughter hated your guts so you had to go. And she knew about other things that still gave her nightmares sometimes—foster fathers and brothers who didn't care about the personal boundaries of the new foster girl.

So, yes, she definitely kept her dreams uncontaminated by reality. And this job was far better than anything she could have dreamed up on her own. If she got it, she would owe Daniel for recommending her, more than she could ever repay.

"I'll check your references tonight." He tapped the list she'd given him. "But after what Daniel said, it all looks good. I'll give you a call tomorrow."

Please, she silently prayed as she grabbed her bag, *hire me and make this dream real.* "I really like Noah. He's a great kid."

"I'm lucky to have him." Love filled Matt's voice when he talked about his son. "And he obviously likes you. I hope you have time to see his latest Lego masterpiece before you go."

"Of course."

They stood at the same time, suddenly close beside each other at the edge of the coffee table. For the briefest of moments, she let her eyelids drift shut as her senses drank him in—that fresh rain scent, the heat radiating off his body, the gentle wash of his breath across her hair.

Noah was so cute, and the setup was amazing. But Matt? Well, *he* was the cherry on top of *her* sundae.

And if she got this job, she would make sure *nothing* screwed it up.

Chapter Two

"You sure you don't mind me hijacking her from your San Jose store?" Matt asked Daniel over the phone.

"It's a great opportunity for Ariana."

Ariana had a lilting quality in Daniel's voice. But she'd told Matt to call her Ari.

"She's always been more interested in child care than moving up the ladder at Top-Notch," Daniel continued. "She worked her butt off getting through college. The scholarships I sponsor are open to all my employees worldwide, but every year, Ariana aced the essay submission and earned the Bay Area scholarship."

"She told me she graduated last May."

"With honors."

She hadn't told him that. In fact, she'd almost downplayed her degree, maybe because she understood that a degree was worth a heck of a lot more with practical experience to back it up. In that, they were alike. He'd graduated and jumped in feet first. And Ari'd had eight years of experience working with kids while she was going to school. She'd be a huge asset for Noah, with both her experience and her education. There was so much to admire about her.

For his peace of mind, there might actually be *too* much to admire.

"It's a win-win, Matt. You're going to love her."

His friend didn't mean it in the sexual sense, but Matt couldn't stop remembering the vision she'd made sitting on his sofa, the end-of-day autumn sun setting her golden hair on fire. He'd wanted to—

Damn it, he had to stop thinking about what *he* wanted. She would be here for his son.

"Noah already loves her," Matt told Daniel. "All she had to do was admire his latest Lego creation and he was putty in her hands."

Ari had handled his son's interruption brilliantly, teaching Noah a lesson without getting angry or annoyed. Considering that the women Ari babysat for couldn't say enough good things about her, Matt knew he had to have her.

For Noah, of course.

"The kid takes after his old man, always coming up with new inventions." Daniel's tone was laced with affection. As godfathers, each and every Maverick adored Noah. "And Ariana has more patience than a saint," Daniel added, "which will help when taking care of a five-year-old boy with boundless energy."

"My only concern is that she's so young." That was a lie. He was also concerned about how *boundlessly* tempting she was.

Matt was always in control of his emotions where

women were concerned, especially after what had happened with Noah's mom. Yet Ari kept sneaking under his defenses, entering his thoughts far too often. He had to put a stop to it. He was a decade older, for God's sake, and about to become her boss.

"We were already out there trying to make our mark at twenty-four," Daniel pointed out, "but she's still hands-off to you."

Humor laced Daniel's warning, but Matt's guts jumped like a guilty man facing the witness stand. "Of course. She's Lyssa's age." To all the Mavericks, Lyssa was still the kid sister they needed to look out for.

"And Ariana's had a pretty rough go of it too."

As a foster kid, she'd been alone in the world. At least he'd had the Mavericks. And if Daniel suspected Matt was imagining anything unprofessional with Ari...

"I won't screw this up with her," Matt said, as much to remind himself as to reassure his friend. "I've been through so many nannies that I'm not sure where else I'd look if things didn't work out this time."

Matt had caught the last nanny screeching at Noah for spilling a glass of milk. It had been all he could do not to throw her bodily out of his house. He'd experienced enough of that crap when he was a kid and didn't put up with anyone treating Noah that way. Ever. He'd handled that problem immediately. Which meant that he and Noah had been going through nannies at the rate of two or more a year.

Yes, Matt was picky where his son was concerned, but half the problem was Noah's mother. Irene had a knack for creating havoc in her wake. She flew in and out of Noah's life like a firefly, lighting him up, then letting him down. Matt still hadn't figured out how to best deal with Irene—and the way she always let Noah down made Matt feel like he was letting his kid down too. Maybe a young, enthusiastic nanny would help counter Irene's bad influence.

"Then take her," Daniel said. "She wants this."

Ah hell, why did his friend have to use those words, forcing Matt to battle images of Ari on his bed, her hair fanned out across his pillows, her skin creamy...

He jammed his brain the way a copier chews up a scrap of paper, crumpled the fantasy, and threw it in his mental trash bin.

No more fantasies. He needed Ari for Noah.

Every other need had to go.

"I'm offering her the job."

"Then you can finally relax. Because she'll be the best nanny you've ever had, guaranteed."

Matt already knew that. It was his need to put this crazy attraction behind bars that had him on edge.

* * *

Ari's heart missed a couple of beats when she read the caller ID on her phone. It was only nine p.m., but she had an early shift at the store in the morning, and she was already beneath the sheets. She slept on a Murphy bed that came out of the wall. It was the only way to get a sofa and a bed into her small studio apartment at the same time.

"Hello?" She couldn't keep the breathlessness out of her voice.

"Ari, it's Matt Tremont. You've got the job, if you want it."

"Thank you." She tried to sound cool and calm even though she was about to burst with joy. "I'll do my best for you and Noah." He was entrusting his son to her. "I'll treat him like he's my own."

"The ladies you work for had wonderful things to say about you."

She snuggled deeper under the covers, ignoring the spring poking her back, and in the dark his voice was smooth, deep, and soft, as if he were whispering naughty things. She'd had two lovers, so she wasn't totally inexperienced, but no one had made her feel the things Matt did, even with a few simple words that weren't the slightest bit sexy.

"Their kids adore you," he continued. "You're never late, and you're always willing to stay longer if they need you." He paused, letting her take in the glowing praise. "Not one of them had a single complaint."

The compliments warmed her. She'd taken care of some of the kids for years, from diapers to kindergarten. And she was going to miss all of them.

"Daniel says I'd be stupid not to jump on you." Dead air followed his statement. As if the call had dropped, or he was holding his breath.

Yes, please, jump on me. But she wouldn't mess this up. Especially when the words didn't have a double meaning for him—it was just her one-sided sparks going off again.

"I'd be honored to take care of Noah. Would Sunday evening be okay to start so that I'd be there to get Noah ready for school in the morning?"

"Good idea. We can slip you right into the routine. Can you make it by dinnertime?"

"Depends on what you're serving."

She made the joke before thinking, but thankfully Matt laughed and said, "Tell me what your favorite is."

Her favorite would be licking Rocky Road ice cream off *him*. A wave of heat rolled through her, and her legs moved restlessly as she tried not to breathe heavily.

"As long as it's not SpaghettiOs or chicken nuggets, I'm good." She said it with a laugh, but all joking aside, those had been her diet staples as a kid.

"There's not a single SpaghettiO or chicken nugget in the house."

"Thank you," she said softly. "I'll see you on Sunday."

Once they'd hung up, she relived the conversation like the silly teenager she'd never been, weaving it into a crazy, sweet fantasy. Come Sunday, she'd be nothing but professional.

But tonight, she would let herself dream...

Chapter Three

Seated beside Ari at the dinner table on Sunday evening, Matt realized just how exquisite torture could get.

"This is definitely not SpaghettiOs," she said with a laugh as she sliced into the moist salmon filet.

"What's spaghetto?" Noah asked.

Matt dragged himself back onto the same spatial plane as his son, feeling yet another kick of guilt at his overtly sensual thoughts. The three of them were seated in the dinner nook, an annex off the kitchen with a swing door between. The formal dining room could seat thirty-six, but he used it only for holidays and business parties.

Ari was the first nanny who'd wanted to join them for dinner. The others preferred the hour off from their duties.

"SpaghettiOs are little round *Os* of pasta and sauce in a can," she explained.

"Can I have some spaghettos?" Noah's speech was exceptional for his age, with no childish lisp even on difficult letters, but he couldn't seem to wrap his tongue around the word.

Matt sure didn't plan on eating canned spaghetti. He'd left that kind of food behind when he'd gotten the hell out of the rough part of Chicago. Ari had left it behind too. But SpaghettiOs and chicken nuggets said a lot about where she'd grown up. The same kind of place he had. He could only hope it was nowhere near as bad.

"Well," Ari said, scooping up more broccoli, salmon, and rice pilaf. "Spaghetti is a lot better with homemade sauce that has good things in it like bell peppers, mushrooms, and onions."

Noah screwed up his face. "Onions are yucky."

Ari dropped her jaw, and her pretty hazel eyes went wide. Matt was as caught by the slashes of topaz in the depths of her irises as he was by her scent, something light and floral.

She shook her head in amazement. "Onions make everything taste better. And garlic."

"Ewww." Noah wrinkled his nose with disgust.

"Don't you like pizza?"

He nodded. "Cookie makes pizza the best."

"Our cook," Matt explained. "She's Russian with a pretty complicated-sounding last name. So she asked us to call her Cookie."

Giving Matt a little smile of thanks for the explanation, Ari turned back to Noah. "I bet Cookie puts onions and garlic in her pizza sauce."

"Really?" Noah raised his eyebrow in a gesture that should have been too old for a five-year-old boy to pull off. But he was rather advanced, if Matt said so himself.

"Yep. Now you better finish your yummy salmon. Because it's *so* good." She forked another bite, savoring it with a purr. "Eat up."

While Matt could barely keep his libido under control from just sitting at the same table with her, Noah did as he was told, making yum-yum sounds the way she had.

When Ari laughed, delight sparkling in her eyes, Matt knew he'd been an idiot to think he had things under control. It didn't matter that she was sweet and innocent and ten years younger than he. His thoughts weren't brotherly, fatherly, or even boss-y. Everything she said captivated him and mesmerized him, as easily as she charmed Noah.

Desperate to get his mind off her charms, he reached into his pocket and pulled out a new smartphone, setting it by her plate. "I'd like you to use this." When she didn't immediately reach for it, he added, "You said you can't get texts on your phone, but if I'm in a meeting where I can text but not talk, I need to be able to get hold of you when, where, and however I can."

She finally picked it up. "I must be the last person in Silicon Valley who doesn't know how to use one of these."

"I'll show you," Noah offered.

She grinned at him. "Thank you."

"You can switch your number over and transfer

your contacts," Matt added. "Of course, you're free to use it for personal calls as well."

"Thank you," she said again. Then she waggled the phone at Noah. "We can use this on our adventures to look up the names of birds and check out maps. Cool, huh?" Noah nodded enthusiastically.

Matt liked that she didn't take anything for granted. He'd known plenty of people who took without even a thank-you, but she was unique in so many ways. God help him, he wanted to explore her uniqueness in every way he could...

Daniel was going to *kill* him for his thoughts. And Matt's foster mother, Susan, would be appalled.

"So, Noah," she said, "I've been planning all the fun things we can do together. Have you ever seen a dinosaur?"

"In a movie. It was real scary." Noah's eyes were wide and round.

"Movie dinosaurs can be scary because they roar." She roared and Noah laughed.

Matt's heart squeezed. Watching his son laugh always made him catch his breath with wonder. He loved the kid so damn much.

"There's a dinosaur skeleton at the California Academy of Sciences in Golden Gate Park that is so awesome, you're going to fall in love with dinosaurs." She looked at Matt. "It's kind of expensive, but the membership is tax deductible."

He couldn't believe she was actually considering

his expenses. Didn't she know just how much money he had? It wasn't like when he was a kid and he went to the museum only on the rare days when they opened it up to the public for free. But he realized that she'd probably used the free days too. "A membership is great. But you don't have to worry about ticket prices. I have enough money for whatever activities you think Noah would like."

"That doesn't mean I should waste it when it makes more sense to get a family membership we can use for a year."

Family. Matt knew how lucky he was to have Noah and the Mavericks as his family. Will, Sebastian, Evan, and Daniel were his blood brothers not by birth but by adversity. Bob and Susan, Daniel's parents, had taken them all in as teenagers when they needed it most, providing the love and nurturing none of them had found at home. There was Lyssa too—something told Matt that she and Ari would become fast friends. Will had fallen in love with Harper and her brother, Jeremy, and Sebastian was head over heels for Charlie and her mother. Only Evan's wife, Whitney, had never felt like family. Nor had any of Matt's nannies. But he could see Noah falling under Ari's spell.

Matt couldn't allow himself to do so as well.

Pushing his plate away, he propped his elbows on the table, fingers laced. "What else do you have planned?" None of the previous nannies had suggested outings.

Ari mimicked him, pushing away a plate so clean that not even the parsley garnish on the salmon was left. "Do you like the zoo, Noah?"

He bobbed his head, trailing his child-size fork through the remains of his salmon and broccoli. "Gorillas are my favorite."

"Me too." She grinned. "How about mummies?"

"Aren't they scary?"

"No, at least not the ones at the mummy museum. And later in the year we can visit the elephant seals at Año Nuevo."

"Is it safe for kids?" Matt had heard the giant bulls could move amazingly fast.

"The docents keep you out of the way of the fighting males." She patted his hand to put him at ease, and though the touch was light and easy, heat spread like wildfire through him. She didn't seem to notice his reaction as she asked Noah, "Have you ever walked across the Golden Gate Bridge? We could even ride bikes."

"Noah's still got his training wheels," Matt cautioned as Cookie barreled through the swing doors to remove their empty plates.

"That was delicious, Cookie. Thank you."

The matronly woman's lined face creased in an answering smile. She'd been with them since Noah was born. "You are welcome, miss. We have ice cream for dessert."

"Yes!" Noah enthused in his little-boy voice.

Ari laughed and Matt joined her, her humor infectious. She was like a fever heating up beneath his skin.

"I will be right back." Cookie marched out in her soft-soled shoes. Noah jumped up with his usual enthusiasm and, almost on Cookie's heels, ran into the kitchen to help.

"Does she live in too?"

"She's got a huge family, and her husband wouldn't hear of it." He didn't have a maid staff either, just a cleaning company that came in once a week. Which meant it would be just the three of them. All alone. With only Noah's bedroom between his and Ari's.

Every cell inside Matt burned hotter.

"It might be fun if Noah met my friend's little boy sometime. They could play together. Is that okay with you?"

He glanced at the swing door, the sound of Noah's laughter seeping through the crack. "I should explain a bit about Noah. He's shy around new kids. He's a cerebral boy, likes books and building Legos."

"I loved books when I was a kid. I still do. That's a good thing."

"I loved them too." Books had saved him in a lot of ways. But his bookwormish ways had also left him prey to other kids, and to his father. As a kid, Matt had been belittled for his brainiac ways. It was one of his worst fears that the same thing would happen to his son. "Not all kids understand that."

"Jorge's a great reader. They'll have a lot in common."

"Yes, but—"

She put her hand on his, as easily as she had when she'd reassured him about the elephant seals. It had the same effect, like a charge shooting through him, lighting up his body. But this was about Noah.

"Did something happen that has you worried?"

Matt had always been careful to hold his cards close to his chest when it came to personal information. But maybe telling Ari about the incident would help her appreciate why he was so intent on protecting Noah.

"It was in preschool last year." He'd just lost another nanny, and he'd picked up Noah that day. "I thought at first he was reading in the classroom with the other kid since they both had their hands on a book." He'd hung back out of sight, glad that Noah was making friends. Then, in barely a blink of his eyes, it turned ugly. "The kid slapped the book out of Noah's hands, making fun of the story he was reading."

He almost shuddered, remembering the kid's words. *Only sissies read books like that.* And he'd heard his father's voice. *Only little weenies keep their noses buried in books.*

"That's terrible. I'm so sorry for Noah." Ari's hand was still on his, helping to keep him in the present.

"The worst was the kid's mom. None of them saw that I was there yet, and Noah"—he had to smile at the memory—"told her that her kid was really mean." Then he imitated Noah's big-boy voice. *"And that's not right."*

"Yay for Noah. But how did the mom react?"

"She had the gall to say that if he hadn't been reading a book meant for girls, it wouldn't have happened. That was when I finally stepped into the room and she realized I'd seen and heard it all." He'd wanted to charge in and shake the woman like she was a rag doll, until all her stuffing fell out. It had taken all his control not to yell at her and her rotten little kid. Not to be like his father. Because he *never* yelled in front of Noah. "I told her I needed a private word with her. And then I made it clear that she'd better never let her kid near mine again. The next day, I found out they'd transferred to another school."

"You did good, Matt." When she squeezed his hand lightly and smiled, he was amazed to feel the tension begin to drain out of him at her warm approval. "Although, I must admit I would have liked to see the other kid's mom trembling in her high heels when you took her down." She finally removed her hand from his as she asked, "And now you've got me really curious—what was Noah reading?"

Trying not to let himself miss her touch, he said, *"Purplicious."*

"Noah has good taste in books. And I love how he handled himself."

Matt's stress instantly flooded back. "I shouldn't have let it get that far. He should never feel belittled."

"Of course not. But he was still pretty amazing,

standing up to an adult like that."

Matt had to tip his head to the side to stare at her, like a movie robot who didn't understand humans. He hadn't, not even for one minute, thought of it that way before. "You're right, he did handle himself pretty well." And Noah hadn't exhibited lasting effects, thankfully. So maybe, with Ari's supervision, a day with her friend's son might actually be good for him. "You said Jorge likes to read?"

"Voraciously."

"What about playing with Legos?"

"How do you think I became a master?" she replied with a grin.

Noah pushed through the door with a bowl of ice cream. Cookie followed with two more.

"What do you think, buddy?" Matt asked. "Would you like to meet Ari's little friend Jorge?"

"Yes!"

Ari's laugh did things to his insides. It wasn't just her pretty face or her lovely, lithe figure. It was her liveliness with Noah, her freshness, her love of life, her exuberance, her try-anything attitude.

Then again, those were some of the same qualities that had first drawn him to Noah's mother.

And that had ended in disaster.

Chapter Four

Matt and Noah gave Ari a tour after dinner, and the house was even more mind-boggling than it had initially seemed. The upper floor overlooked the front hall with a wide balustrade and was ringed by eight bedrooms, each with its own bathroom and sitting area. Matt said he wanted plenty of space for his family when they visited. Ari's room included a desk and a computer, though she'd brought her own laptop—and, best of all, a whirlpool tub.

The main floor consisted of the living room she'd interviewed in, complete with a grand piano; a formal dining room; and the kitchen, containing a huge pantry and a walk-in fridge. Matt displayed his favorite art in a special room, and Noah had his own playroom with lidded boxes full of toys, a chalkboard, and erase board. The great room came with all the latest entertainment equipment and a sun porch that opened on to the pool, the hot tub, and Noah's playground.

The most marvelous thing in the whole house, though, was the library, which rivaled the Beast's in *Beauty and the Beast*, with enough books to keep reading straight through for a decade. Ari's fingers itched to touch the volumes, and she saw some of her favorites, from Tolkien's *The Hobbit* and the three volumes of *The Lord of the Rings* to Stephen King's *The Stand*, all of them looking like collector's editions.

She longed to stay in the library, but Noah dragged her downstairs, where they walked her through the soundproofed basement with its fully equipped gym, the game room, and the screening room.

She couldn't believe she would actually live here. She'd never had so much space in her life, never had her pick of anything she wanted to eat from a restaurant-size walk-in fridge, never been able to just walk outside and jump into a heated pool.

And she'd *definitely* never known a man like Matt Tremont.

When the tour was finally over, Noah said, "Do I gotta go to bed, Daddy?"

Matt turned to her with a gorgeous smile. "Does he gotta, Ari?"

They were so adorable, and so much alike, that her heart squeezed in her chest. She appreciated that Matt subtly deferred to her, putting her in charge in Noah's eyes.

"You gotta," she said to the little boy. "Since it's Sunday, you need to take a shower to get ready for the week."

She waited for the inevitable fight little kids put up about washing. Instead, he told her, "I've never taken a shower before. Only baths."

"I'll show you how to work the taps."

She felt Matt's gaze on her as they headed through Noah's huge bedroom and into his bathroom. With the shower stall open, she adjusted the dual shower heads. "It's easy. Just turn this dial." She demonstrated while Matt took in her every move. The water was warm instantly, with a safety valve that kept it from scalding. Matt thought of everything. She gazed down at Noah. "Pretty easy, right?" She turned off the shower. "Bet you can do that."

He nodded. "Uh-huh."

Grabbing soap and shampoo from the tub, she put them on the built-in ledges in the shower. "I'll get your jammies while you wash." She tapped Noah's nose with a light finger. "Or I can help, if you like."

He insisted, "I can do it by myself," but she left the bathroom door slightly ajar so she could hear if he called.

"He's never done this alone before." Matt leaned against the wall next to the doorjamb, his arms crossed over his muscled chest, his face a little tense. A moment later, Noah shrieked, and Matt dove for the bathroom.

"It's cold, Daddy, it's cold!"

"Here's how you make it warmer." Matt's voice sounded strained from within the bathroom.

Meanwhile, Ari opened bureau drawers, finding pajamas with a racing motif that matched the comforter. The sound of the shower muted as Matt half closed the door again and crossed to her, the pulse at his throat still beating quickly.

"Don't worry," she said softly. "We might need to clean up some water off the floor when he's done, but he's a big boy." One of the moms she'd worked for had been super cautious with her first child, the way Matt was with Noah. "It's amazing what they're capable of."

He didn't nod, didn't agree, simply said, "They grow up fast."

She wanted to smooth the line from his forehead and tell him that Noah would always need him, that the note of *I can do it* in his son's voice would never change that fact.

But the part of her that wanted to touch him was all woman, so she kept her hands to herself. "They do grow up fast," she agreed. "One minute they're toddlers, then the next thing you know they don't want you to hold their hand at the bus stop anymore."

"Susan warned me. I didn't believe her."

"I met her at the youth home in San Jose, right?"

"Yes, Susan and Noah's grandfather Bob were both there." The tension in his face softened with love. "She's Daniel's birth mom, but she and Bob took all of us in and made us family, so Noah calls them Grandma and Grandpa."

Ari knew the basic Maverick story, since Daniel wasn't the type to hide his past or the seedy Chicago neighborhood he'd come from. Daniel and his sister,

Lyssa, were the biological kids, but his mom had raised all the Mavericks since they were in their early teens. Ari could see the adoration shining in Matt's eyes when he spoke of the man and woman who had taken him in. He'd been lucky to find them. Though she'd heard there were good people like Susan and Bob in the foster care system, she'd never met any of them personally. She had been lucky to find lifelong friends, however. Rosie and Chi would always be her sisters of the heart, just as the Mavericks were Matt's brothers even without blood tying them together.

The water shut off and the shower door opened. "You doing okay, Noah?" she called out. "I've got your jammies."

As Matt watched her progress to the bathroom door, her heart beat faster, her breath came quicker, and her skin warmed from more than the shower steam.

She handed the pajamas through the door without opening it, giving Noah some big-boy privacy. A couple of minutes later, she asked, "Ready?" and he made an assenting noise. Sitting on the edge of the bath, she toweled his hair dry. It was thick and needed little more than ruffling to bring up the curls. "Almost dry. Brush your teeth, then you get your story."

When Noah started to put his toothbrush away after only a few seconds, she urged him to do more. "Your teeth will look like a dinosaur's if that's all you do." He scrubbed a little harder.

"Why don't you read Noah his story tonight?" she suggested to Matt. She didn't want to force too much change on the little boy all at once, and she also wanted to hear Matt read, to watch him the way he'd been watching her.

Reading had been the lifeline that got her through dark days. And tonight she wanted to bear witness to Matt sharing his love of books with his son.

The sight would be all the more poignant after the emotional story Matt had told her at dinner. His pain was almost something she could touch, and she'd envisioned him wanting to charge to the rescue only to have little Noah rescue himself. She wasn't sure Matt saw it that way, but eventually, with her help, he would. Noah was an amazing little boy.

And his father was an amazing man.

Matt hauled Noah up and slung him over his shoulder, making his son squeal with delight all the way to the bed. Ari settled into a wicker chair by the window, curling her feet beneath her as she watched father and son.

Matt's big body dwarfed the twin bed as he leaned against the headboard with Noah nestled into him and the book open between them. He flipped a couple of pages. "Here we are. The fearsome giant has come down from the mountains into the village." He deepened his voice. *"Gregor the giant roared while the villagers ran. His footsteps were a great thumping that toppled all the vegetables on the grocer's cart."*

Noah pointed at the page. "He doesn't look very mean, Daddy."

Matt glanced down at Noah tucked beneath his arm. "Maybe he's not really a scary giant. Maybe he stubbed his toe on the way down the mountain and that's why he roars."

"Look." Noah tapped the book. "He's on one foot, hopping because his toe hurts."

They studied the illustration, then Matt began to make up their own story. "What if Gregor the Giant actually wants to ask for help? But why would a giant need a tiny villager's help?"

Noah gazed up at him. "Because..." He bit his lip, thinking. For all his energy, Ari could see that he was also a pensive child—cerebral, as Matt had put it earlier. According to Daniel, Matt had been the same. "I know!" Noah finally said. "He needs help because his little boy is sick."

"Do giants have little boys?"

"Of course. They're just like you and me, Daddy, except they're real big."

The new story unfolded before Ari's eyes, about Gregor the Giant and his brave but sick little boy Noah. She was captivated by the love they shared and how their minds worked so beautifully together. Matt's love shone through every silly character voice he made up, every time he chuckled with Noah, every new and outrageous story element they added. He was the essence of fatherhood, the epitome of love.

Unbidden, she realized her eyes were growing damp. Ari sniffed softly, and Matt looked up, holding her gaze as he spoke another line in the Giant's voice. *"Thank you for helping my little boy. I will give anything you desire."* His words burrowed deep inside as his eyes held her captive. "But now, young master, it is time for you to sleep."

"No," Noah crowed.

"Yes," Matt said in the deep giant voice and laid aside the book they hadn't actually read. He scooched Noah down in the bed. "Good night."

Ari uncurled from the ball she'd formed on the wicker chair and came to Noah's other side. "What a story," she said, smoothing his dark curls. "I can't wait for another one tomorrow night." She kissed his forehead. "Sleep tight."

"Night, Ari. Night, Daddy," he said, already sounding sleepy as Matt kissed him and said, "I love you."

Matt followed her out, closing the door halfway, leaving Noah with the beam of a night-light. She stopped, leaning against the far wall across from the balustrade. "You're some storyteller."

"He'd sleep with books if I let him. Just like I wanted to when I was a kid." He propped a shoulder against the wall beside her. "You're good with him, Ari. I wouldn't have considered letting him shower by himself yet, but you made him feel capable."

She blushed with the compliment, but also from the closeness of his big, male body in the hall. She was average height in her sneakers, but he made her feel petite and feminine. "You're a wonderful father. Making up that story with him—you've got a gift."

"No gift. Just that he's everything to me." When he settled more comfortably against the wall, she pretended it was because he didn't want to let her go yet. At least until he asked, "What are your after-school plans tomorrow? The zoo?" Of course he'd want her itinerary for her first full day of caring for his son.

"I thought we'd get to know each other for a couple of days before we head out and about."

The house was so quiet now, even the normal creaks and groans absent. Though it was all in her head, it felt as though the silence settled around them like intimacy.

"When we're ready for trips to the museum or zoo," she continued, "is there a number to call to arrange an outing with your driver?"

"You can give Doreen your plans each morning. As my full-time employee, she also makes sure all the cars are gassed up, washed, and maintained."

Earlier, Ari had gotten the tour of the six-car garage, one space housing only a man's mountain bike and a child's bicycle on training wheels. Matt had told her the spot was available for her use, though she was embarrassed to park her ancient Honda next to all the luxury cars with their waxed-to-a-sheen paint jobs.

"I usually drive myself to work unless I have meetings in the city," he said. "And though I do have to visit factories domestically and abroad, I still try to stay local as much as possible." He obviously didn't want to leave his son for long periods or too often. "Videoconferencing is the miracle of the modern age."

When he smiled and his clean, masculine scent filled her head, she almost forgot all the questions she had for him. *Think about Noah.*

"Since you mentioned Noah was reading *Purplicious*, it's obvious his reading skills are developed even if he likes you to read to him before bed."

"Yeah, he loves story time. But he's a good reader, pretty advanced." Matt dipped his head a moment, looking at the carpet. "Books are so important to a kid."

"I know. In foster care, books from the library were just about all I had." And before that too, living with her mother.

When he looked back up and said, "I practically lived at the library as a kid," she could have sworn a spark lit between them.

"Me too." Which was why she had to know, "Were those first editions of *The Lord of the Rings*?" She was practically hyperventilating at the thought…or maybe that was simply from being so close to Matt.

"Yes." He smiled big. "You're free to read them. Books are meant to be read, even if they are first editions."

"I have them memorized," she admitted, her fingertips itching at even the thought of holding the volumes.

"Most people I know just watch the movies." He looked impressed that she wasn't one of them.

"Movies are a couple of hours, while books transport you for days or weeks. You can live in the pages of a book."

"Yes." His voice was low, his gaze roaming her face again. "Most people don't understand that. Books can be—"

"A lifeline," she finished for him. "And you've given that precious love of reading to Noah." She felt herself trembling slightly, as if they were on the brink of a deeper connection than just boss and nanny. Pulling herself together before she could do or say something foolish, she asked, "I was wondering, may I speak with Noah's kindergarten teacher about his progress?"

"Of course. You have permission to do anything you think will benefit him. As long as he's safe. Keeping my son safe and happy is the most important thing to me."

"I'll always keep him safe," she said, remembering his story about the bully and the book, and his fears for Noah. "He seems like a very happy child."

"He usually is, thankfully."

They were both suddenly so quiet that she could hear a clock ticking down in the front hall. She could feel the heat of his body, smell the clean scent of him as though she had her face buried against his chest.

Neither of them moved, but his gaze lighted on her hair, her eyes, her cheeks. Her mouth.

She couldn't quite keep her body from straining toward him. Especially given the heat she swore was burning in his eyes. He could have been holding his breath, he was so still. And she waited...

"Now that you're off the clock"—he pushed away from the wall, took a step away from her, and then another—"you probably want to finish unpacking."

She could have sworn there had been a moment where they'd shared something. But he'd ended it. Abruptly.

Obviously, he'd remembered she was just the nanny.

She'd have to make sure she remembered that too.

Unpacking the few things she'd brought had taken ten minutes. Besides the stash of books she'd collected from thrift stores, she had a few changes of clothing, enough so that she didn't have to do laundry more than twice a week. She'd learned to travel light after so many moves, first with her mother, then from foster home to foster home. She'd left a few things behind in her studio apartment. Thankfully, Matt was paying her enough to keep it, since there was no way she'd let it go in case her brother, Gideon, came looking for her.

Not wanting Matt to know she had so little to her name, she said, "I thought I'd try out the whirlpool tub in my room. It looks awesome."

A heavy pause followed, one that was long enough

for her to realize—too late—the suggestiveness of her comment.

"Yes," he finally agreed. "The tubs in this house are great."

Praying she hadn't stepped over some nanny boundary and promising herself to be more careful in the future, she said, "Good night."

When her bedroom door closed, she sagged against it.

If Daniel ever suspected she had the hots for his business partner, he'd tell Matt to send her packing for sure.

Chapter Five

By the end of the first week, Matt was seriously concerned for his sanity.

Ari's tantalizing scent lingered in a room after she left it. The upstairs hallway smelled like lavender bath salts, and he couldn't erase the image of her naked in all that bubbling water. Story time with Noah had become torture, with Ari curled up in the wicker chair by the window, listening with rapt attention. He sometimes lost himself in midsentence, unable to keep his eyes off her. Dinner was equally dangerous. She told him about the day's activities, and he could barely remember a thing. Not when he was so drawn to the heat of her body, the glow of her hair, the sweetness of her skin, the way her mouth moved.

And how badly he wanted to taste her.

If Ari had been merely pretty, he'd have gotten over it. Especially since her exuberance and her unconscious charm had initially reminded him of Noah's mother. That should have warned him off if nothing else did. Irene was like Holly Golightly in *Breakfast at Tiffany's*—silly and carefree, always getting herself into trouble, but so sweet you couldn't help forgiving her. Until one day you couldn't take any more...and you realized you'd never be more than a fun, and temporary, distraction. Irene flitted in every few weeks or months, showering Noah with extravagant gifts, then disappearing just as quickly, leaving behind a devastated little boy who couldn't understand why his mommy always left him.

But Matt couldn't help but feel that there was so much more to Ari. The questions she asked, her interest in Noah, the way she listened to the bedtime stories, her gaze soft with affection for his child. The fact that she wanted to talk to his son's teachers and find activities that would enhance his capabilities, to actually learn who Noah was as a person, was not only beyond anything any nanny had ever given—it was beyond what Noah's own mother had given him.

When she'd told Matt she'd keep his son safe, it felt like a vow.

But it was the moment she'd told him how books had been her lifeline that he couldn't forget. Her words could have been his own. No one else had ever understood just how much the pages of books transported him. He forgot the neighborhood, his life, the bullies, his dad's angry words. He was somewhere better. He didn't know how bad Ari's childhood had been, but books had obviously done the same thing for her.

"So how are things going with your new nanny?"

Matt started at Sebastian's question. The Maverick

Group's headquarters were on the twenty-ninth floor of Sebastian's high-rise in downtown San Francisco, and this was one of the rare occasions when they were all there at the same time. All five Mavericks had their own offices, along with Cal Danniger, their business manager, and Noah Bryant, their lawyer.

"Ari's great with Noah," Matt said. "She takes him interesting places, teaches him. I've never had a nanny so involved."

"Sounds like she's got a lot of energy," Evan said, leaning against the reception desk, arms folded over his chest. "Isn't she a lot younger than your previous nannies?"

"She's definitely full of energy and enthusiasm," Matt replied.

They were spotlighting him, and he cursed the heat coursing through his body at the mention of her. She was a heck of a lot younger than he was, she'd come out of a difficult past as a foster child—and, most important of all, she was *off-limits*! He knew he had his head in all the wrong places.

"You've got a winner in Ariana." Daniel sprawled in a leather chair, legs spread, hands on his knees. "Your home has got to be like a breath of fresh air for her."

Matt was once again reminded of her scent. Which then reminded him of her nightly soak in the tub...and all the images that assailed him when he was just down the hall, unable to get her out of his head.

"She's special," Daniel went on. "She always took the new employees under her wing and showed them the ropes."

"Then why did you let her go?" Will looked up from scrolling through his phone. "Jeremy keeps talking about how pretty she is, by the way. Sounds like he hasn't forgotten meeting her in San Jose when we were all rebuilding the youth home."

"Don't talk about how pretty she is," Daniel said. "You'll give this guy"—he hooked a thumb at Matt—"ideas."

"*Ideas* are the farthest thing from my mind," Matt lied, every eye on him. It was a lie he was afraid his closest friends would see through if they looked hard enough. The Mavericks were protectors, and they were all keeping an eye out for Ari. There'd be hell to pay if he screwed up.

"Anyway," Daniel continued, "having been a foster kid, she appreciates the importance of surrounding children with love and kindness."

The Mavericks had been raised with Susan and Bob's love and kindness. But the years before that had shaped them too. When high school came to an end for all of them, they'd made a vow to get out of that filthy Chicago neighborhood, and they'd each done it in their own way.

Will had turned his uncanny sense of what people desired into an importing empire. Sebastian's sensitivity and charisma brought him worldwide renown as a self-help authority. Evan had his numbers, Matt had his inventions, and Daniel had his home improvement conglomerate.

Each and every one had their demons to battle too. Matt could self-analyze enough to admit that his dad's cruel words still played a huge role in who he was today.

No son of mine is going to be an effing weenie.

Your friends can't do all the sticking up for you your whole life, ya puny little weakling.

Buck up, you idiot.

He'd eventually bucked up. But he'd also sworn never to tear his son down the way his own father had tried to demolish him. He'd always controlled himself ruthlessly, never yelled at Noah—never yelled at anyone in front of him either. And he'd vowed to protect his son from anyone who did, whether on a playground or at school. He worried that he wouldn't be able to step up for his son every single time, like the day that kid had slapped the book out of Noah's hands…but he pushed those fears out of his head. He *would* be there for his kid, just the way Susan and Bob had been there for each of the Mavericks.

The elevator dinged and the middle set of doors opened on Cal Danniger. "Did I miss a meeting notification?"

"Nope. We're grilling Matt about his nanny," Sebastian drawled.

Cal stepped out of the elevator, letting the doors

close behind him. As business manager, he handled all their mutual holdings under The Maverick Group umbrella. While they were hands-on, it was impractical for the five of them to manage the ventures the entire group was involved in. Cal was their trusted guy.

"Don't tell me you lost another one. How long did she last? A week?" Cal shook his head in feigned disgust. While he wasn't a Maverick, they all looked on him as a sort of cousin, given that he'd worked for them from the inception of The Maverick Group.

"I haven't lost this one," Matt growled. And he wouldn't.

Not as long as he kept his hands to himself.

"I don't get what's so wrong with them all," Will said.

"I caught the last one speaking harshly to Noah." Matt could still feel his blood boiling over that. He'd fired her, had her pack up her things and get the hell out of his house inside of ten minutes.

"Are you really that bad a judge of character *every* time you hire someone to take care of your kid?" Sebastian asked.

He was a damn good judge of character, but dealing with children was different than managing a QC department or running an assembly line. "Noah is special. I want the perfect nanny for him, and I've got high standards. What's wrong with that?"

"Luckily, Ariana's perfect," Daniel said. "So don't mess it up."

Evan pushed away from the reception desk. "Glad you're here, Cal. Do you have a status report on the Link Labs endeavor yet?" They'd signed the agreement almost six months ago, and so far things had been progressing better than expected. Matt had brought the venture to the group, but Evan was their financial guru, and he was all about the numbers and quarterly reports.

"I've got it all in my office," Cal said, heading down the hall with Evan.

Matt was damned glad he was off the hot seat. Sooner or later, if they kept talking about Ari, he was bound to give himself away.

The bigger problem was that more than his base nature was getting to him. His fantasies were no longer merely about begging her to let him join her in that tub. Sometimes they were about joining her with Noah, going to the zoo, simply being with her.

Ari was becoming an obsession.

"Evan's looking a little haggard." Sebastian slouched in his chair, his gaze on the hallway.

Will frowned. "Living with Whitney will do that to a guy. He needs a good woman like Harper." His eyes turned bright with that look of love he got whenever he said her name.

Will had never looked happier or seemed more content, not even when he'd made his first billion. Only Harper had done that for him. Along with her brother, Jeremy. They'd be married in Chicago at Bob and Susan's house over the Christmas holiday, and Matt had a feeling Jeremy might have a little niece or nephew within a year.

"It really sucks how things have worked out for them," Daniel said. "I'm not a fan of divorce, but sometimes I'm not sure there's another way."

Matt agreed, but he was afraid Evan couldn't see the light. "He'll never do it. He's too loyal." Then he turned to Sebastian. "How's Noah's dinosaur coming?"

Sebastian's fiancée, Charlie, was a brilliant artist who worked primarily in metal. And she'd promised Noah a dinosaur for his garden.

Just hearing her name had his friend smiling with a look in his eye that could have been the twin of Will's for his fiancée. "New commissions are being thrown at Charlie every day, but she loves working on Noah's present. All I can say without spoiling any surprises is that you should think about getting the garden ready soon for some absolutely brilliant sculptures."

"You and Will are just too disgustingly happy," Daniel groused good-naturedly.

Sebastian trained his eagle eye on Daniel. "What about you? You've been spending all your free time working on your cabin in Tahoe lately. Is there someone you've got hidden up there that you're not telling us about?" He cocked one devilish brow.

Daniel laughed and shook his head like they were nuts. But he tugged at the open collar of his shirt, as if somehow, impossibly, it had become a little tight. "I just want the roof on the cabin before winter this year."

"Right," Will said, obviously having noticed the collar-tugging as well.

To save himself, Daniel turned the spotlight back on Matt. "What about you? Anyone caught your eye recently?"

Jesus, he'd thought their interrogation was over.

"Nope." But if Daniel's collar had been tight, Matt's was strangling him.

Because Ari had caught him from the first time he'd ever set eyes on her.

Chapter Six

October in the San Francisco Bay Area could be warm, especially in the early part of the month, but Matt's pool was heated all year round, and Ari intended to make the most of it. Three times during their first week, she'd given Noah swimming lessons, and he was doing extremely well. He wasn't afraid of the water in his face, but he hated his water wings.

"Sorry, sweetie," she called out as he clung to the far edge of the pool. "You can't take them off. Let's try it again—swim to me." She held out her arms in encouragement as Noah did another lap of the shallow end.

He splashed through the water toward her, the water wings making his strokes awkward. Matt had insisted he wear them for safety reasons, but from everything she'd learned in her courses—and she'd even looked up the question online—there was a good basis for kids his age to swim without flotation devices when they were under adult supervision. She hoped Matt could see that tomorrow if he joined them, since he devoted his weekends to Noah.

The week had been fabulous. Noah was adorable, and his laughter twisted her heart around his little finger. Their driver, Doreen, took them anywhere Ari wanted to go. They'd visited the Oakland Zoo one afternoon, gone to the mummy museum another day. Once, they'd played with Jorge and Rosie, and just as Ari had predicted, the two children had become fast friends. When she told Matt about it, he'd seemed pleased.

But she especially loved story time each night, when she sat in the wicker chair and watched Matt read to his son. She got her fill of his gorgeous face, his tender smile, the love in his eyes. Then, after they'd tucked Noah in, Matt made time to talk with her about the day.

Her fantasies about him were only a dream. One that would never come true. But in her experience, dreams were often better—because no one left you in the end or threw you out when they were tired of you.

And really, the nanny and the rich guy? It wasn't just a fairy tale—it was a full-blown cliché.

In the water, Noah threw one last burst of power into his arms to reach her. She scooped him up and held him high, her muscles straining. He was a growing boy and getting heavy. "You're an amazing swimmer!" Setting him on the pool deck, she hoisted herself up beside him. "Okay, since we're getting out, we can take the water wings off now."

"Yay!" He immediately pushed them down his little

arms, then ran for the towels on the chaise lounge where Ari had left them.

"No running by the pool," she cautioned him, and was glad he slowed down to a fast walk.

After drying herself off and putting on her terry-cloth cover-up, she sat on the edge of the chair and helped Noah dry off his thick, curly hair. The late afternoon sun sparkled on the rippling water in the pool. She was in the most beautiful place on earth, with a thicket of live oaks just beyond the lawn and a row of flowering bushes. Nothing could be better.

Then Matt unexpectedly stepped out of the house, and her heart actually stopped. Just *bam!* Her breath caught and her skin tingled, and it felt like all the stars fell out of the sky.

In jeans, he was a masterpiece worthy of a museum. But in a black suit, his tie off, and the top two buttons of his white dress shirt undone... Sweet Lord, he was someone you could see only on a movie screen. Someone to gaze at and drool over but never touch, because he couldn't possibly be real.

Seeing his father, Noah squealed and squirmed away from her. "Daddy," he shouted in his high, sweet voice as he ran along the pool's edge. "Guess what I just did!"

"Don't run," she called out, Matt echoing her words.

But Noah was too focused on his daddy to listen as he cut the corner of the pool. Her heart in her throat,

Ari started running too. But she wasn't fast enough to stop Noah from tripping.

Someone was shouting, maybe screaming—it could have been her. Then Noah's little voice cried, "Daddy!" as he fell, his skull heading toward the concrete lip of the pool.

The water exploded with a great splash as Matt dove into the shallow end just as Ari reached the edge. But Noah fell before she could catch him.

She'd never believed in miracles until that moment, when Matt seemed to grab Noah right out of the air before he actually plunged into the water. He held the little boy's body in his arms as though he were a rare jewel, while Noah squalled.

Then she saw the splash of blood on Noah's forehead, and her ears rang with terror, her voice dried up.

"Call Doreen now!" Matt ordered. "Tell her we need to go to the hospital."

He might have shouted. She might only have been reading lips. Cradling his precious son in his arms as Noah cried, Matt slogged to the stairs. Water streamed from them both as he climbed out.

Ari had already grabbed her phone. Doreen answered immediately, and Ari shouted instructions she couldn't actually hear over the roar in her ears.

"I think he hit his head." Matt ran his shaking hand over Noah's scalp. "It's okay, buddy. Daddy'll take care of you."

He carried Noah across the deck while Ari followed. Matt's sodden suit left a trail over the sun porch, then the floor, and Doreen met them at the front door.

"The car's ready." Matt's driver took in Noah's pale face and Matt's ruined suit, then ran down the front steps to open the car door, her blond ponytail bouncing, so perky and out of place in the moment.

They piled into the backseat, Noah in Matt's arms and Ari crowded against them, her hand on Noah's forehead.

She couldn't feel a lump, and she prayed he'd suffered no more than a scrape and a bruise. He'd taken a tumble—and scared the living daylights out of them—but his daddy had saved him.

Then she lifted her gaze from Noah. And saw Matt's stricken face.

* * *

How could I have let this happen?

Matt shouldn't have surprised them. And he should have been more strict with Noah about never running by the pool. But Noah sped everywhere, and he was always excited when Matt got home.

"He's going to be just fine," Ari said softly.

She was trying to soothe him, but just as he hadn't stopped Noah's tumble into the pool's edge, he couldn't stop the jumble of his guilt-ridden thoughts either.

He swallowed hard, his teeth grinding together.

Noah no longer whimpered and lay quietly in his arms as Doreen guided the big car through the streets. Thank God the hospital wasn't far.

"It's probably just a scrape."

He could barely hear Ari's words when he was so frozen with terror and when he kept seeing Noah falling on repeat inside his head.

"It was an accident," she said softly. "That's how kids are, always rushing."

But accidents didn't happen to Noah. Matt had vowed to always protect his kid. *Always.* He was worth more than an oil baron or a social media king, and if he couldn't protect his kid no matter what, then what was the use of all that money?

He wanted to yell at Doreen to drive like the wind. An ambulance would have had sirens, but would also have taken longer to get to them.

All the while, Ari's voice in his ear kept him just on this side of sanity. "All kids fall when they're running. They fall when they're riding their bikes. They have little accidents."

They had huge ones as well. Like Jeremy, Will's soon-to-be brother-in-law. He'd been hit by a car at the age of seven while riding his bike, and he'd never been the same. He was a great kid, but he would always *be* a kid, even at eighteen. That accident had robbed him of the chance of ever growing into a man.

The car swayed into a turn, and Matt held Noah tighter. Everyone thought Matt was too powerful to break. But his son was where he doubted himself. Because Noah was the most important thing in the entire world.

And if he couldn't step up to protect this precious child, then what the hell good was he?

Doreen drew the car up beneath the Emergency Room portico, and Matt climbed out with Noah still clinging to him.

"Daddy? I'm cold," Noah whimpered as Matt carried him through the automatic doors. His soaked bathing suit had dropped a few degrees in the air conditioning.

Ari tore off her terrycloth cover-up. "Put this on, sweetie." She tucked the terry robe around Noah. Then she rubbed Matt's arm. "You must be freezing."

He was so cold his teeth wanted to chatter. But it wasn't his wet clothing. It wasn't the air conditioning.

It was his failure to protect his son.

* * *

Fifteen minutes later, they were in an examining cubicle separated from the other cubes by a curtain. Matt could hear the low murmur of voices, but his focus was solely on Noah. A nurse had brought him scrubs to change into, and a pair for Ari as well since she was shivering in her swimsuit.

"Can I have another lollipop?" Noah asked.

"As soon as I've finished the exam, but only if your father says it's all right," the doctor said. Matt tried to take solace in the experience lining her face. She gently probed Noah's scalp, his arms, his legs, then finally stepped back. "You've just got a few scrapes and bruises." At Matt's nod, she held out the jar for Noah to choose a purple lollipop. "I'll let Jami, my wonderful assistant, clean up that scrape on your forehead."

Ari put her hand on Noah's knee as the nurse came over with alcohol wipes, the pungent smell making Matt's eyes water.

He lowered his voice for the doctor's ears only. "Doesn't he need a CT scan to make sure he doesn't have a concussion?"

The smile the doctor gave him reminded him of Susan. "Mr. Tremont, he's fine. I'd be willing to bet he scraped his head against the pool's edge rather than actually hitting it. There's no bump. Just take him home, give him some SpaghettiOs, and let him rest." Noah had started chattering about SpaghettiOs and mummies and gorillas the moment the doctor gave him the first lollipop and began her exam. "You have nothing to worry about."

If he could think rationally about what had happened, if he could stop replaying that recording in his brain of Noah falling, he might be able to see that the doctor and Ari were right about the scrape. But he never wanted his son to feel the kind of pain he'd experienced himself.

Matt would never forget falling off his bike when he was trying to get away from the neighborhood bullies who'd made his life a living hell. To this day, he remembered their laughter and that long walk home, his arm cradled against his stomach. He'd known his dad was going to be madder than ever. *Don't be such a freaking weenie* and *How the hell did I raise such a wimp?* were two of his favorite refrains. That day, his father told him to buck up, his mother nodding furiously behind him. Somehow, that was even worse, the fact that his mother hadn't believed it was her job to protect him, and that she'd agreed as his father said, "We can't afford no freaking emergency room for a stupid sprained wrist just because the idiot couldn't stay on his bike."

It was the school principal, not his father, not even his mother, who had ended up sending Matt to the doctor, where an X-ray revealed the break in his arm. His dad had been hugely pissed about that bill. He'd even demanded the school pay for it since they were the ones who'd sent Matt to the hospital. He'd stopped only when they mentioned Social Services.

It was the Mavericks who finally saved Matt—along with Susan and Bob, who looked out for him and turned him into a worthwhile human being. Never his parents. And now he would do anything to protect Noah, spend every penny. He would never let his son be bullied, never let him get hurt.

But what if Matt couldn't always rescue Noah, just like he hadn't rescued himself when he was a kid and the other Mavericks had needed to protect him? What if he wasn't capable of stepping up when push really came to shove? What if he wasn't there when his son needed him most?

As if she could sense his inner turmoil, the doctor said again, "He's fine. Your wife is taking care of him too."

He focused on Ari still rubbing Noah's leg while the nurse pressed the square SpongeBob bandage to Noah's forehead as his son chattered cheerfully. And the words he'd been about to say—*she's not my wife*—never made it past his lips.

The doctor squeezed his arm. "Take your family home and spend some quality time together. And stop worrying about Noah."

Didn't she get it? He would never stop worrying about his son.

Never.

Chapter Seven

They'd both long since changed out of the scrubs the nursing staff had given them as Ari and Matt got Noah ready for bed. The little boy's color was back, and the SpongeBob bandage on his forehead was a badge of honor.

"I was real brave, wasn't I?" He stood on the small stool in his bathroom so he could reach the sink as he brushed his teeth.

"You sure were," Ari said. She turned to Matt with a smile, but his features were strained, his mouth a flat line.

Nothing she'd said had eased his guilt. Tonight definitely wasn't the time to talk about getting rid of the water wings. At this point, she was half afraid he'd say Noah couldn't swim at all anymore. Matt would wrap his son in cotton wool if he thought it would keep him safe.

Her heart split in two for him. She ached for his pain, his self-recrimination, but she also wanted to show him how resilient little kids were. Yes, you had to watch out for them, but you had to let them run free too, or they suffocated. Kids bounced back—she knew this for a fact, having bounced plenty during her own childhood. Heck, Matt had too. He'd come from a terrible childhood—and look how he'd thrived.

She wished she could help him get over what had happened. It was beyond painful to watch Matt silently visualize every horror, imagine all the what-ifs—and beat himself up for what had almost happened.

But it *hadn't* happened. That was key. How could she make him understand? Not only that all was well, but that it was okay not to hold Noah quite so tightly.

He'd eaten SpaghettiOs with Noah tonight, laughing whenever his son said something funny. But he couldn't mask the strain around his eyes when Noah wasn't looking.

"What would you like to read tonight, sweetie?" With Noah's hand in hers, she hunkered down by the bookshelves, the colorful choices calling out to them. Books truly did open up worlds—all those times when she'd felt alone, without a family, she'd taken temporary refuge in the books she devoured.

Noah grabbed a book and held it up for his father. "This one." *James and the Giant Peach.*

"I can't wait to hear your daddy read it to you."

When Matt's eyes met hers, Ari saw utter bleakness. There would be other scrapes, bumps, and bruises, because Noah was full of energy and would keep on running, because that's what little boys did. How would Matt handle it?

She didn't have any answers tonight, only knew that he needed to relax enough to read to his happy son. She almost grabbed his hand and shoved the book into it, but finally Matt curled his fingers around the spine.

Ari took her usual spot. And despite his mood, Matt got into voice, reading with exaggeration, big highs and low lows, Noah hanging on every word.

Her heart overflowed. She hugged her knees, letting the sight of father and son become part of her.

She hoped to someday sit watching her beautiful children with their father. Maybe it was having a mom who wanted her next fix more than she needed new shoes for her daughter—but Ari had always vowed to be a great mother, giving them everything she'd never had herself. She knew it was exactly how Matt felt about his son.

When Noah finally fell asleep, Matt laid the book on the table, then slid out from the bed covers so he wouldn't wake him. Pulling the covers over Noah's shoulder, Matt leaned down to kiss him, lingering as if he needed to breathe in his son's little-boy smell.

After Ari kissed Noah, Matt followed her out, pausing at the door to take one last long look at his sleeping child. Finally, he flipped out the light, leaving the door half open as usual. But instead of their nightly ritual of discussing the day, Matt mumbled a good night and turned away.

Maybe she should let him brood. Maybe anyone

else would leave him alone in his sorrow. But Ari just couldn't.

"He's safe, you know," she said quietly. "Perfectly safe and sound with only a scratch that's already healing."

He stopped, his back stiff, his hand on the wall as if to brace himself. "It could have been so much worse."

She took two steps closer. "Do you blame me?"

He turned sharply, his dark, bleak eyes meeting hers. "Of course not. He saw me and he ran. It wasn't your fault. It was mine. I shouldn't have surprised you both. I should have taught him never to run by the pool. I should have done something, *anything*, to make sure he didn't fall."

One more step, close enough to breathe in his scent, to feel his heat, to touch his face. She wanted to surround him with her warmth, as if that could ease his tension. Cupping his jaw, she forced him to look at her. "Can't you see that if I'm not to blame, then you aren't either?"

His muscles rippled under her fingers as he clenched his teeth and gritted out, "Protecting him is my job. The most important thing I do. And I let him down."

"No." She couldn't bear to watch him tear himself up any longer. "You were there for him. You caught him. And he knows you love him every single second."

For a moment, hope flashed in Matt's eyes. But just as quickly as it came, it was extinguished.

"*Matt.*" His name was the barest whisper on her lips. "Don't do this. You're a good man. A great father."

"You barely know me."

"I know enough."

But when she looked up into his eyes, she could see that he wasn't listening. He could hear only the harsh and critical voices inside his head. She'd had to fight those enough times herself to understand just how hard it was to do it on your own. So she did the only other thing she could think of to slice through those voices.

She closed her eyes, went up on her tippy toes.

And put her mouth on his.

* * *

Matt knew he should fight it, but everything in him needed Ari's touch, her lips on his.

She reminded him of all the things he wanted…and all the things he wasn't in control of. He couldn't control what she did to him—how badly he wanted to taste her, touch her, lose himself in her, and forget everything else. He wasn't able to stop Noah from reacting to everything with enthusiasm and excitement, and the truth was that he didn't want to. Of course he wanted his kid to run to him and throw himself into his arms—Matt just wanted Noah to stay completely safe while he did all those things.

He's safe, you know.

Ari was right. Noah was safe and sleeping. In the morning, he would be the same happy kid he'd been today before the fall by the pool.

And—*amazingly*—Ari was kissing him.

His self-control as an adult had always been strong as steel. First, to protect himself from his parents' "lessons" on being tough, from his father's angry ridicule and his mother's total indifference, no matter how difficult or painful the situation. And then again, after Irene had flitted away and he'd learned to keep his walls up for everyone but the Mavericks. The women in his life had sent him a huge message, and he'd never allowed another woman close. He'd bedded them, but he'd never let them stay.

But with Ari in his arms, how could he help but give in to the dreams he'd had from the first moment he'd set eyes on her?

She tasted so damn sweet, smelled as fresh as wild flowers, felt as fragile as a new bloom. Then she moaned, a soft sound that twisted him up inside. When she opened her mouth, deepening their kiss, he was a goner. He turned with her, pushing her up against the wall, and kissed her with every ounce of need that had been building in him.

At long last, he could forget the accident, his guilt, his fear. In this moment, there was only Ari's mouth under his, her body soft and yielding against him.

On her toes, she wound her arms around his neck, her curtain of hair falling over him. He went deep, playing with her tongue, drawing on her sweetness until he couldn't breathe.

Until he couldn't think of anything but her.

Sliding his hands down her torso, he splayed his fingers to cup the undersides of her breasts. Her body strained against him, almost begging. He slipped his thumbs over the peaks, stroking until they were tight and hard. There was no question that she wanted this as badly as he did, the moan in her throat ripe with desire and need.

If he wanted to stop, it had to be now. And yet the hard lessons he'd learned about women were suddenly like distant voices in a dense forest, just far enough away from him to ignore.

He dropped his hands to her hips and hauled her up, spreading her legs around his waist, letting her feel what she did to him, her hot center riding him through the thin leggings she wore.

He rocked into her, wanting her innate beauty. Her hopefulness. Her kindness. Wanting more than the physical. It was how thoughtfully she spoke, how caring she was, how selfless and yet how strong. So unlike the examples of his past.

Most of all, he wanted to believe that he was a good man, and in this moment, with her body so close, her lips so sweet, he almost could. Because he already knew that Ari would accept only the most worthy.

Somehow he managed to pull back enough to murmur, "I shouldn't do this."

"You should."

"You're my na—"

Her kiss cut off the rest. "I want this, Matt. I want *you.*"

He should let her go. Apologize for taking advantage of her. But the only words that came out of his mouth were, "Come with me."

"Anywhere," she whispered.

"Hold on tight." To him. To this moment.

He cupped her against him and walked with her to his bedroom, shoving the door closed behind them. Shutting out the world and guilt and duty. For tonight, there was only the two of them.

And the forbidden desire that consumed them both.

Chapter Eight

The moon cast a bright swath across the room, the thick carpet, the massive bed. Beside the mattress, Matt let Ari's feet slide to the floor. "I don't want to hurt you." He rained kisses along her neck and collarbone before adding, "If this is the first time."

Even now, he was such a gentleman. "You don't need to worry." There'd been two guys she'd cared about as a teenager, but with both relationships, in the end they hadn't mattered enough to each other to stay together. Standing in the circle of Matt's arms, she realized that was all they'd been: boys. Not men like strong, loyal, loving Matt.

"Ari…" he murmured into her hair, his hands trailing down her arms. "I want to make you feel so good."

Just being here with him was more than she could have ever hoped for. Fantasized, yes, but never hoped it would be real. Moments earlier, he'd been conflicted about wanting her, but she couldn't stand the thought of his walking away. Not now. Not when they'd both finally given in to what she'd felt between them from the start.

"I want you to feel good too," she said softly, "but even though I'm not a virgin, I'm not… I haven't had much…"

He pulled back to cup her face in his hands, and in the heat of his eyes she was glad to see that desire was still winning out over duty or worries that she was his nanny. "All you need to do tonight"—he kissed her again—"is let me take care of you."

She'd already known he was a caretaker—but now he showed her that it applied to everything he did, even pleasure. Emotion bubbled up, wanting to burst out of her as he gave her what she craved, pulling up the soft cotton of her T-shirt, inch by mind-altering inch, his fingertips setting her skin on fire. Then he tossed the shirt aside and stared at her as if she was the most beautiful thing he'd ever seen.

"Damn, you're pretty." He cupped her breasts through her bra. "I've dreamed of how you'd feel." He swished a thumb over first one hard nipple, then the other, sending sparks racing down to her center.

Ari shivered with a need she'd never known before, her core clenching for his touch, his mouth. She swore he must be able to read her mind as his hand followed the trail of sparks, down, down, down, to cup her where she was hot and so very ready.

"I couldn't stop dreaming of how you'd taste."

She opened her mouth for breath, but he'd stolen all of it. He was a man, not a boy. He didn't fumble, he didn't beg. He seduced her with a man's desires, with words that made her tremble.

Hooking his fingers in the waistband of her leggings, it seemed as though inner conflict held him in its grip again for a long moment. She held her breath to see which way he'd go.

Finally, he eased them down, looking at her as though she could say no at any moment. As though he would actually stop if she asked him to.

"Please," she whispered, a million miles away from *no*.

When the pants slid to her bare feet, she held on to his arms and stepped out of them.

"Beautiful." He ran his hands from her rib cage to her hips. *"Beyond* beautiful."

She blushed all over, her skin turning as pink as her cotton panties and bra.

"Kiss me," he urged. "Show me how much you want this. How much you want me."

She leaped to kiss him the way he demanded, opening her mouth beneath his, diving in. She wanted to climb his body, wrap herself around him. She felt primal, as though she was devolving into her animal nature. And he devolved just as quickly, growling deep in his throat, his hips thrusting against hers, his hands holding her tightly to him, taking her mouth like he couldn't get enough, like he'd lost all control.

She was fumbling for his belt when he pulled back abruptly and held her hands still over his still-latched buckle. "Look at me, Ari."

The command in his voice shot a thrill through her as she raised her eyes to his burning gaze. She'd never felt so desired. Sex had only ever been about the end game—get in, get off, get out—at least for the boys she'd known. Matt made it intimate and special, like in her dreams.

"Promise me you want this, or we'll stop."

She didn't have to think, didn't so much as hesitate. "I've never wanted anything more."

His grin was slow...and utterly devastating. "In that case," he said, "keep taking off my belt."

She didn't fumble, his eyes on her giving her bravery and grace. She pulled his buckle loose and had begun to unzip him when he laid his hand over hers again.

"Just the belt until I tell you I'm ready for more."

Her fingers trembled with the need to hold him in her hand. And her whole *body* trembled with the sensuality of his erotic commands.

She ached to rip off his clothes and dive on him, but she loved that he made her wait. Then, finally, he said, "More," his eyes lit by fire.

She left his jeans for the moment and slid her hands beneath his shirt, resting her palms on his stomach. "Like this?"

When he growled his assent, she skimmed her hands slowly over his abdomen, to the chest hair beneath the pads of her fingers, to his flat nipples. His skin jumped beneath her touch, and his hard body flexed against her belly.

Gathering his shirt, she pushed it over his head. *Oh God*, all that awesome flesh, all that power, was right before her eyes, his chest broad, his muscles taut.

"You make me crazy. *This* is crazy." His voice rumbled against her ear. "But I want to savor it. I want to savor *you*. Don't rush." He slid his hands down her bare back, cupped her bottom, holding her long and hard against him, letting her feel what she did to him.

He was the definition of sensuality, enjoying every touch, every taste, every moment of her—making her feel like no other woman had ever mattered, only her.

He couldn't know how badly she wanted to matter to someone. And in this moment, she truly felt like she mattered to *him*.

Her hands trembled as he put them on denim, helping her unzip and shove his jeans all the way down. Once they were gone, she stepped back, *dying* to see his erection, so hard, so big, outlined by only a thin layer of cotton.

"For you. Only for you, Ari." When she shivered with the thought of him inside her, he soothed her. "Don't be scared."

"I'm not." Not of whether they'd fit—he would be perfect—but of something else entirely. "I don't want to disappoint you."

He lifted her high, and she wrapped her legs around him. The cotton between them barely a barrier, she felt the steel of him between her thighs.

"You could never disappoint me." He knelt on the bed and laid her down in the middle. She sank into the thick comforter. "Don't you know you're special?"

She could barely think, certainly not well enough to answer a question like that.

He didn't wait, simply ate her alive, kissing her until her lungs were starving for breath. He pressed her down into the bed, his weight like a blanket, like heat, like the stars above.

Slowly he kissed his way down her chin, her throat, her collarbone, until he reached the edge of her pink bra, flicking the clasp open with expert fingers. Inch by inch he eased the cups aside, caressing her with his tongue and the short whiskers along his jaw. His lips closed over her nipple and he sucked hard.

Ari cried out, arching deeper into his mouth, her hands fisting in the comforter. Her legs fell open, and his hips slipped between them, the hard pressure of his erection turning her insides to liquid and fire.

Now she knew that she'd only played at loving before. Because making love with Matt was beyond anything she'd ever experienced. His mouth on her, his hands all over her, his body between her legs—this was man owning woman, possessing her body, touching her soul.

He pulled the bra straps down her arms and blew a warm breath over the wet peak of her nipple. She shivered with need.

"Ari."

She wanted to cry at the way he said her name, so tenderly, so gently, so reverently.

Working his way down her stomach, he layered every inch of bare skin with kisses. Her belly jumped in anticipation…and a little fear. She'd done this before, but with those two boys, it had felt clumsy and messy and wrong, and she'd just wanted it to be over.

But…*ohhhh*…Matt's mouth on her skin felt so right. So incredible.

"I'm dying to taste you." He tugged off her panties. "Dying to touch you. Inside and out."

She panted, rolling her hips as he slid one finger, then two inside, finding a spot so sensitive that a rush of heat bolted straight through her. Then he loved her with his mouth, his fingers, taking her to a sweeter place than even heaven could be.

Riding the storm of his mouth, his touch, his heat—it was almost too much. So good it hurt. Her body bowed with pleasure, her hands wrapped around his head, holding him to her. Until the moment she thought she couldn't take any more.

And he pushed her over the edge into madness.

* * *

Matt didn't want to let Ari come down off the high, because the moment she did, he would too. And he couldn't stand returning to the last dark hours he'd been trapped in. Nor did he want to have to face that being with her like this was wrong. More than anything, he wanted to stay right here, steeped in soul-deep pleasure. So he roughly pushed aside the voices in his head calling him a bastard for taking her.

He licked her sweetness softly, stoking her fire higher, then hotter still, even as the first climax rolled through her. She gasped and moaned as she went straight through one release to the next, her legs quivering as she squirmed on the bed, fisting her hands in the comforter.

"MattOhGodPleaseAgain"

Her words bled into each other in the sexiest of songs as she came hard against his lips and tongue and fingers. Matt had never seen anything, or anyone, as beautiful as Ari in his bed, naked and trusting him to give her pleasure.

Every night she'd slept in his house, Matt had dreamed of this. Loving Ari, kissing every inch of her perfect skin, roaming his hands over her curves, the slope of her hip. But the reality so far eclipsed the dream that he couldn't trust himself not to push her too far or too fast on this one stolen night.

After he slid up her body to taste her mouth and feel her in his arms, she finally found her breath again. "Now I know what it means to say you've 'died and gone to heaven.'"

Damned if he didn't feel power swell inside him at the sure knowledge of how much he'd pleased her. Since he was a teenager, he'd studied the female body the way he studied the schematics for a new robotic.

He'd noted what women liked and kept the techniques that elicited the best reactions.

But being with Ari was so natural. He saw, he wanted, he kissed...and he lost himself in the tasting. When he was with her, he forgot everything but her scent, her skin, her breathless voice begging him to make her feel good.

"It's not always like that." He played his fingers through her hair, nipped at the smooth skin on her shoulder, letting her feel him, right *there*, throbbing against her. "Not always that good."

Touching her didn't merely banish the terror of the afternoon—her arms around him actually made him feel whole. She was sweetly sexy, unconsciously seductive. And she was kind as well as caring.

"I know it's not always good." Her eyes were still closed as she laughed, a little sound she seemed to choke off. "It's *never* been this way for me."

She'd obviously been with inexperienced men who didn't care, didn't learn, only took and never gave. But Matt wanted to give her so much more. All night long. Because in the morning...

No. He wouldn't think about the morning.

There was only now. A handful of stolen hours to show Ari how much he wanted her.

But he didn't want to simply *do* things to her. He wanted her totally engaged, so he rolled to his back and brushed the damp hair from her face. "I want to feel your hands on me."

He relished her low intake of breath at his sensual command, loved the way her pupils dilated with heavy arousal, not only at his request, but at the sight of him as her gaze flitted down his naked torso to the aching hardness beneath his boxers. She swallowed, then put out her hand, her fingertips brushing him.

He hissed a breath between his teeth at the sexy yet tentative touch. He wanted to press her hand to him, stroke himself with her palm. But she had to come to him on her own.

"Earlier, you said how much you wanted me," he began in a low voice.

"Every second." He reveled in the fire leaping to life in her eyes as she added, "Every day."

"Then take what you want, Ari."

Shifting sinuously closer, she wrapped her fingers around him, navy blue cotton and all.

The sensation was so glorious, he couldn't stop from bucking in her hand. Despite her inexperience, she instinctively stroked him from base to tip. And this time he wasn't the only one whose breath hitched with pleasure. She was such a gift. One he wasn't sure he'd ever done anything good enough to deserve.

So when he thought he saw insecurity flash across her face, he tipped his fingers under her chin to raise her gaze to his. "There's nothing you could do that I won't love."

She drew in her breath, held it, biting her lip. He wanted to bite it for her. "Feel what you to do me,

Ari."

God, the things she did to him.

She released her breath in a sweet sigh that washed over his mouth. He wanted to taste her again with a ferocity that burned in his gut. But Ari stole the thought right out of his brain as she slipped her hand inside his boxers, hot skin to hot skin.

Then she climbed on top of him, and he truly lost his mind.

Chapter Nine

Matt was like steel against her palm. Ari had never been an aggressor, yet with Matt she wanted to explore, test, savor. She wanted to do all the things she'd never even imagined until she'd met him.

Sitting astride him, her legs spread, her hand on his erection, she leaned across his chest and kissed him. As she used her body and hand to stroke him, he thrust his fingers into her hair and held her mouth to his, kissing her so deeply she felt as if she were falling right into him.

Before, sex had been physical, something she'd thought she wanted though it never turned out the way she dreamed. But Matt was a million times better than any dream. The hot, hard feel of his naked flesh in her hand, the taste of his mouth, his body rocking against her—it was all brand new. She'd never felt this needy before, as though her skin were on fire and her body molten. She'd never known desire like this. Only for Matt. He made her feel beautiful.

Even more, he made her *fearless*.

When they surfaced to breathe, she said, "I want to

see all of you."

His smile grew slowly, wickedly—like the devil who'd just won the temptation game. "Take what you want, Ari. *Anything* you want."

She all but tore off his boxers, then stilled at the sight of so much hot, hard flesh. "You're so big." Her voice dripped with awe. "So beautiful."

He laughed, the warm sound washing over her. "Are you sure that's the right word?"

"It's exactly the right word." She curled her fingers around him, so thick he almost didn't fit. Maybe she should have been frightened, but her arousal climbed higher, surpassing even the long, glorious minutes he'd used his tongue and fingers to play her body like a fine instrument. "*Beautiful.*"

She stroked his tip, rubbing a drop of moisture over him, before sliding down, down, down to his base. She loved the hiss of his breath, telling her the pleasure was as infinite as what he'd given her, and she couldn't wait another second to feel him inside her. She needed him to take her, to own her, body and soul.

As if he could read her mind, he rolled with her, his hips parting her legs, the muscles of his arms rippling as he held himself above her.

"*Mine.*" He slid his hand along her cleft, where she was slippery and hot for him. "Tonight you're all mine."

"*Yours,*" she echoed against his lips as their mouths found each other again.

Even as he kissed her, turning her wild inside, he was reaching into the bedside table for protection. Pushing himself off her, he slid it on, his eyes as hot as the erection in his hand, throbbing with a fever.

Fever for *her*.

His muscles taut as he leaned forward on one hand, he stroked her sex with the blunt tip. Electricity thrummed through her, too much, and she grabbed his arm to ground herself.

"So pretty," he murmured. "So perfect." He pressed a soft kiss to her shoulder. "Your skin." To the swell of her breasts. "Your body." Then back to her mouth where he murmured, "Your mind."

No one she'd ever gone to bed with had wanted her mind before, let alone someone as brilliant as Matt. She wanted to tell him how much that meant to her, that tonight was so much more than hot sex. So much more than a way to take his mind off the pain he'd suffered today.

But he was kissing her with such fire—and with the insistent friction of his shaft against her sensitive folds, he pushed her straight toward the bliss he'd given her twice already. Yet another ledge she wanted to jump from. Into ecstasy, into heaven.

With him this time.

"Please."

His eyes were midnight dark with desire. "I'm going to tease myself to death." He laced his words with a smile. "But I want you so ready you beg."

"I'm already begging." She hadn't known it was possible to need anyone this much.

"Not just with words." He stroked his fingers over her sex again. "With *all* of you."

Her body moved, matching his rhythm. Pressure built inside her as she rocked into him, against him, wrapping her arms and legs even tighter around him so that she could get as close as possible. And then he slid the thick tip of his shaft inside, and her breath stopped.

"Tell me, Ari." He held himself perfectly still over her, unmoving even as she was desperate for him to take her. *All* of her. "Tell me this is what you want."

"Yes. Please. God. More." She hoped she made sense, but the stars exploding before her eyes were stopping her synapses from firing properly. "I want more. I *need* more."

"You beg so exquisitely." Finally, he eased himself all the way in, every inch of hard heat he gave her making sensation burn hotter. More intensely. "*You* are exquisite."

⋆ ⋆ ⋆

Matt wanted to hold out, to push Ari further, to take her to places she'd never been. But she was so ready for him that he couldn't stop himself from thrusting hard and deep, over and over, until she was coming in another beautiful climax.

He groaned her name, clenching hard inside her as everything spilled out of him, all thought, all feeling.

There was just her taste on his lips, her scent ruling his head, her body gripping him tightly, owning him as much as he owned her in that moment.

Spinning out of control with pleasure beyond anything he'd ever dreamed possible, he took her mouth as deeply as he took her body, palming her face and plundering her, staking his claim.

Nothing had ever felt like this. Like heaven, like bliss, like beauty.

Like *Ari*.

He'd loved her wide eyes as he gave her sensual orders, their color deepening in the moonlight. There was sex, and then there was being totally engaged in the act, relishing every touch, every look, every breath. He sensed that in the past, she'd gone with the flow, acted upon rather than acting—but he'd refused to let her simply react to him.

He nuzzled her hair, and she murmured something indistinguishable, a satiated sound. He'd have to move soon before he grew too heavy on her, but for the moment, he wanted only to match his breath to hers, feel her skin along his, savor being inside her.

When they finally separated, it felt like losing a part of himself he'd only just found. But knowing they couldn't stay locked forever, he moved into the bathroom to dispose of the protection they'd used. By the time he returned, she'd fallen into the easy breathing of sleep.

Moonlight washed her features as smooth as a

sculpture. She looked so young that his chest clenched with renewed guilt.

But he'd allowed himself to have her just this once, and he wouldn't give up so much as a minute of their one night together, damn it. Pulling up the covers, he gathered her close and let himself relish every single second she was in his arms.

* * *

Ari woke in the dark knowing immediately that she was in Matt's bed, in his arms. Warm and safe.

Home.

If he'd sent her back to her room, the writing on the wall would have followed her all the way down the hall. But she was snuggled against him like a lover, not a one-night stand.

She'd always packed light and had gotten used to moving on, but that didn't mean she didn't love the times she got to stay. Lord knew she wanted to wake up beside Matt as the sun rose, and she fitted herself more deeply into his arms, playing light fingers over his chest, outlining his heart. He'd made her feel special, with his hands, his mouth, his body, his words. There had to be emotion or it was just sex. And what they'd done couldn't possibly be *just sex*.

His hand closed over hers, over his rapidly beating heart.

"Now you've done it," he murmured. "Woken the sleeping—"

"—giant," she finished.

"Are you ready for the consequences?" he asked in a teasingly sexy voice.

Not wanting to be coy or play games with him, she said, "I'm ready for anything with you."

That was all it took for him to pin her to the mattress with his body. God, how she loved his weight and his erection hard against her thigh, loved how his lips took hers, his tongue mimicking the way he'd taken her just hours before.

His fingers slipped and slid over her sensitive flesh, until she writhed beneath him and he groaned his own need against her mouth. "Ari." He kissed her deeply, passionately and fiercely, before her name fell from his lips again. "*Ari.*"

Another condom from the bedside table in his hand, he sat back. In the moonlight through his bedroom window, the sight of him was rich, like a feast with mouthwatering scents and tastes that made your eyes roll back in your head.

He tore open the packet. "Put it on me. I want to feel your hands driving me even crazier than I already am for you."

Never having put on protection before, she accomplished the task with slow precision. So slow that his breath quickened and his hands clenched. When she was finished, he hauled her up until she straddled his hips, her knees on either side of his.

"Take what you want, Ari."

It was an order. It was a plea. His words made her catch her breath, releasing another rush of need.

It was partly how he made sure the choice was hers, but his sensual commands were also who he was—a man who took control. And who also made sure that control spun out into boundless pleasure.

She kissed him hard as she slid down until he filled her completely. And this time, they moved with her rhythm, her pace, the control all hers. Until he cupped her hips to thrust deeper, and the world tipped sideways as they cried out together, two bodies fused into one.

Chapter Ten

Matt hadn't spent a whole night with a woman since Noah was born. Not since Irene had handed over his infant son and admitted she couldn't hack motherhood. *Sorry, I thought it would be fun.* But though it had gutted him to know that neither he nor their son had been enough for Irene, he also knew she wasn't cut out for such responsibility. She was like a butterfly who refused to be netted by a family. So he'd taken Noah and never looked back, swearing he'd be a better father than his dad had ever known how to be, a better parent than his mother had wanted to be. He became Noah's protector.

Women had come and gone since then, some lasting a few weeks, some only a night. But none of them stayed in his house or slept in his bed. He hadn't wanted Noah to get attached to someone who wasn't going to be around long. Not when they'd already had that with Irene.

But now there was Ari. And as much as he'd known he should send her back to her room—hell, that he should never have carried her into his bedroom in the first place—he hadn't been able to.

Not when the night had shifted into something he couldn't define. Something he'd desperately needed.

And not when he'd wanted to stay with her in the heart of pleasure, where nothing else mattered.

But now the sun was up—and the bright light screamed the difference between last night and today.

Damn it, he'd screwed up. Royally.

He'd wanted Ari so badly he couldn't think straight. Couldn't even remember that he'd brought her home for Noah, his number one priority. Matt's work, his inventions, his business—he'd throw them all away for his son. Just as he'd give up every penny in his bank account if it meant making Noah smile, hearing him laugh, bringing him joy.

But money had never brought any of those things. And lately, Noah laughed because of his beautiful, bright, talented nanny...

...who was making delicious little noises that started Matt's primal head thinking on its own. With sleepy, throaty sounds, maybe a moan, she rubbed sinuously against him in her sleep.

Sweet Lord, he wanted her again. He was *this close* to pulling her leg over his and taking her from behind, giving them both more of the most sinful pleasure he'd ever known. But he couldn't keep taking her, consequences be damned. She was here for Noah. She was only twenty-four to his thirty-four. She was wholesome, fresh, and innocent—and even though he wasn't her first, he'd still debauched her.

She'd kissed him in a gesture of comfort. And he'd let things blaze out of control.

Susan would have his head if she ever found out. Daniel would simply kill him. The Mavericks would disown him. And Matt would deserve it. He'd broken a solemn promise not to take advantage of Ari.

But even as his gut told him how wrong he'd been to take her the way he had, his heart shouted how right she'd felt in his arms, every single second of their lovemaking.

If only she wasn't working for him…

If only she wasn't Noah's perfect nanny…

If only he hadn't made that vow to Daniel and the Mavericks…

The worst would be Susan's disappointment in him. His family's disappointment. He was a Maverick, and a Maverick *never* broke a promise. It was his job to step up, to protect his son, his family, the people who worked for him. Instead, he'd stepped off a cliff.

And God help him, he'd loved every moment of his fall.

But no matter how much he wished it were otherwise, a man couldn't seduce his nanny without consequences, regardless of how rich and powerful he might be.

One hand fisted in the covers, he tugged them from the tangle of their legs. He wanted to be gentle, but they were so entwined that there was nothing gentle about it, no other choice but to throw them off. Then he damn near vaulted from the bed.

Where the hell were his jeans?

Awakened so abruptly, Ari stared at him, then sat up with the sheet clutched to her beautiful breasts, her hair a sexy mess that made him want to crawl right back in there with her.

The guilt choked him as he finally found his jeans and pulled them on commando. He made himself face her, so pretty, so perfect. So innocent. "I'm sorry. Last night was a mistake." The words fell from his lips before he could find a way to make them softer. Or less harsh. "I shouldn't have let that happen. It was entirely my fault. I took advantage."

Ari tipped her head to the side, and he wondered if she could hear the staccato beating of his heart. She wasn't the kind of woman who hid her emotions, but nor was she an open book.

Especially not when she replied with a far more even tone than his, "You didn't let anything happen. Nothing was your fault. And you didn't take advantage of me." She paused, her eyes holding his. "I wanted you, Matt."

Hearing his name on her lips made him remember every time she'd said it last night.

Every time she'd *moaned* it.

"I felt the same last night." He wouldn't lie to her, but he also needed to remind them both. "But you work for me, and I put you in a compromising position. It was wrong. And I apologize for doing that to you."

She blinked, but she never looked away. He wished he knew what was going on behind her pretty eyes. There were so many things she could do. Freak out. Cry. Quit.

Instead, she held out her hand. "Could you please hand me my clothes?"

The sight of her bare arm reminded him vividly of her creamy skin beneath his hands, her luscious scent fogging his mind. Just like that, he was hard again, his body crazy for her even when his brain knew it was a bad idea.

He didn't even want to consider what his heart wanted—or what it couldn't have where she was concerned. Because this was so damned wrong.

He found her leggings, her shirt, her lingerie, and the simple act of touching the pink panties and matching bra sent him deeper into overdrive. His hands shook as he handed over the bundle.

"I have to go in to the office this morning," he told her, shoving his hands in his pockets so he couldn't reach for her. "Testing." It was the truth, but it was also damned convenient under the circumstances.

"I'll get dressed."

Without an ounce of self-consciousness, she slipped out of bed, stepping into the pretty pink lingerie that made his mouth water. All that gorgeous skin, the breasts he'd cupped and tasted. *Everything* he'd tasted.

He wanted to drop to his knees and tell her he was an idiot to end things like this.

But he couldn't. For her sake, because she mustn't ever feel she had to sleep with her boss to keep her job. For Noah's sake, to keep the best nanny he'd ever had. And because Matt had promised his friends he'd never take advantage of her. He couldn't change last night, but he could make sure he never did it again.

She tugged on the leggings, then pulled the shirt over her head and flipped her long hair out. His fingers itched to run through the silky tresses. With a bone-deep desire that was almost crippling, he wanted to beg her to return to his bed, to never leave him.

But before he could drag either of them deeper into the mess he'd made, she gave him a soft smile. "I don't regret what happened last night."

"It isn't regret," he had to tell her, feeling like the lowest life form. Because, God help him, he couldn't bring himself to wish away a single thing they'd done. "It's just that I couldn't live with myself if we did anything more to compromise your relationship with Noah."

She gave him a look that made him wonder if she knew that reason was only the tip of the iceberg. But instead of pushing him on it, she simply said, "Noah and I will be fine. I promised I would take care of him, and I'll never break that vow." Brushing her hair back from her face, she added, "What we did wasn't wrong. And it wasn't your fault either, so stop feeling guilty.

There's nothing to worry about, okay? Now, I'll go get Noah up."

She stunned him. She was letting him off the hook for everything.

So why didn't he feel the least bit happy about it?

* * *

Last night, Matt had touched her so deeply, so intimately, that he'd actually rocked her world. Ari had never truly understood that saying until he'd literally knocked her world off its axis.

Only to apologize at first light and tell her it had been a mistake.

With her bone-deep sigh echoing in the hallway, Ari checked on Noah, who was still sleeping, before padding down the hall to her suite.

No matter what Matt believed, it wasn't a mistake. Not for her. But her mother always said men were different, that their emotions didn't get involved. Realizing that might be true for Matt hurt deep in Ari's heart, as if one of the valves had stopped working and she couldn't catch her breath.

I'm sorry. Last night was a mistake.

I shouldn't have let that happen.

It was entirely my fault.

I took advantage.

While she'd been painting rosy pictures of dreams coming true, he'd been getting ready to apologize. As though she were a schoolgirl taken advantage of by an older boy who wanted only one thing.

But Matt had wanted more than that, hadn't he? She'd sworn she felt it when he kissed her. When he stroked every inch of her. When he held her and made her cry out in ecstasy. When he told her he appreciated not only her body, but her mind too.

Ari stripped down, tossing her clothes on the bathroom floor. His scent was all over her, and she couldn't go to Noah smelling like sex with his father. Noah deserved her undivided attention, so she stepped under the dual hot sprays of the shower.

She'd remained calm in Matt's bedroom, but now, as she ran through everything in her head on an endlessly repeating loop, she couldn't help but worry—would he fire her? Was he afraid she couldn't let go, that she'd turn all stalkerish? That she'd tell Daniel?

She hoped he knew she wasn't that kind of person, that she'd never hurt him. He'd said they couldn't sleep together again, and she'd respect that. She was his kid's nanny, and she would never shirk that duty. Not even when her heart had broken in two as Matt stood awkwardly by the bed, his hands in his pockets.

Maybe she should spell it out. *Don't worry, I won't turn into a crazy one-night stand.* She didn't want to be fired, didn't want to leave Noah. Not when she could be so good for him.

I could be good for Matt too.

But he was off-limits now.

One day, when she fell in love, she wanted it to be

with a man who was good for her too. For a few precious hours, she'd thought Matt could be that man. But now she knew better: He didn't *want* to be that man.

Her chest ached deep inside as she stood beneath the hot needles of the shower spray. Good thing she had plenty of practice in getting over bumps in the road. Even the big ones.

Or else this morning would have destroyed her.

* * *

Ari and Noah ate breakfast together in the kitchen. Cookie loved to talk while she cooked or did the dishes. "Matt does not normally go to the office on Saturday. He always spends weekends with his boy."

But he wasn't here today, and Ari was all but certain he'd gone to the office to avoid her. She definitely needed to clarify her position when he returned, both from the personal and the job perspective. She'd also have to make sure he didn't continue to beat himself up with guilt over something she'd wanted with every cell of her body. She would never regret their one and only night together. Not when Matt had opened her eyes to how incredible lovemaking could be when it was with the right person.

Ugh. She couldn't keep going there. His use of the words *mistake*, *fault*, and *took advantage* had made everything perfectly clear.

"Can I have another waffle, Cookie?" Noah held up

his plate.

Cookie made thin waffles slathered with fresh homemade jam and big chunks of strawberry. She looked at Ari for permission.

"Let's share one more," Ari said. "Halfsies."

Noah bounced on the stool Ari had pulled up to the counter opposite Cookie. "Halfsies," he sang out.

Her heart ached with how much like his father he was—the cleverness, the eyes, the smile. But she vowed not to nurse her hurt. She'd learned long ago that things didn't always work out the way you wanted. People left you, forced you out of their houses, or tried to do bad things to you while you lived under their roof. But it was how you felt about everything that made you who you were. You either wallowed in misery...

...or you got over it and kept holding on to hope.

Ari might not give up her dreams, but she *would* get over having them crushed.

Deep in the night, she'd hug her memories of their beautiful night close to her heart, the touches, the kisses. But during the day, she'd be totally practical and realistic. From here forward, she'd never forget that Matt was just her boss. Period. End of subject.

"Let's go for a picnic," she told her little charge. She wanted the warmth of the bright autumn sun. "We can pack sandwiches." She glanced at Cookie. "If Cookie doesn't mind us using her kitchen." It would be good to have Noah do things for himself sometimes.

"Oh no. That is my job. I will make cheese and tomato sandwiches." Cookie's broad face lit with a smile. "I have a special basket to put my goodies in."

It would be ungracious to refuse, so Ari smiled her thank-you and plucked Noah off the stool, swung him high, then down to the floor. His hand in hers, they headed out to the stairs so she could get her tennis shoes. But they were stopped by a roar outside. A semi was backing through the gates into the wide driveway, just as a red sports car buzzed around it and jammed to a stop.

Noah dropped her hand and ran to the entrance hall, stretching on his toes to pull down the handle and swing open the front door. "Mommy!" He hurtled down the steps like a careening freight train, Ari's heart pounding its way up her throat to choke her.

Oh God, could there be a *worse* day to meet Matt's ex?

Even at the best of times, Ari wouldn't have been ready to compare herself to the bombshell who climbed ever so elegantly from the expensive, sporty car. But today of all days, when she was doing everything she could to rebuild her crushed heart…

The stunning woman scooped Noah into her embrace. He wrapped his legs around her waist as she cradled him lovingly against her hip and peppered his face with kisses. Her thick, dark hair was cut in a chic bob, her fashion-model figure draped with clothes Ari was sure had cost a year's salary.

Ari didn't want to be jealous. It was a totally wasted emotion when Matt wasn't with this woman anymore—and when he didn't want to be with Ari anyway. Plus, his ex seemed so in love with her little boy that it was honestly hard to find anything wrong with her.

The woman shaded her eyes from the sun. "Hello. Who are you? Another of Matt's nannies?"

Noah clung to his mother, laughing, giggling, joyful. Ari's chest squeezed tighter around her heart as she walked down the steps. "Yes, I'm Ari." She made herself smile. "Noah's new nanny."

"You must have guessed I'm Irene, Noah's mommy." She tipped the boy's face up and kissed his nose. "It's been ages, and I've been out of the country." Her voice dipped down into baby talk. "I just had to see my little man."

"It's so nice that you could stop by, but Matt's not home—"

"Good, then my timing is impeccable." Irene raised her brow in a perfect arch. "Matt always gets his shorts in a bunch when I bring my little boy a fabulous present." She looked down at Noah. "Do you want to see what it is?"

"Yes!" Noah squirmed in her arms, and she set him down, taking his hand.

Irene flourished her other hand at the two men who had climbed down from the semi's cab. "Open it up, boys," she called.

At Irene's command, they opened the back doors.

"What is it?" Noah strained to see inside.

"Wait and see," Irene told Noah, her mouth curved in a satisfied smile, as if she'd bought the present just for the effect.

It shouldn't have hurt to see his small hand in his mother's elegant, manicured fingers. This was what Ari wanted for all children—parents who loved them even if those parents weren't together. But this morning it reminded her of last night's dreams. And this morning's apology. Reminded her that she didn't really matter.

Because she was just the nanny.

Chapter Eleven

The two men pulled out a ramp and used dollies to roll down a massive round thing with metal legs that looked like an enormous beetle. Moments later, Ari recognized the beetle as a trampoline—one that would stand at least five feet off the ground.

"Take it through the side yard to the playground," Irene called. Noah ran after the men as they trundled the trampoline around the side of the house.

"Did you also order a mesh cage so Noah can't bounce off?" Ari had glanced into the truck as she'd passed. It was empty.

"A cage?" Irene's eyes were framed by thick lashes as she watched Noah, his body vibrating with eagerness as the men quickly set up the huge trampoline on the grass next to the sandbox. "You can't *cage* a little boy. They have to run free. Do you put him on a leash when you go to the park?"

Ari didn't dignify the question with a reply. Instead, she pointed out what any rational person would already have noticed. "That's a long way for a five-year-old to fall."

Irene *tsk*ed. "You'll keep him safe when you're up there with him. That's what Matt pays you to do, isn't it?"

"Yes, that's *exactly* what Matt pays me to do. Which is why there's *no way* I'm going to put Noah on a trampoline like that in the first place." Matt might worry too much, but in this, he would be perfectly justified. "It's too tall for him to even climb on."

Irritation flashed in Irene's big blue eyes. "There's a rope ladder. Besides, you can boost him up."

"No," Ari said emphatically. "Not without netting."

One of the men scrambled up and began jumping on the trampoline. Noah shouted in excitement. "Can I try, Mommy? Can I, can I?"

Before Irene could get out the word *yes*, Ari said, "No."

"I'll help him," Irene insisted. Thankfully, though, she wasn't exactly kicking off her heels and making a run for the trampoline.

"Not while I'm here." Ari would stick to Noah like glue if that meant keeping him safe from his mother's dangerous gift. "He could fall off before you had a chance to grab him." Ari pointed a finger at the delivery man, then jerked her thumb back, gesturing for him to get down. He rolled off the side, his heavy work boots thudding on the ground.

"Party pooper," Irene said. "You're just like Matt. He took away the skateboard I gave Noah last year. *And* the kiddie parachute I bought him. The canopy was a huge Superman."

"You gave Noah a *real* parachute?"

"Haven't you ever jumped out of a plane? There were kids out there jumping, and they had the best time. Free-falling is one of the most amazing sensations *ever.*" She sighed like she'd just had an orgasm.

But Ari couldn't imagine that free-falling had anything on making love with Matt.

Oh God, she couldn't be thinking like that, especially not around Matt's ex!

She turned her focus back to the issue at hand. "That's crazy. Children shouldn't be jumping out of airplanes."

"Spoilsport." Irene scrunched her nose. Even then she was stunning. "I can see you're the perfect nanny for Matt, just as overprotective as he is. And here I thought he only hired you because you're cute. Come on, if you're so worried about Noah, we can both get on the trampoline with him."

Working to ignore how insulting the word *cute* had sounded, as though Ari were nothing more than a new pet meant to entertain the family, she reiterated, "Not without a net."

"I'm his mother."

"And I'm his nanny, hired by his custodial parent."

Irene sighed. "All right, Mary Poppins, you win."

Ari hunkered down in front of Noah, who looked like his world had just ended. "It's too big for you, honey. You could bounce off and land on your head."

She smoothed her fingers over the bandage on his forehead. Irene hadn't even asked about it.

"But I wanna try," he whined.

"Don't you worry." Irene swung him up in her arms and marched back to her car. "I thought your daddy might be too much of a stick in the mud to let you have fun with the trampoline, so I brought you plenty of other prezzies."

"Ma'am, you gotta sign."

"Put it right back on the truck," Ari said, ignoring the clipboard the man held out.

"No can do, ma'am. You gotta talk to the store about returns."

"Then have *her* sign for it." Ari nodded at Irene.

Ari had always assumed that having a loving parent meant everything would be okay. But for the first time she realized things were more complicated than that. Because while Irene clearly loved her son, that didn't necessarily mean she was good for him. Not when she seemed to bring just as much recklessness and instability with her as she did adoration and love.

* * *

After they'd carried the seemingly endless number of boxes and bags into Noah's playroom, Irene ordered coffee, which Cookie brought, accompanied by pretty bone china cups and coffee cake on matching flowered plates. Ari apologized to Cookie, saying they wouldn't need the picnic lunch, and got a knowing smile in return, as if she was used to Irene's unannounced visits. Noah wolfed down cake with a milk chaser, then dove on yet another present.

"No," Ari said for what felt like the millionth time when he unearthed an array of firecrackers in a bag that read *Catalonia*. Talking with Irene was like saying no to a child over and over.

"But I got them in this marvelous town in Spain. They have a wonderful tradition—"

"I'm sorry, Noah," Ari said. "Those are really dangerous." Seeing that he was on the verge of a tantrum—heck, Ari felt like having a tantrum herself—she added, "Why don't you build a giant's castle out of the new Legos your mommy brought you?"

Thankfully, she was able to divert him before the explosion. But Irene wasn't at all diverted from her purpose. "You really are a Mary Poppins, aren't you? I didn't mean Noah should set off the fireworks all by himself. You and Matt can help him. Before we had Noah, it's just the sort of exciting thing Matt would have *loved* to do with me."

Ari tried to ignore the implication about all the other exciting things Matt had loved to do with Irene. And really, no matter what she thought of the woman—or how much her heart clenched inside her chest—she couldn't pretend his ex wasn't stunningly beautiful. What man wouldn't want to do exciting things with Irene? And for more than just one stolen night...

"If we'd ever gotten married," Irene continued, "I would have made sure we had the most incredible fireworks show."

"You two were never married?" Ari couldn't keep the surprise from her voice.

Irene flapped her hand. "God forbid. Matt's adorable and"—she fluttered her eyelashes—"we're still *such* good friends." She winked as if to make it perfectly clear just how deep that friendship still ran. "Even with the baby coming along, I wasn't ready for marriage. But I thought having a baby would be such fun." She widened her eyes dramatically. "I just didn't realize they were so much *work*. And I got so bloated and ugly." She grimaced. "I couldn't do *anything* fun anymore." Then she smiled brightly. "The baby shower was a blast, though. Even if all the presents were for the baby." She planted her hand on her chest. "I'm an absolutely *terrible* mother. Matt's so much better at the whole parenting thing." She waved with a flourish.

Ari had the uncharitable thought that the gesture was just like the Wicked Witch. But Irene wasn't really wicked. She was just…careless and thoughtless. After spending less than sixty minutes with her, it was obvious that having fun was more important to her than actually raising a child.

Ari's mother had had nothing and Irene had everything, but still Ari saw the similarities: Fun was the most important thing to Irene, just as the next fix had been more important to Ari's mom than keeping food in the fridge or taking care of her kids.

"It's so much better for Noah this way, don't you think?" Irene looked at Ari as if she expected her to actually agree that leaving her child was a good thing.

"Mommy, come help me."

Noah already knew how to build the blocks on his own. He had his father's inventive spirit, and he could follow the instructions. But he obviously wanted his mother's attention.

And Irene was good at giving a few moments of bright and cheerful attention, even if she was as terrible at being a full-time mother as she said. She lay on her stomach on the floor beside him, propped her elbows, and began sorting through bits and pieces, reading instructions, and making Noah the center of her world. He soaked up all that love, laughing, playing, enjoying.

"We went to the zoo last week," Noah told her, recounting all the animals they'd seen in Oakland.

"That sounds like such fun." The tiny frown creasing Irene's forehead made Ari think she was a little jealous that her son had had fun with someone else. "In fact, let's go to the zoo in San Francisco this afternoon just as soon as we're done building your new castle. They have the most marvelous gorillas there. Ari, could you please arrange that for us?"

Ari nodded, texting Doreen to ask her to please have the car ready in the next hour or so for a trip to the San Francisco Zoo. Noah and his mother talked about everything Noah had done with Ari in the past week, and Irene made plans for all the things they would do not only this afternoon at the zoo, but also the next time she visited, which she assured him would be in a couple of weeks.

Matt should have told her Noah's mother stopped by every two weeks. Warned her, anyway. But maybe if Irene was a little jealous of the fun things Noah had done with Ari, she might come around more often.

In any case, Ari knew she needed to stop judging Irene. Yes, there were some obvious lapses in her judgment. And she could be a bit condescending with "the help," as Ari and Cookie so clearly were to her. But at the same time, she was very sweet with Noah, listening to his chatter as though it had the potential to rearrange mountains or bring world peace, while she handed him pieces and praised him for the absolutely amazing, fantabulous job he was doing. Ari's heart lit up seeing the glow on Noah's face, the joy brimming in his eyes and bubbling over in his voice.

A cell phone rang from deep within Irene's ginormous, expensive leather purse. "Can you toss me my phone?"

After witnessing Noah's joy, Ari barely even resented being cast as Irene's personal assistant. She rummaged down into the expensive bag, searching for the phone's lighted dial and the source of the old Blondie song *Call Me*, then handed it over to Irene.

"Angela, honey, talk to me. It's been ages."

Propped on her elbows, the phone to her ear, Irene crossed her legs at the ankles, swinging them back and forth, flashing the red soles of her shiny black high heels while Noah plugged away at the giant's castle. Some of his glimmer died as he lost her focused attention.

"Yes, I'm in California, so of course you should count me in. I wouldn't miss it for the world!" Irene flipped her wrist to look at her watch. "I have to pack and shower and make myself gorgeous, but I can do it." She listened, nodding. "Send your driver. I have no desire to manage the drive to SFO on my own. You're a doll. Smooches." Hanging up, she flopped over on the carpet, then rolled into a cross-legged position. "You are *not* going to believe this." She waited until she had both Ari's and Noah's complete attention. "Angela got an invite to a private fashion extravaganza with three of *the* top designers. In Paris. This will be epic." She clapped her hands. "We're taking her daddy's personal jet." She patted Noah's cheek. "I have to run, sweetie. But we'll do all those fun things we talked about when I get back. Promise." She leaned in, offering him her cheek. "Give Mommy a smooch."

"But I want you to see the castle." His lower lip trembled, and Ari saw tears glimmering. "And we were going to the zoo."

"Oh honey-bunny, I wish I could, but I've got to pack and shower. So many things to do before Paris." As if she'd only just noticed her son's impending tears, she cupped his chin. "I'd take you with me, but you know your daddy would hate that."

Ari's hackles rose like a mama bear protecting her young. Irene had given Noah exactly an hour and a half. Ninety minutes of love and attention before the timer dinged. But getting into a battle in front of Noah would make things worse.

Irene rolled to her feet, smoothed her designer outfit, then held out her hand to Noah. "Walk me to my car so you can give your mommy a big good-bye kiss."

Ari could see how much self-control it took the five-year-old boy to blink back his tears before he scrambled to his feet and took his mother's hand. Outside, Irene hauled him up in her arms and covered his face with more kisses, while Noah threw his arms around her neck, hugging tightly as though he'd never let go.

After less than sixty seconds—Ari couldn't help but count silently in her head—Irene pried him off. "Run to your nanny. She'll help you finish building your toy."

He stood staring at his mother for a long moment before finally trudging back to Ari's side. For the first time, he didn't reach for her hand, and when she bent down to take his, it was limp.

Irene climbed into the car, blowing kisses. "I'll be back soon. We'll do the zoo. Promise. Love you. 'Bye!"

Ari remembered the trampoline too late, and before she could remind Irene to have the store pick it up, Matt's ex was gone with a squeal of tires as the sporty red car roared through the front gates, like a hurricane blowing through and leaving its wreckage behind.

"It's not too late," she told Noah. "We still have time for that picnic Cookie was going to make us."

"I don't want to go," he grumbled, his mouth in a frown as he stared down the empty drive.

"Okay. Then why don't we finish the castle so your dad can see it when he gets home?"

"I hate the castle." He scuffed his shoe on the drive. "Why wouldn't Daddy let me go if Mommy wanted me to?"

There was no way Ari could explain to the little boy that Irene would never take him on a trip like that, because no matter how well behaved he was, he would get in the way of her fun. Ari was beyond fumed that Irene had the nerve to blame it on Matt.

She knelt in the driveway. "It's very hard for little boys to pick up and go like that. You have school on Monday. And your mommy will be very busy with all her designer friends."

His lip trembled again. "But she was going to take me to the zoo."

"I know." A bubble of anger rose up in Ari's throat, and she had to work to swallow it. She didn't say that he and his mom would do it next time, because she didn't believe Irene would actually follow through. For Irene, there would always be something sparkly and new that took precedence over Noah. "We'll think of something fun to do instead."

He jerked his hand out of hers. "No!" he shouted, stamping his foot. "It's not fair. I want to go with her. I want to bounce on the bouncy thing. Daddy isn't nice to me! And neither are you!" He ran up the steps into the house, slamming the front door behind him.

Ari double-cursed Irene. And by the time she got to the playroom, Noah had blown through, kicking the castle apart. She climbed the stairs to his room to find him curled in a ball on his bed. She sat beside him, but he rolled away, giving her his back.

"Everything's going to be okay," she whispered. It was the same thing she'd told his father less than twenty-four hours ago. The same thing she'd told herself this morning, even as her heart continued to ache.

"It's not." He sniffled and sobbed, his arm over his face. "Why doesn't she like me?"

She was close to tears herself. "Oh, sweetheart, of course she likes you. She loves you." But what excuse was she supposed to give for the way Irene had behaved? "She's just so busy." And careless and thoughtless. And downright cruel. "She loves you, sweetheart. As much as your daddy does." Then she added what was already in her heart. "As much as I do."

All her words did was make him sob harder, hiccupping with his distress.

Knowing he needed to get it out, she let Noah cry, rubbing his back, until finally he fell asleep. And all the while her heart broke for him, for the mother he wanted and could never have. She knew about wanting your mom to be someone you could count on—wanting it even when you knew it was never going to happen.

Her heart broke for Matt too. She was sure that every time Irene visited Noah, it ended like this—in tantrums, stamping feet, and tears. How helpless and powerless Matt must feel.

Just as helpless and powerless as Ari felt against her growing feelings for Noah's father, who had made all of her dreams come true for a few precious hours in the dark.

Chapter Twelve

Matt went straight to the playroom when he got home from the lab. He tried to spend weekends at home with Noah, but with the new product Trebotics International was releasing at the end of the month, the quality inspection this morning couldn't wait. He'd hoped his absence would make things easier with Ari too, giving them both a few hours to think straight about what they'd done last night and accept that it could never happen again.

Only, he hadn't been able to push her into a corner of his mind any more than he'd been able to keep from taking her to his bed last night. Every other thought was of how beautiful, how soft, how sweet—and how sexy—she'd been.

You can't have her, he reminded himself. *Last night can never happen again.*

But all it took was one smile from Ari, seated beside Noah on the playroom floor, for Matt's heart to stutter in his chest. In the sunlight through the window, her hair a fiery gold, she was the angel he'd seen by the fountain during the unveiling of Charlie's sculpture.

He'd used the excuse of work to walk away from her this morning, but now he was all out of excuses. He knelt on the carpet beside them and a gazillion Lego pieces, finally noting that Noah hadn't looked up, not even to say hi. "What are you working on, buddy?"

"Nothing." His son's voice was sullen.

Matt's gut twisted again with fear as well as guilt. "Is everything all right after yesterday?" he asked Ari, his pulse racing. Could a concussion bring on mood swings? Had the doctor diagnosed his injury correctly?

"He just woke up from a nap. He's still sleepy. Right, Noah?" She reached out a hand, and Noah flinched. The movement was slight, but Matt was hyperaware after yesterday's fall.

"You don't usually take naps anymore," he said to his son.

Noah shrugged and kept robotically plugging parts into his latest creation. Matt frowned. Something was definitely off. But if it wasn't yesterday's fall, then what?

Ari moved gracefully to her feet. "I'll get your dad some coffee, okay, Noah? We'll be right back." She gave Matt a penetrating stare and gestured for him to join her.

By the time he met her in the kitchen, Matt had finally guessed the problem. "Irene was here, wasn't she?" He recognized the signs, and they tore him up inside, knowing exactly what Noah was feeling.

Ari pursed her lips. "Yes. I didn't want to talk about it in front of Noah."

He swore under his breath. "Tell me what happened." Every beat of his heart felt like a nail driving deeper.

Closing her eyes briefly, she shook her head. It was the kind of gesture everyone made after Irene descended on them like an atomic bomb. "She brought him Legos, firecrackers, and a trampoline."

"*Firecrackers*?" Even for Irene, that was crazy.

"The trampoline is outside. I wouldn't let him use it, and he's upset. It's not child-size, and there's no net." She sighed. "But we were getting over that. Until Noah's mother got a call inviting her to Paris for a fashion show right *after* they'd made plans to go to the zoo together this afternoon. She had to leave right away to catch her plane, so no zoo."

Between Noah's accident yesterday and the huge mistake he'd made with Ari, Matt had already been on edge. If Irene had been standing in front of him, he would have yelled until she was reduced to tears, no matter how many times he swore he'd never do that. She flitted in, created an uproar, then flitted out again, leaving him to pick up the pieces.

Leaving was the only thing about her that he could count on.

And Noah was like Humpty-Dumpty, who couldn't be put back together again.

"I'm sorry," Ari said. "I didn't realize how upset

he'd be. Poor guy cried himself to sleep. He thinks she doesn't love him."

Jesus, it killed him that he couldn't figure out how to protect Noah from his own mother. Matt had never wanted his child to feel unloved or unwanted the way he had. But Irene never stuck around to see the aftermath of what she'd done, and when he told her, she simply rolled her eyes and said Noah seemed perfectly happy.

"Don't apologize," he told Ari, his voice gruff as he worked to contain his fury at his ex. "It's not your fault. I should have warned you about Irene." But he barely wanted to admit his terrible choice in girlfriends to himself, let alone tell his new nanny. Especially when he'd been lusting after Ari despite knowing better.

Yet she had clearly handled the whole situation well, calming Noah down enough to play with his Legos. Sometimes it took days for what he'd dubbed The Irene Effect to wear off.

"Actually, that's not all." He braced himself as she said, "She told Noah the reason she couldn't take him to Paris was because you wouldn't let him go with her."

Damn Irene. "I need to mend fences with Noah." He ran his hand through his hair. Because while he needed to deal with the mess Irene had left, that didn't mean he could use it as an excuse to avoid Ari. She deserved better than that. "We need to talk about Irene after Noah's in bed. About last night too." He paused, trying to read her expression, but couldn't get a better handle on what she was feeling than he had that morning. "Is that okay?"

"Yes," she said softly. "I'll leave you two alone for now."

The last time he'd talked with her after Noah had gone to bed, he'd lost control. Ari was pure temptation. But tonight he vowed not to touch her. He wouldn't beg to kiss her. He wouldn't remember the softness of her skin or how sweet she tasted.

No matter what.

Not even if he lost his mind trying.

⋆ ⋆ ⋆

Thankfully, Noah settled down by dinner, and at story time Ari was hugely relieved to see him reading with his father as though nothing had ever happened. She marveled at how quickly—and deeply—the little boy had burrowed into her heart. His happiness mattered to her big-time.

It was unimaginable that Irene had chosen to give up Matt and her beautiful son for the freedom to hop private planes and attend fashion shows in Paris. Ari would have done *anything* to have a family like them.

Once Noah had fallen asleep, Matt and Ari headed downstairs together to talk. In the living room, he gestured to the sofa while he went to the sideboard. "Would you like something to drink? A glass of wine?" he asked as he poured himself a finger of scotch.

"White, please."

"I should have explained about Irene." He was obviously more ready to tackle the subject of his ex than what they'd done last night. "But she hasn't been here for months. I wasn't even sure she'd show up again."

Ari hated how carefully he avoided brushing her fingertips as he handed her the glass.

"You deserve to know what happened so you understand how it affects Noah when she drops in."

"He was so sad it broke my heart," she said softly.

"That's what I hate." He rolled the glass in his hand, and despite knowing better, she couldn't help but want to be the glass, his hands all over her, heating her. "Nothing I say makes it better. You really helped today, Ari. He doesn't normally recover so quickly."

"A five-year-old shouldn't need to *recover* from his mother's visit." Maybe she was speaking out of turn, but she understood only too well how hard it was when a parent acted carelessly with your feelings.

He set his glass on the side table, elbows on the arms of the wingback chair, and steepled his fingers. "When she found out she was pregnant, she thought it was a 'total gas.'" He laughed without an ounce of humor. "I would have married her for the baby's sake, but Irene wanted to wait and see how things went."

Ari curled her feet up under her, propped her chin on her hand, and sipped her wine. She wanted to put her arms around him, to erase the pain that laced every word of his story. But after this morning, when he'd made it perfectly clear what a huge mistake their lovemaking had been, she didn't dare touch him.

All she could do was ache.

* * *

Matt didn't say that Irene had initially wanted to terminate the pregnancy and he'd talked her out of it. He only said, "She was pretty cavalier about the whole thing." He stared at his glass on the table beside him. "She did have some fun with the attention the pregnancy brought."

"Until she had the baby shower and all the presents were for Noah instead of her."

He snorted an abrupt laugh. "That's Irene. Admitting things like that doesn't even bother her."

"At least she's honest about who she is, I suppose."

He was impressed at how much Ari had already figured out. "She told me right up front that she'd make a crappy mother. She bitched and moaned when I said she couldn't drink or have the occasional cigarette. But she gave them up for the duration."

Maybe he'd told Ari enough already, but he'd never really talked about this with anyone before. Not even the Mavericks—at least, not beyond the basics. Susan and Bob knew more, but they were worriers, so he was careful to edit with them too. Ari, though… Ari was different. He got the feeling she understood in a way no one else ever had.

"We met at a Silicon Valley party. I'd started Trebotics." He'd made his first few million, and he'd reshaped himself physically and mentally from the weakling his father had believed him to be. "She was young, only twenty-three. And she made me feel young too." He'd had women before Irene, but she was so fun-loving that she made him want to be fun-loving too. "She never took anything seriously, and for someone like me who took *everything* seriously, it was…different."

Irene was a slap in the face to everything his parents had taught him—which in retrospect was probably a big part of her allure. His father would have said she was worthless and flighty and Matt was ruining himself by taking up with her. Though his father was gone by then, dead of a massive coronary during Matt's first year in college, being with her still felt like he was getting one up on his dad.

But the Irene he'd thought he wanted turned out to be an illusion. She loved her fun to the point that she had no sense of responsibility. She was caring until she forgot about a friend and snubbed her for another. She lived on the surface of life without any deep thoughts or deep feelings.

"When she found out she was pregnant, I realized I wanted my son more than anything. So I was willing to take her too. But when the baby came along, she decided he wasn't any fun—crying, needy, wanting to be held all the time. Noah was a month old when she handed him over to me." He should have known Irene would never last, but he'd actually been shell-shocked—partly because he had no clue how to take care of a baby either. He'd asked when she'd be back and her answer was simply, *I don't know*, accompanied by a careless shrug of her shoulders. Whatever trust there'd been between them had died in that moment. Because it wasn't just his son who wasn't enough for Irene. It was Matt. And that destroyed his final thread of hope that he'd one day have a real love like Bob and Susan had.

"I've been trying to understand her," Ari said, with a frown that indicated she wasn't getting very far. "Thank God Noah had you. A lot of kids have no one."

"I wish I could be enough for him," he said in a low tone. "But every time she flits in for an hour or two, then suddenly discovers something more 'important' to do, he ends up feeling like he doesn't matter. Sometimes I think he'd be better off if she were gone forever." He could feel his teeth grinding. He always kept his emotions under control and lost his cool only when his son was threatened, by a nanny or a bully or a bully's mother. But Irene made him want to break his vow to keep his cool in every situation. "She comes back just often enough to keep Noah on her hook."

Ari reached out, then just as quickly retreated, dropping her gaze. It was obvious she wanted to offer comfort.

She couldn't know how badly Matt needed that comfort, how much he wanted to wrap himself around her and breathe in her scent like a calm breeze washing over him.

* * *

The room had grown darker and more intimate the longer they talked. Matt was only a touch away. But no matter how badly she wanted to, Ari couldn't touch, not even when his pain for Noah was like a physical wound in her own body. She hurt for Matt as well, for the hopes he'd had five years ago and the dreams that had died.

"I can't believe she actually brought him firecrackers and a trampoline," he said. "But the Superman parachute is still the ultimate. All I can think is that she wants him to be a daredevil like she is."

Ari could almost see him shudder at the thought. Matt's biggest fear was that something bad would happen to his son, but while she obviously wanted Noah to be safe, little kids still needed to run free and try new things. Which meant they were going to get hurt sometimes.

"Maybe a little daredevil isn't so bad," she said gently. Before Matt could object, she explained, "I don't mean jumping out of planes and lighting firecrackers in the backyard. Just small things like learning some tricks on a scooter. Or a pogo stick." She thought about the water wings that hampered Noah when he was swimming, but decided this still wasn't the right time to bring that up. Not tonight.

Picking up his tumbler, Matt swirled the liquid. "He begged to see *Jurassic World*, but I should have known he'd be terrified of the dinosaurs. The only reason he wants to try the daredevil stuff is to impress Irene. He wants her to love him so badly that he'll do anything, and I want so badly to protect him from turning himself inside out for her."

Matt was so kind, so loving, and such a great dad—even if he was sometimes as overprotective as Irene was careless. Ari wanted to climb onto his lap and wrap her arms around him, feel him close and warm and solid against her.

Instead, all she could say was, "Being scared of roaring dinosaurs gobbling up people isn't the same as wanting to try things like the trampoline." Though Noah could probably do more than his dad would let him. "I was terrified of the flying monkeys in *The Wizard of Oz* when I was a kid."

"You were afraid of the monkeys, not the witch?"

"They had big, awful grins."

"For me it was *Natural Born Killers*."

She gaped. "Your parents let you watch *Natural Born Killers*?"

He shrugged. "My dad said you had to be tough to get along in this world. My mom agreed with him."

"That's crazy. How old were you?"

"I was twelve." He grimaced. "In reality, it's probably not any worse than a lot of video games. It was just seeing it up there on the big screen."

She could see that he was trying to move them beyond the specter of *Natural Born Killers*, but Ari still thought it was crazy to take a kid, even a twelve-year-old, to see a couple cut a bloody swath across middle America.

She might not be able to wrap her arms around him, but she could make sure he heard the truth. "You're doing a great job, Matt. No matter what else happens, Noah will always know how much you love him."

He stared at her for long moments before he finally said, "Thank you for being so good with him under difficult circumstances."

She blushed at his praise. And the way he looked at her. As if there was more he needed to say. More he wanted to *do*.

God, how she longed to be in his arms, where nothing else mattered but how much pleasure they could give each other. And where she'd finally felt like she mattered.

It was long past time to shift the conversation to what they'd done together the night before. It might feel easier in the short term just to ignore it, but she couldn't let it fester between them—and he obviously didn't want that either, since he'd brought it up earlier.

"About last night—"

He held up a hand. "I can't apologize enough for what I did."

Frustration ate at her. Didn't he see that she'd been

a totally willing partner in their lovemaking? And that he hadn't coerced her into anything?

In a deliberately measured voice, she said, "As I mentioned before, it wasn't just you. *I'm* the one who kissed you first last night. And I won't regret what we did." A muscle jumped in his jaw as he listened, and she had to wonder if he might be equally frustrated. "In any case," she made herself continue, "I want to reassure you that what happened between us hasn't changed anything about my dedication to Noah or this job."

He looked distinctly uncomfortable. "I know you'd never walk away from us." He grimaced as if he'd said the wrong thing. "From Noah, I mean. And I'm the one who needs to reassure you. You should know how much I want you to be Noah's nanny. Last night didn't change that."

She swallowed hard, working to keep her emotions leashed as she nodded to let him know she understood. Last night he'd told her how much he wanted *her*, and not just for his son. Twenty-four hours later, they were back to square one.

The only square they were allowed to stand in, it seemed.

The silence lay heavily between them before he finally broke it. "It's late. I should let you go to bed." The word *alone* hung unspoken in the air. "Good night, Ari."

She'd known from the start that fantasies were all

she could ever have, so she made herself say, "Good night, Matt," and walk away.

* * *

Matt poured himself another finger of scotch. He didn't need it, but if he didn't do something with his hands and mouth, he'd follow Ari upstairs and put them all over her.

He couldn't believe he'd told her about *Natural Born Killers*. What the hell must she think of him now, after Irene had descended like a phantom of all that could go wrong—and then he'd started spilling about his parents?

It had been his birthday. Matt had wanted to see *The Mask* with Jim Carrey. He remembered sitting in that movie theater with his parents, his eyes squeezed shut against all the blood, the casual death, and he'd actually been ashamed. His dad had punched his arm hard when he realized Matt's eyes were closed, and hissed, "I'm not wasting all that money on a movie for you to sit there with your eyes closed, ya little weenie." His father continued to pinch him every time he thought Matt's eyes were closed.

Sissy. Weenie. You could learn a lesson here about sticking up for yourself.

And while his mother hadn't said a word, she'd closed her eyes during all the gore too.

She'd died of cancer a couple of years ago. He'd paid for her care, her hospital bills, and for the house payments after his father's death—but she'd never asked Matt's forgiveness for the role she'd played in his upbringing. A mother's job was to protect her children, but she hadn't even tried. She'd never even asked to meet Noah. On her deathbed, she'd laid claim to turning Matt into the man he was—how everything they'd said, everything they'd done had toughened him up, prepared him for life, for success.

But the only thing they'd prepared him for was *survival.* He'd somehow managed to survive his parents, but it was Susan and Bob who'd prepared him for life, who'd hugged him the way his parents never had. After that birthday, he'd stayed at Daniel's more frequently. He'd never actually moved in—his father would never let him go—but more often than not, he was underfoot at the Spencers'. And the Mavericks had become his family.

He was blessed to have Noah and the Mavericks and Susan and Bob. He'd betrayed not only Ari's trust by taking her to bed, he'd also betrayed his family's trust in him to do the right thing.

What's more, Ari was sweet, kind, and so good for Noah. So no matter how badly Matt wanted her, he couldn't afford to lose her by crossing that line with her.

Ever again.

Chapter Thirteen

Sunday was Cookie's day off, as well as Ari's. But instead of heading out right away to see her friends, Ari ate breakfast with Matt and Noah.

"Can I break the eggs?" Noah was asking Matt at the stove as Ari pushed through the swinging door.

"I don't want you to get too close to the stove in case the bacon fat spits on you. Why don't you sit at the counter with Ari?"

Noah climbed up beside her, and she pushed the pitcher to him so he could pour himself a glass of juice. She half expected Matt to say the juice pitcher was too heavy for him. Noah clearly wanted to help, and he could have broken the eggs without getting anywhere near the bacon. But Matt tended to be overly cautious.

She chatted with Noah about his favorite cartoon, while Matt drained the bacon and scrambled the eggs. Then he finally sat at the counter beside them.

"Do you have big plans for the day?" he asked in a voice that was far too polite, especially considering how intimate they'd been.

She told herself she'd eventually get used to it. After her heart mended.

But not only were they acting as if Friday's lovemaking had never happened, Noah didn't say a word about his mother either, as though there'd been no visit from Irene yesterday. Ari had even removed the bandage from his forehead. New day, new attitude. If it didn't feel right that they were all shoving too much under the rug...well, Ari shoved that feeling under the rug too.

"I'm going to visit Rosie and Jorge."

"Jorge's fun," Noah said as he pushed his scrambled eggs around his plate as though he were excavating.

"Sounds like a great day."

She hated how forced Matt's smile seemed. God, any minute now they'd start talking about the weather.

"What about you two?" she asked.

Matt looked at Noah. "We'll figure something out. Whatever we do, at least we've got great weather, don't we?"

She barely held in her wince at his mention of the weather as Noah nodded, then shoveled his eggs onto his fork and chewed with big bites.

She wanted to make suggestions for them. And she wanted to go with them. But she wasn't family—she was just the nanny.

After finishing her eggs, she laid her napkin on the table. "Thanks for breakfast. Can I help with the dishes?"

Matt waved her offer away. "Don't worry. I'll handle it. Enjoy your day."

When he didn't ask her to change her plans to hang out with them instead, a sharp pang in her chest said she wasn't totally in control of her dreams. All those times she'd let go of foster families or old boyfriends hadn't actually been all that hard. But with Matt…

She sighed. After they'd made love, after he'd made her feel like she mattered, it turned out that letting Matt go wasn't easy at all.

Get a grip, Ari. After all, she'd walked into his arms with her eyes wide open, hadn't she?

She kissed the top of Noah's head and forced herself to smile at Matt as she waved good-bye. In the huge garage, as she unlocked the door of her ancient car, the shiny frame of Noah's bicycle caught her eye, the training wheels on the back. Behind it was the mountain bike.

She needed a distraction to take her mind off her one and only night with Matt. And Noah needed a distraction to take his mind off his mom. What better way than learning to ride his bike without the training wheels? They could surprise Matt after Noah had mastered it. It might help him reevaluate his position on the water wings or letting Noah help cook breakfast or…heck, any number of things.

And it might end her fixation on how seductively her sexy boss kissed. Because she needed to concentrate on being the best nanny Noah had ever had. Even better than Mary Poppins.

★ ★ ★

Ari had been here only one week. How was it possible that the house could feel empty without her? Matt had itched to ask her to spend the day with them, but he'd have driven himself to the edge of insanity keeping his hands—and mouth—off her all day long. Hell, he'd barely been able to sleep last night. It had taken all his willpower not to walk down the hall and beg her to come back to his bed, back into his arms. Back to the place where everything finally felt *right*, if only for a few precious hours in the dark.

No question about it, she was worth a beating from his brothers. But it was Susan's gaze he couldn't face if she knew he'd taken his nanny to bed, abusing the trust of his employee.

"So, buddy, what shall we do today?"

"The zoo." A pout hinted on Noah's mouth.

Ari had mentioned Irene's broken promise. There were obviously residual effects of her casual thoughtlessness.

"I haven't been to the zoo in ages." He always tried to do something fun with Noah on their weekends together. "I heard about a great place close by from a guy at work. With a puppet theater and a petting zoo. You can even talk to the parrots. How does that sound?"

"Fun!" Noah's eyes bugged with excitement.

"I just need to drop off some work papers on the

way, okay?"

Half an hour later, they were in the car. Doreen had the day off, and he enjoyed driving Noah himself. He had the guilty thought that it would have been so damn sweet with Ari beside him, leaning between the seats to inspire Noah with endless questions or comments, teaching him with everything she said and did.

Wending their way through surface streets to reach the San Jose office, Noah chattered about school, the mummy museum, meeting Ari's friend and her son. He was glad Noah was distracted, because the neighborhood wasn't the best. He was pretty sure he saw a drug deal going down in an alleyway, and an inappropriately dressed lady attempting to attract business, even on a Sunday morning.

He'd seen worse in his old Chicago neighborhood. A stabbing or a shooting on a Friday night was common. But when Noah came along, he'd realized the true importance of having made it out of that life. His mission was to make sure his son never lived the kind of childhood Matt had, the kind of life all the Mavericks had experienced. If not for Susan and Bob, he didn't know where they'd all be. The Mavericks were his blood brothers. But Susan and Bob had been their heart.

Turning a corner, he almost hit the brakes. Golden-blond hair, skinny jeans, and an innately sensual walk that stopped his heart—he'd know that rear view anywhere.

What the hell was Ari doing *here*?

She stopped at a corner apartment building, its flaking paint faded to gray and the awning ready to fall off its struts. His foot unconsciously lifted off the accelerator, and the car slowed as she opened the outer door and disappeared inside.

This was where her friend lived?

This was where she'd brought Noah?

It couldn't be. She'd vowed to keep his son safe, and he trusted her to keep that promise. Ari wouldn't bring Noah here. So what was up? Had she lied about where she was going? Maybe she planned to meet up with a man instead of her friends.

After what they'd done Friday night, Matt's mind twisted imagining another man's hands on her, another man's lips covering hers…

"Daddy?"

Damn it. He'd stopped paying attention to Noah. "Yeah, buddy?"

"Do parrots bite?"

"We'll find out today." His son was priority number one, not what had happened with Ari the other night. But he still couldn't strip the image of her with another man from his mind—or the jealousy that knifed deep into his gut.

Because even if he couldn't have her now, for one perfect night Ari had been *his*.

⋆ ⋆ ⋆

Noah adored the puppet theater, and he'd gone back to the petting zoo three times, hunkering down to stroke his hands along the goats' sides. They learned that parrots could bite and their beaks had tremendous pressure per square inch. Matt approved of how carefully the docent handled both the birds and the kids surrounding them. When the talking parrot repeated what Noah said, he giggled, his hands over his mouth. By the end of the day, they'd vanquished Irene's ghost completely—at least until the next time she dropped in to stir things up. Happy, laughing, joyful Noah chattered all the way home.

"We have to tell Ari about the llamas, Daddy." Matt had lifted him up to pet them.

That had been Noah's refrain all day long: *We have to tell Ari.*

It was impossible to stop thinking of her when Noah clearly wished she had been with them too.

If Irene was the specter...Ari was the dream.

A dream Matt couldn't let himself have. Not just because she was his son's nanny, but also because he didn't have anything to offer her beyond wild, beautiful, fabulous sex. Matt didn't have what it took to cement a real relationship that would last, not after Irene or a childhood like his. He could still see Ari's horror when he'd told her about *Natural Born Killers*.

It was close to dinnertime, and Matt stopped for takeout pizza. The closer they got to home, the faster his heart beat with anticipation for the mere sight of her car parked in the garage.

Damn it, he had it crazy bad for her.

They found Ari in the kitchen, the refrigerator door open as she surveyed the contents. He'd told her she was free to indulge in anything available.

God, how he wanted to indulge in her.

No. He needed to keep his perspective. Needed to remember that their night together had been a mistake.

But when Noah rushed to her, and she closed the fridge and knelt to hear a blow-by-blow replay of everything he'd seen, all with a child's wonder, Matt's heart blossomed watching her with his son.

She was the caregiver he'd always wanted. The others had been too stern or too lax, too standoffish or too uninvolved. One had adored the luxury of his house, using it like her own mansion when he wasn't home, hosting pool parties for her girlfriends. Another had designs on moving permanently into his bed. But to all, Noah had been merely a job.

To Ari, Matt's son was a special person who deserved all her attention.

"I brought pizza." He held up the box. "There's enough for you to join us if you'd like."

"Thanks." She smiled at him as she grabbed plates and napkins, poured milk for Noah, then got sodas for him and herself. Lord, what her smile did to him. So much.

Too much.

They sat at the kitchen bar, and as soon as she took

her first bite, she moaned, "Oh my God, this is *good*." Then she scooped up a string of cheese and licked it off her finger.

Matt's body went into hyperdrive—and his mind went to places no man's thoughts should go when his son was sitting so close.

"Did you have a good time with your friends today?" Matt hoped he sounded conversational rather than desperately hooked on her.

"Jorge and Rosie were great. Our friend Chi stopped by too, which was a nice surprise."

She didn't appear guilty, as if she'd been holed up in a filthy, run-down apartment with her secret boyfriend all afternoon. And yet jealousy—and concern—still ran rampant in his head.

Noah shoved his last bite of pizza into his mouth, then scrambled down from his seat. "Let's see a movie, Daddy. Ari." He clapped his hands. "*The LEGO Movie*!"

"More Legos?"

"Yes!" He raced off, expecting them to follow.

"Have you ever taken him to LEGOLAND?"

"No." He grinned. "But only because he'd want me to leave him there. Forever."

By the time they entered the great room, Noah had the TV on and the movie queued up on streaming. He threw himself down onto a big bean bag he'd pulled in front of the TV. "You can come down here with me, Ari." He waved his arm at her.

"Actually, Ari and I need to do some adult talk

while you're watching."

Noah harrumphed like a disappointed old man, but he settled in for the movie. Ari sat in the center of the sectional couch near the window, and though Matt wanted her next to him—as close as she could get—he forced himself to sit on the other side of the L-shaped couch.

"Did something happen today?" Ari kept her voice low. "Something about his mom again?"

"No. He didn't even mention her." He didn't want Ari to think he was some crazy stalker, but he also didn't want it to come up later that he'd seen her in town and hadn't told her. "I saw you on our way to the park. I had to take a detour into San Jose to drop off some papers. It wasn't the best part of town."

"Oh." She picked up a pillow and curled her arms around it, her legs pulled up, her feet bare, her toes colored with red polish. He couldn't stop the thought that she'd curled herself around him just like that less than forty-eight hours ago.

"I know you were visiting your friend, but the building didn't look exactly..." He searched for the least offensive word. "Safe. If you want Noah to visit your friend and her son, it would be better to have Doreen bring them here."

"Rosie's place is in Willow Glen. She rents a cottage from a little old lady, and it's really nice. There's a park nearby too." She breathed deep. "Where you saw me...that's my apartment. The rent's really cheap, and if things don't work out here, I need to have someplace to go back to."

She *lived* in that neighborhood? Horror rose in his throat. Terrible things happened in neighborhoods like that. He'd grown up in one. He hated the thought of her ever being there. Did Daniel know?

"You don't have to worry that I'll fire you."

But he was her employer, and he'd slept with her, and then in the morning he'd told her it was a huge mistake. No wonder she had a fallback plan, given that most guys in his position would probably can her just to make things easier on themselves.

"It's not because of what happened between us," she said softly. "I just learned early on that I need a place to go. Just in case. And also..." She hesitated, then suddenly rushed on as if she had to get the words out before she rethought them. "My brother, Gideon, might come looking for me. I've been sending out letters and emails trying to find him. And that's the address I use."

She had a *brother*? She hadn't noted any next of kin on her application. Daniel had never mentioned a brother either. Or that she was searching for him.

Maybe he shouldn't get any more embroiled in her life. But in this past week he hadn't just desired her, he'd also come to care about her. Which was why he needed to know, "Why would he be looking for you?"

For a long moment, only the sound of the TV filled their silence. Finally, she said, "My brother joined up right out of high school, when I was eight. My mom and I moved around a lot. When she died, they couldn't find him."

And she'd entered the foster care system. "I'm sorry."

She shrugged, and he knew that shrug. It was what you learned to do when you were used to losing everything. It was the shrug you gave when you had to suck it up and move on with your life, even if it felt like there weren't a hell of a lot of reasons to keep moving anymore.

"How did you lose your parents?" he asked softly.

She swallowed. "My dad died in a car accident when I was real little. Mom never got over it. The only thing that made her feel better was drugs."

A deep ache curled around his internal organs. His hands itched to comfort her. If Noah hadn't been glued to the TV in the same room, he might have given in. But he could only listen, the way she'd listened to his story about Irene.

"She started losing jobs all the time. We moved around a lot. Gideon remembered the good times, and he used to tell me about them. But I didn't remember my dad. I only remembered my mother…like that. When Gideon turned eighteen, he joined up so he could take care of us. He said he'd send money."

"But he never did?" It must have been a huge double blow.

"I'm sure he tried. But we got kicked out of our

place right after he left." She pressed her lips together. "I don't think my mom's landlord ever told him where we'd gone. I'm not even sure if my mom gave the guy any information to pass on."

His heart broke for her. She'd never even had a childhood. His chest ached with his inability to reach out and fold her into his arms.

"How old were you when she died?"

"Twelve." She blinked slowly. "It was a drug overdose. They tried to find Gideon, but Jones isn't exactly an uncommon name. I didn't know which branch of the service he'd gone into. I didn't even know if he was still in the military."

Jesus, what she'd been through—a drug-addicted mother, losing her brother, losing her home over and over, never feeling safe. He saw clearly now why she empathized so easily with Noah's pain over his mother's aborted visit. And with him.

In so many ways, their childhoods mirrored each other—the instability, never knowing how his dad would react, a mother who was emotionally absent. They'd both been abandoned. But he'd found the Mavericks and Susan and Bob. Whereas Ari had gone into the foster care system.

"I'm so sorry," he said again, knowing his words were completely inadequate. "How were your foster homes?"

He got another shrug. "I got moved around a lot, but I was used to that after living with my mom." She deliberately left out every detail but that one.

Yet another thing they had in common—Matt never gave people the details of his shitty childhood either. He didn't want their pity. And he didn't like to have to go back there, even in his head, if he didn't have to.

"But I met some really good friends," she continued in a brighter tone. "I don't know what I'd do without Rosie and Chi."

He saw so many things now. Her desire to help with the youth home for foster kids coming of age was rooted in her own experience. He called Bob and Susan his foster parents, but they were far more than that. They were Mom and Dad. A kid needed tremendous luck to find people like the Spencers.

But though Ari hadn't been lucky, she was resilient. She'd taken care of herself all on her own. She'd grown and thrived. She was bright and enthusiastic and full of joy, laughter, and hope. They came from the same beginnings, but while Ari had the strength to step out into the light, too often Matt still remained in the darkness of his past.

That was the biggest reason why he needed to leave her alone. Drawn to Ari's brightness as if he needed to feed off her, Matt knew he could so easily drag her down. Just as Irene had always accused him of doing to her.

But God, how he admired Ari for the woman she'd made herself into. "You're amazing."

She tilted her head, her lips parted. And he felt the

denial coming. But he wouldn't let her say it.

"My parents were alive," he told her, "but we barely had enough money to eat sometimes. We lived in Chicago, and usually my coat and boots had holes in them when I walked to school." There'd been so much worse, but he wouldn't burden her with his father's cruelty or his mother's indifference. He just needed her to know she wasn't alone. "I understand how hard it is. But the Mavericks and I had Daniel's parents. Without them, I wouldn't be here."

She shook her head, her hair falling over her shoulder. "You'd have found a way."

Without Susan and Bob's solid presence, without the Mavericks going to bat for him, he would have remained the kid his father hated. The Mavericks and the Spencers had helped him to value his love of learning.

Who had helped Ari?

"Rosie and Chi sound like your Mavericks. They kept me sane in an insane world. We all need people to help us through."

He allowed himself one gentle touch, taking her hand in his. He couldn't be with her again, but there was something else he *could* do. Something that would mean the world to her.

"I can help you find your brother."

Chapter Fourteen

Ari wasn't a speechless kind of girl, but Matt stole the words from her lips.

I can help you find your brother.

Matt Tremont was a man who made the impossible possible. Look where he'd come from—a childhood where there wasn't enough to eat and his feet had nearly frozen through the holes in his shoes. That had to be why he was so good to the people who worked for him, respectful with Doreen, and sweet with Cookie. Now this, an offer to help return her brother to her.

She simply nodded, with all her gratitude shining in her gaze.

"What have you learned so far?" He squeezed her hand, and his comfort touched her deep inside.

Finally, she found her voice. "I started looking for him about three years ago." With her college tuition, books, and day-to-day living, even with Daniel's fabulous scholarships, it had taken a long time to put a little money in a savings account.

After her mom died, she'd been shuffled between

so many foster homes she couldn't count the parents or the kids. She was like a transient, losing everything again after a few weeks or months. Between her mom and foster care, she'd learned to live and pack light. She'd run out of places to hide her meager stash from the other kids. Another lesson in traveling light: They couldn't steal what you didn't have. One of the fathers had tried to molest her, but she'd been able to get out of there fast, mostly because she'd had so little to take with her.

She'd not only survived, but she'd been lucky to find Rosie and Chi, her best friends in all the world. After high school, when Daniel had given her the job at Top-Notch, she'd lived paycheck to paycheck, and she'd clung to the little studio like she did to Rosie and Chi. In a world where she'd never had anything, the small room was *hers*, a hideaway, a place to run to. And it was the only place where Gideon could find her, if he ever got one of her letters.

"I didn't know whether he'd gone into the Army, Navy, or Air Force, so I called them all. I even went to recruiting offices for help. Finally, someone was able to tell me that he was in the Army, but he'd gotten out nine years ago." She'd spent hours on library computers until she'd saved enough from Daniel's scholarships for a laptop she'd waited for six hours in a Black Friday line to buy. "I've used free people searches and a few cheap subscriptions. I sent emails and letters, or called if I could find a phone number." She felt as helpless after three years of searching as she had in the beginning. "But nothing."

The frustration of all those years welled up in her. But Matt's hand was still on hers, warm, reassuring, the soft cadence of his voice soothing. "I've got a private investigator. Rafe Sullivan has access to special databases." Before she could say she didn't have the money for an investigator, he added, "He's on retainer whether I use him or not."

She still didn't know how to thank him. "I tried everything. Gideon Jones. G. Jones. Gideon R. Jones. G.R. Jones. Gideon Randolph Jones."

"Randolph?"

It was a relief to smile. She felt like she'd put too much emotion into the air, clouding everything. "My mom loved old Westerns, and Randolph Scott was her favorite cowboy."

She'd watched with her mom, who usually wasn't capable of doing more than lying on the couch. Ari loved books, and her mother loved movies. They couldn't afford cable, so they'd watched TV on an ancient black and white that still had rabbit ears. That TV was the only thing they took with them when they left yet another apartment, and it had worked for years, even if it was a little snowy.

Oddly, those Saturday afternoon matinees had been some of their best times together. Her ribs squeezed tight around her heart. Gideon had watched too. He hadn't been like regular brothers who found their little sisters totally annoying. Maybe it was because he was so much older. He was her big protector, watching over her. Always there. Until suddenly he wasn't anymore. He'd been gone twice as long now as she'd even known him, but he would always be in her heart. And she would keep on looking for him, no matter what.

"It'll be okay, Ari." Matt looked deep into her eyes. "We'll find him."

Oh God, she was going to cry. He was so good to her. Without any strings attached. Not that she wouldn't give him anything he asked for.

She needed a moment, alone, without his kind eyes on her, or the waterworks would really start flowing. "Popcorn. Noah needs popcorn. I'll be right back."

She dashed for the kitchen. There had to be microwave popcorn *somewhere.*

"Ari."

Matt's voice stilled her. Hands on the two open doors of the fully stocked pantry, she stared at shelves of canned goods, sacks of flour, sugar, oatmeal, boxes of cereal—enough food to feed an army. She felt him so close behind her that her hair ruffled with his breath.

"Family is the most important thing in the world. I want nothing more than to help you find your brother."

"Thank you." She sniffed softly as she turned to face him. "No one's ever done anything like that for me." She bit her lip as a tear slid down her cheek. In

Matt's arms, for a few wonderful hours, she'd felt like she mattered. But this was more. "Thank you," she whispered again. From the bottom of her heart, from the well of her soul, and from her gut, which had suffered the worst. "I'll never be able to thank you enough."

He brushed the wetness from her cheeks. "We haven't found him yet."

"But you will." She blinked through her tears into his breathtakingly handsome face and what she saw in his eyes made kissing him again completely unstoppable.

Up on her toes, she wound her arms around his neck and hung on through the storm raging inside her as she kissed him. No one had ever tasted like Matt. No one had ever felt so hard or so perfect against her. No one had ever consumed her. She wanted him ferociously.

Fearlessly.

Matt backed her up against the shelves. The cans wobbled, but he cupped her face and kissed her openmouthed, stealing her breath, making her knees weak. With her palms to the backs of his hands, she held him close. She didn't hear the clatter of cans falling on the shelves or the doors banging against the wall—there was only him, his delicious scent, his roughened hands, his hard body pressed against her.

She couldn't help herself. Didn't even want to. Not when the only place that felt right anymore was in his arms.

She was his.

All he had to do was take her.

* * *

Matt wanted Ari so badly that he was almost beyond reason. She was so beautiful. So sweet. So perfect.

But somehow, some way he had to find the self-control to do the right thing…even if nothing had ever felt more wrong than the two of them going to separate bedrooms tonight.

It nearly killed him to step back from her. His breath was harsh and hard in his throat as she stared up at him with half-closed lids, her lips red and lush from his kiss, her skin flushed.

There was so much more to her than a typical twenty-four-year-old. She'd suffered, she'd overcome, and she'd kept her humanity.

Yet again he had to remind himself that she was not only his son's nanny…but that he was a man who would inevitably suck all the joy out of her. Because while she had overcome her past, he still lived with all its vivid scars.

"Ari, I promised you I wouldn't—" he began, but she shook her head to cut him off.

"I should probably go to bed now," she said in a shaky voice.

She was right. It wasn't safe for the two of them to sit in the family room on the couch together. Even with Noah in the room, Matt would drink her in. Want her. *Need* her.

God, yes, he needed her.

But he wasn't good enough for her.

* * *

God, that kiss.

Ari put her fingers to her lips. Even after she'd made herself walk away, she still tasted him, still felt his hard body against her.

As she turned over in her dark bedroom, the covers tangled around her legs. The soft sheets caressed her skin, and she imagined his flesh on hers.

That kiss hadn't been about comfort, or even gratitude. It was pure desire. Instinctive need. Hot emotion ready to boil over.

She knew all the arguments. He was her boss. She was Noah's nanny. This was supposed to be business. He was paying her. She was a decade younger than he was. He couldn't take advantage of her. She didn't need to hear him say it all.

But after that kiss, none of it mattered. Not after the way he'd looked at her. As though he wanted to sink inside her right there against the shelves.

And as though helping her find her brother was now as important to him as it was to her. She was positive that Matt would find Gideon.

And she would help Matt find his way to *her*.

Chapter Fifteen

Over the next couple of weeks, Matt had to make two business trips, but he was home on the weekends. Ari took Noah to school, returned to set lunch and dinner menus with Cookie, then made up lesson plans for the afternoon.

There was plenty of playtime as well. Noah loved his huge sandbox and was quite the little builder, making tunnels to drive his trucks through and shoring them up with big cardboard tubes. He built sand skyscrapers and roads and stuck in red, green, and yellow lollipops for signal lights. Someday, he told her, he wanted to build real skyscrapers, and she encouraged him to dream big. After all, look at what his father had accomplished.

Noah was interested in everything. When Cookie was baking one afternoon, he wanted to help. The three of them had a wonderful time, even if there was cake batter all over the backsplash because Noah lifted the beaters before they were turned off. And he'd learned another lesson by helping to clean up the mess.

They kept up their swimming too, but when Ari

mentioned the water wings to Matt, his answer was, "When he's a little older. Maybe next summer." She had to bite her tongue to keep herself from saying, *Next summer? He's a strong enough swimmer now.*

The trampoline still remained, though Irene hadn't called Noah or texted. She'd flown off to Paris and disappeared. Ari's heart ached every time Noah asked when his mom would be back.

When Ari suggested a net would make the trampoline safe, Matt's answer was, "I'm getting rid of it. The removal company said they'd be here within the week." There would be no bouncing in Noah's future. The only thing she could do was wean Noah off his training wheels and hope Matt saw the light, finally understanding his son was capable of so much more.

That was life with Noah. But there were also her evenings with Matt when he was in town. They talked about Noah and Ari's favorite parts of the day and after dinner, the three of them would play a game or go for a walk. After story time, when Noah was asleep, Matt would give her an update from his private investigator, Rafe Sullivan, who was tracing Gideon's military record. The information Matt relayed to her each night made her feel as if they were actually getting closer to finding her brother.

And every single moment they were together—and most of the moments they weren't—Ari dreamed of Matt kissing her. Touching her. Whispering sensual commands like, *Go to my room, strip off your clothes, and be waiting naked for me when I get there.*

Alas, he always said a polite good night and went to his room alone. There were no intimate evening conversations. No glasses of wine. No more baring of souls and confidences.

But she *did* catch him watching her when he thought she didn't notice. With a very male get-her-down-to-her-bare-skin look that made her whole body tingle with awareness. It was just enough to help keep hope alive that he might someday stop looking at being with her as a mistake.

She'd dreamed about those looks every one of the three nights he'd been gone on his latest business trip and was impatiently waiting for his return tonight. She and Noah were spending the afternoon at Rosie's so the kids could play. Chi had dropped by too, and they all sat on Rosie's tiny patio, drinking lemonade and watching the boys.

"Is Jorge still using training wheels on his bike?" Ari asked.

With her Latino heritage, Rosie was a beauty, with thick, curly dark hair and cocoa eyes. "He's been off them since he started kindergarten in September. But I still watch out."

"You're just a nervous mama," Chi said.

Chi was short for the Asian name her first foster parents refused to pronounce correctly. But Chi had liked the new name. She said it was like Tai Chi, calming yet powerful. Her silky black hair hung straight down her back, and she had smooth, flawless skin. She'd been in foster care since she was eight. Rosie lost her parents when she was eleven. They'd all found each other at Ari's second foster home. When they'd eventually been split up, they'd sworn to stay best friends. And they had, through thick and thin.

"I'm not nervous," Rosie huffed, smiling as she did so. "Why do you want to know about the training wheels, Ari?"

"I'm weaning Noah off his." He was more interested in his sandbox buildings so far, though, and they hadn't spent much time on it yet.

"He's a smart, agile kid. He'll be on two wheels in no time." They all reached in with their lemonade and clinked glasses to Noah's eventual success. Education was fabulous, but firsthand experience like Rosie's was the best kind of backup to go along with Ari's gut feelings.

Ari still had dreams of teaching someday, but right now there was only Noah and Matt. Maybe when Noah was in school full time…

If she was still working for Matt, that was. She couldn't bear to think of a time when she wouldn't be.

She pushed those thoughts away when Chi said, "Thanks for recommending me to your ladies." She nannied part time while she was working on her degree.

"Only for my bestie." Ari tapped her fist to Chi's upper arm. "You'll be great for the kids."

"So how's the billionaire working out?"

"It's amazing. I get to eat anything I want. I live in a suite that's three times the size of my studio. Noah is a doll. And I'm getting paid a ridiculous amount of money. What more could a girl ask for?" Okay, so Ari *could* ask for more—another night in Matt's bed followed by a morning where he didn't kick her out of it.

"Doesn't hurt that the billionaire is awesomely hot," Rosie said to Chi in an aside behind her hand.

"Ooh." Chi's eyes grew big. "Has he hit on you yet?"

Ari's blush was enough to give her away.

"Oh my God." Chi gasped. "He *did* hit on you."

"He did not." Smack between the two of them, Ari was in the hot seat.

"Look at that." Rosie pointed. "Her cheeks are totally red."

"Come on. We know there's something. Dish," Chi demanded.

Ari glanced at the boys, who were happily engaged. "It was only once." Twice, if she counted the kiss in the pantry. "And he didn't hit on me." She squeezed her eyes shut before admitting, "I hit on him." She licked her lips and admitted in a low voice, "I didn't just hit on him. I went to bed with him."

Both of her friends were silent a long time. A *very* long time that spoke volumes about how crazy they thought she was.

Finally, Rosie said, "You actually *slept* with him? With your billionaire boss?"

"It was an accident," she tried to protest.

"An accident?" Chi scrunched her forehead. "Like you were both naked and just happened to trip into each other's arms?"

"No." Ari would have laughed, but her stomach was twisted up. "Noah had an accident by the pool."

When both women looked over at Noah, who was playing cheerfully, she said, "He's okay, thank God. But after we took him to the emergency room, Matt was really upset. I just wanted to comfort him."

"So you're saying it was a simple hug for *comfort* that went off course?" Rosie looked at her over the rims of her sunglasses.

"Yes. No." She buried her face in her hands. "Stop giving me a bad time," she begged.

Chi put her hand on Ari's arm. "We don't want to give you a bad time. But we're worried about you. You know what happens to girls who sleep with the boss."

Ari dropped her hands. "I know." She breathed deeply and let it out in a long sigh. "But I honestly don't think he's going to fire me. Even though…"

"Even though?" Rosie prompted.

"I kissed him again the other night," Ari whispered. "In the pantry."

Chi shook her head. "Girl, I'm not being mean. But that's two strikes already. Not only is he your boss, he's a totally over-the-top rich guy who probably goes through women like tissue paper."

Chi was just trying to help, but Ari had to argue, "He's not like that. He doesn't take his money for granted. And I haven't seen any other women coming around. In fact, I don't think he's gone on a date since I've been there."

Before Chi could do more than roll her eyes at Ari's protests, Rosie asked, "How do you feel about everything that's happened?"

"I don't know." *Liar.* She didn't wait for one of the girls to say that. "All right, I admit I've got hopes."

"Oh. My. God." Chi was always the more dramatic of her two BFFs.

"Not just because of how amazing it was to be with him," Ari protested. "But because he's offered to find my brother. Why would he do that if he didn't have feelings for me?"

"Maybe because he feels guilty for taking advantage of his nanny and wants to make it up to her?" Chi suggested.

Rosie sent Chi a dirty look before folding her hand over Ari's. "I'm sure his motives for finding your brother are nothing but kind. Who wouldn't want to help you? But be careful. We don't want you to get hurt."

Rosie had met Jorge's daddy when she was nineteen. She'd fallen hopelessly. When the bastard found out she was pregnant, he ran. Rosie had just finished her AA degree in bookkeeping when Jorge was born, and with Chi's and Ari's help, she'd eked out enough time to find a really great accounting job she'd held for the last five years. It made sense that she'd worry about Ari getting hurt after she'd been hurt so badly herself.

Chi had never dated—had never even seen a good relationship up close, only the bad ones. No wonder she was so quick to assume that Matt's motives weren't pure.

Ari understood her friends' caution. She'd seen her fair share of bad relationships too, but she still couldn't help hoping the fairy tale would actually come true. Hope was the one thing she'd always vowed to hold on to.

"I don't want to be careful," she admitted, looking out at Noah playing blissfully. She didn't only want to build tunnels and roads and castles in the sand with him—she also wanted to build dreams that came true.

Before she'd met Matt and Noah, she'd always told herself dreams were better than reality because you couldn't be disappointed. But if you were never disappointed, maybe that meant you never risked anything.

And Matt—and Noah—were worth risking it all.

"Even if I think you're acting crazy, we'll be here no matter how it works out," Chi said, and Rosie nodded her agreement.

"I love you guys." Ari blinked through the emotion flooding her eyes.

She could dream all she wanted, but the one thing

she could count on was that her friends would be there for her if she bounced herself right off love's trampoline and landed hard enough to break her heart.

* * *

After an inspection of his Florida plant on Friday, Matt's pilot had orders to get him home by six that night. He missed his kid like crazy.

And missed Noah's nanny like crazy too.

Working around the clock should have driven thoughts of her out of his mind. Instead, he pretty much lived for her nine p.m. check-in calls, when she ran him through the day's activities and he let her know about any new lead his investigator was following regarding her brother. And every time they hung up the phone, he'd needed to stand beneath a freezing shower spray for ten minutes to give himself some semblance of control.

His foster mother had always helped him get his head on straight. Taking advantage of the long flight, he called her from the quiet of the luxurious lounge on his private plane.

"I know she drives you crazy, honey," Susan said after he finished telling her what had happened with Noah during, and after, Irene's latest visit.

"You could have a kegger on that trampoline. And of course, she just dumped it and ran."

It shouldn't still make him angry, but during last night's phone call, Noah had once again asked if

Mommy was coming back soon to teach him how to jump on the trampoline. It could be months before Irene showed up. Matt hated being helpless in the face of his son's pain.

"Why don't you get a safety net?" Susan asked, echoing Ari's suggestion.

"Because then Irene would win."

"Matt," Susan said, her tone clearly indicating she wasn't impressed with his behavior. "The trampoline shouldn't be a battlefield."

He knew it shouldn't be a contest for Noah's love. All that mattered was Noah's happiness and keeping him safe. Yes, he could protect Noah by forbidding Irene access to him. But that would only intensify the little boy's feelings of abandonment.

Which left Matt feeling like he was all out of options.

"I know I'm being an asshole about the whole thing." Frustration rode his every word. "I just have no idea how to deal with her flitting in, then leaving him behind like a forgotten toy."

Susan tutted with sympathy. "I know how hard it is on him, but you have to stop blaming yourself, honey." When he'd told Susan about Noah's fall by the pool, she'd said the same thing. "You never believe you're stepping up enough, but honey, I wish you'd see that you constantly take responsibility. You're there for your brothers whenever they need you. You're there for us without question. You're there for your company, your people, even your business partners. And you are there in every way possible for Noah."

"Then why can't I find a way to fix Irene so that Noah isn't brutalized after every one of her visits?" The same way Matt had been with every cruel word his father said, every time his mother refused to stick up for him or help him in any way. It ripped his heart to shreds watching his son. And it was his job to fix it. His inability to do so made him feel like he was just as bad of a parent as his own had been. In a different way, maybe, but the result was the same every time Noah cried himself to sleep, wasn't it?

"You can't fix Irene, honey. You can only be there for Noah. And you are, every single day." Then she clucked at him. "I know what you're thinking, but you're nothing like your father." When he didn't answer, she added, "You listen to me—I'm not the only one who thinks you're one of the best dads in the whole world. We all do."

"Yes, ma'am," he said as if she were his commanding officer. Which, to be honest, she was more often than not.

"Now tell me how that lovely Ariana is working out." Susan had liked her the moment she'd met her, when they were all working to build the youth home in San Jose.

"Noah loves her. She turns everything they do into a learning experience. She's even got him interested in mummies after she took him to the local museum."

"I'm so glad. If you'd come back to me with another nanny horror story, I would have given up and moved out there to take care of Noah myself."

All the Mavericks would love it if Bob and Susan moved out West, but they were born-and-bred Chicagoans. They loved the change of seasons, fall colors, white Christmas, and they were dying with impatience for Harper and Will's holiday wedding.

If not for Susan and Bob, Matt would have avoided Chicago like a plague of rats. At least the Mavericks had moved the couple out of the old neighborhood, and with retirement, the two of them were finally enjoying life.

"You'll see how great Ari is for yourself when you fly out for Will's Halloween party," he said.

At least, they'd see her if Matt didn't screw everything up and lose her before then. He never took a nanny to a Maverick event. Yet he'd planned without question that Ari would go with them. Not only did she know Daniel and the rest of the Mavericks, it seemed natural to include her. Everything about her seemed so damned natural…

For the first time, he found himself wondering—was there a chance that Susan wouldn't actually blame him for finding Ari irresistible?

Although, even that wouldn't change the fact that he wasn't right for Ari, that she needed a man who stepped up *every* time, who had moved past his shadows and would never crush her joy, her hopefulness.

"Oh, I hear Bob calling, sweetheart. We're binge-watching *Sons of Anarchy*, and he's dying for the next episode."

Binge-watching *Sons of Anarchy*? Susan and Bob? Now *that* was scary. "That's really violent, Mom. I'm shocked." *Midsomer Murders* was more their speed. "Maybe I need to speak to Daniel about putting parental controls on your streaming service," he teased.

"Do not even think about separating a woman from her streaming, especially when there are good-looking men on motorcycles involved," she said with a mock growl, then blew him a kiss over the phone. "Dad sends his love."

"Love you both too."

As soon as he disconnected, his cell phone beeped with several texts that had come in while he was talking to Susan. After quickly checking to see if any of them were from Rafe regarding Ari's brother, Matt had to work to bank his disappointment that his friend hadn't turned up any real leads yet. Fortunately, there *was* one thing Matt could do to make things better. Something he hoped would not only make Noah smile, but Ari too.

Chapter Sixteen

Ari was surprised to find two burly men from the sporting goods store installing a safety net on the trampoline when she and Noah returned home. Though Noah was overjoyed, she made sure Matt's name was on the work order.

"Can I, can I, can I?" Noah dashed around the lawn like a satellite orbiting the earth. "Please, please, please?"

She hunkered down in front of him. "Let's wait for your daddy." She was just as excited, though.

Maybe the water wings wouldn't have to wait until next summer. Maybe Matt was starting to see he didn't have to hold on so tightly or be so worried—and that his son would be safe if he let him fly a little higher once in a while.

She heard the car, and Noah ran to the driveway. Moments later, he was back, skipping around his father, herding him into the backyard.

Her pulse pumped harder, her heart beat faster, every nerve tingling for Matt. She'd heard all of her friends' warnings, but she was beyond being careful.

Because she wanted to risk everything for the chance that true love might actually be real.

"Welcome home." Her heart fluttered up to her throat, making her a little dizzy. "Noah got your present." He smiled at her, and that was all it took for her heart to race like a wild thing. "Do you want to do the honors for the first bounce?"

"I'd rather watch Noah. And you, Ari. I want to see you both having fun together."

It thrilled her to be included. As if she were more than just the nanny. As if she were family.

Noah was already running to the trampoline, and she scooped him up, tossing him into the middle before she climbed up. They jumped and rolled and played and his laughter filled the air.

It was glorious. It was freedom. It was like being the kid she'd never had a chance to be. When they finally came down, she was breathless...and Matt's gaze was so hot she swore it set her skin on fire.

If Noah hadn't launched himself at his father right then, she might have jumped on him herself.

"Come on, Daddy, you too." At Matt's back, Noah attempted to push the immovable object. Until finally it moved.

Then Noah grabbed Ari's hand. "Come on," he insisted. "I want to jump with both of you."

They clambered up and jumped high, Noah screaming his delight. Every time Matt landed, he bounced her too, until she was shrieking as loudly as

Noah. She'd never had so much fun, never laughed so hard, never ached so badly with how much she wanted this every moment of every day. With Noah *and* Matt.

Finally out of breath, she lost her balance, knocking into Matt, pitching them both sideways. He landed on top of her, his body flush against hers.

Oh God.

Every part of him was hard. Mouthwatering. Perfect.

Laughing, Noah thought it was such fun to jump around them, jostling them over and over until she thought she might actually lose her mind. Neither of them laughed anymore. Instead, Matt stared into her eyes as if she was the most beautiful thing he'd ever seen.

Before utter insanity descended on her and she wrapped her arms around Matt and kissed him in front of his son, Ari did the hardest thing in the world—she rolled away and crawled down the ladder.

When Noah urged her to come back, all she could do was shake her head, and say, "Boys only now."

Her two favorite boys in the whole wide world.

* * *

Ari was a mess, hair tangled, shirt askew, face flushed, breasts rising and falling with gasping breaths.

And Matt had never wanted anyone more.

It had been nuts to let Noah pull him up there with the two of them. But it had been the other side of insanity to fall on Ari and stay right there, her soft curves crushed beneath him, her big, beautiful eyes staring into his.

Even with her on the other side of the net, he still couldn't catch his breath. His need for her was an ache deep in his body and his soul.

He hadn't bought the trampoline net for this. He'd wanted to cut off his battle with Irene at the knees. To see Noah laugh and Ari smile.

But now he saw himself for the liar he was. He'd also wanted Ari to know he'd listened to her suggestion to buy the net, that he respected her opinion, that she mattered to him. More than he could possibly let her know if he meant to keep from falling back into bed with her.

"Dinner's probably getting cold." Even ten minutes later, Ari sounded as breathless as he felt.

"Yeah, buddy, dinner time. Let's get washed up."

Noah grumbled with every kid's instinct—no leaving the playground, no washing up. Matt used the distraction to regain his control, something he found increasingly difficult to do around Ari. Even with something as harmless as jumping on a backyard trampoline.

Noah grabbed their hands and swung himself like a monkey in a tree, laughing as they walked him into the house. And it felt right—so damned right, the three of them like that.

When Noah ran off to wash his hands, Matt gave

Ari the news he'd received just before his son had dragged him into the backyard. "I just heard from Rafe, my PI. They've located a former member of your brother's squad down in San Luis Obispo. His name is Zach Smith. We should go see him together. I'll tell you more after Noah's in bed."

Ari reached out, then squeezed her fist tight before she actually touched him. He knew she expressed herself through touch, through comfort, a hug, a kiss. Lord, how he wanted that touch. That kiss. Wanted it so damned bad.

"Thank you so much. For finding someone who knew my brother—and for offering to take me to see him. But I know how busy you are with work right now."

"Don't worry about my work." He covered her hand with his. He'd take any excuse to touch her. Sure, he was in the middle of the new product release, but nothing was more important than finding Ari's brother and repaying her for everything she did for Noah.

And for him.

* * *

Ari didn't want to rush story time, but she couldn't stand the suspense. She needed to know every detail of what Matt had learned about Gideon. After Noah was asleep, Matt lit the fire pit on the back deck and gave her a warmed brandy.

She'd never known such decadence before she'd

met him, but then, she'd never known a man like Matt.

Their feet perched on the edge of the pit, they sat beneath a cloudless sky filled with a million stars. The fire was warm against her soles, but it was Matt so close beside her that truly heated her from the inside out.

"It's not a pretty story," he finally said, "which was why I didn't get into it in front of Noah. Shortly before your brother got out of the Army, three of the members of his unit were killed by an IED."

Her stomach clenched. She read the news on the Internet, and she'd seen plenty of movies. An IED was a homemade bomb. "Was Gideon hurt?"

"No. But the guys in his squad were."

The brandy burned as it went down, especially after the chill of learning about the bomb. The worst was possible when it came to war zones, but still, she'd always prayed Gideon was alive—and uninjured.

"I'm hoping the guy in San Luis Obispo can shed some light on where your brother went after he got out."

She wanted to curl her fingers around Matt's…for as many reasons as there were stars in the sky. "Thank you. You don't have to take me down there, but I really appreciate not having to ask him these questions on my own."

"It might not be easy. And I want to be there for you, Ari." His words hung between them for endless moments, his expression intense. "Since I've been away for a few days, I'd like to spend the weekend with Noah, then take care of some critical issues for the new product release, and go down on Wednesday, if that's all right with you. Will's agreed to have his housekeeper, Mrs. Taylor, look after Noah, and Doreen can still drive him to school."

Matt had already arranged everything. All the Mavericks banded together when anyone needed something. Even when *she* needed something. Again, she felt almost like family. "Wednesday is perfect."

"Good." He was still looking at her, so intently that her skin tingled—*all* of her tingled. "I've booked a couple of rooms at Walter Braedon's Regent Hotel in San Luis."

She didn't know much about the Regent chain of hotels beyond the pictures she'd seen of them online. They were virtual palaces. And probably cost as much.

"That's too fancy." She'd noticed he was careful to say he'd booked two rooms, reminding her they wouldn't be sleeping together. "I already owe you so much—"

"You don't owe me anything, Ari. I'm the one who owes you for making my son so happy since you came here. Besides, I've gotten used to five-star accommodations." He gave her a small smile that made her heart beat even faster. "So you'll just have to live with it."

"I don't know how to thank you." He'd done so much for her in such a short space of time. It was almost over the top.

"Stay." His eyes held hers. "Just promise you'll stay with us, Ari." He cleared his throat. "Noah has gotten very attached to you. I can't think how heartbroken he'd be if you left now."

She didn't want to be careful. She wanted to be fearless. But for now, she simply nodded and made herself smile. "Of course I'll stay for as long as Noah needs me."

And then one day, maybe, Matt would finally realize *he* needed her too.

Chapter Seventeen

Zach Smith's house was in a middle-class neighborhood with white picket fences and a bus shelter on the corner that was decorated with a yellow school bus. The lawn was immaculately cut, its hedge trimmed, and the front walk was strewn with toys—a pint-size baseball mitt, a Big Wheel tricycle, a bat. From the backyard, Ari heard shrieks of laughter.

Evidently, he worked nights and his wife worked days so that someone was always with the kids. Matt had made the appointment with him and, thankfully, Zach had seemed more than willing to talk.

As soon as Ari and Matt stepped up to the front door, a stocky, heavily muscled guy with a military haircut opened it. "Glad you're here. I've got the coffee on."

The interior of the house was as neat and tidy as the outside. Except for the toys. Ari stuck out her hand. "Thanks so much for talking with us."

Zach shook hands with them both. "Gideon and me, we were like this." He twined his fingers. "He told me all about you, Ariana."

Ari could barely stop tears from springing to her eyes. Zach couldn't know how much his words meant to her. And Matt couldn't know how grateful she was that he'd found Zach and had come with her today.

She'd held on to the belief that her brother hadn't forgotten her. That faith kept her going through the darkest hours. Finding him would be like the light finally showing at the end of a long tunnel she'd been traveling through for so long.

"Come on in and sit, you two." Though not tall, Zach was a big man, about her brother's age, with expansive gestures. He waved them over to the couch, where he'd set out coffee, mugs, creamer, and sugar on the coffee table. The backyard view out the sliding glass door was of the kids, two boys and a girl, all under the age of ten.

"They just got out of school." Zach wore an adoring-dad look, with a broad smile and laughing eyes. Whatever he'd gone through during his tours of duty, Ari was glad to see he hadn't brought it home with him.

"Man, your brother was a kick," he told her. "Huge prankster. You wanted to forget about it all for a while, you hung out with Jones." Smiling with the memory, he shoved mugs at them while he sat in the side chair that gave him a sight line to the backyard. "But he had another side to him he didn't show most guys. And it really broke him up when he couldn't find you or your ma. He wrote letters and sent emails, but it's hard when you're over there, ya know."

"My mom and I had to leave the apartment we were in." Ari didn't say they'd been kicked out, didn't mention that drugs had torn them all apart. She felt the subtle shift of Matt's body beside her, as if he were moving closer, wanting her to know she had his support.

"He figured that. And later he got a letter saying she'd passed." He shook his head. "It was six months after, and he started writing letters like crazy, even more than he'd written before." Zach shook his head. "But no one could tell him who to contact about what happened to you."

Gideon *had* looked for her. She knew he wouldn't give up—just like she would never give up her search for him.

"Thank you for telling me that. It really means a lot to know he tried so hard to find us." Matt's hand covered hers, and he squeezed it in solidarity as she said, "To find me."

"Do you have any idea where he is now?" Matt asked.

"We lost touch. It happens like that when you get stateside." Zach rubbed both hands along his thighs, his gaze down as if he were seeing things he'd long ago put out of his mind. Then he breathed deeply, let it go with a sigh, and his smile returned. "I was Smith. He was Jones. They called us Alias Smith and Jones, like that old Western TV show. You couldn't have one without the other. It's like they say in the movies, band of brothers and all that. Because all you've got is each other."

"I know what that's like," she confided. "I have a really close bond with my friends from foster care."

"I can see the similarity," he said with a nod. "We thought it'd be a cakewalk, ya know. Do your time, collect your paycheck." He snorted at his own naiveté. "But then there was 9/11 and everything changed. Me and Gideon were attached to the same squad. We got bumped up to team leaders. We didn't think about getting out, because we were doing important stuff over there." He puffed out a breath. "We re-upped," he said, then clarified with, "Reenlisted," though Ari already knew what he meant. He gazed at her with a deep sadness in his eyes. "Kiddo, if he'd known about your ma, he woulda come home, but he got that letter a few months too late."

Kiddo. That's what Gideon had always called her. Hearing Zach say it brought tears welling up again.

"I know he would have come home for me. I'm just not sure he would have found me." After all, she'd been searching for three years and gotten nowhere. "The only thing I know is that he got out about nine years ago."

Zach nodded. "We both did. It was a fu—" He cut himself off. "Sorry, kiddo." He gave her a sheepish grin. "My wife gets on my case about the language 'cause of the kids. Anyway, it was a mess over there."

"And there was something about Gideon losing some guys?" After nine years of a total black hole of information about her brother, she had to know everything.

"IED. Lost his team. Three of his people. Damn near broke him in two. It wasn't his fault, but I'd'a felt the same if it were my guys. That's what got him in the end. The guilt, ya know."

"And what about you? Why did you leave?"

He swore softly, then just as quickly added, "Sorry. But hell, we couldn't have Alias Smith all by himself. It was Alias Smith and Jones or nothing." He drifted deep inside himself again. "It was time, ya know. The longer you're there, the higher the risk. I figured, without Gideon, my number just might be up."

"When did you last see him?" Matt's voice was low.

"I only saw him once after we got stateside."

Outside, children laughed. The sun was still shining. Yet inside, Ari felt as though darkness had fallen.

"He just vanished?" she asked.

"He didn't want to see me." Zach's expression was tight, but not with anger. With understanding. "I made him remember. And remembering tore him up."

For a moment, her hopes plummeted. Zach had said in the beginning that they'd lost touch, but it went deeper than that. And she'd been so hopeful there'd be more clues to follow after they talked with him.

"What did Gideon say the last time you saw him?" she asked, absolutely refusing to give up now. She'd made it this far—surely Zach had to know more than he thought he did. "Was there any indication where he thought he'd go?"

Zach sighed deeply, sadly. "He wanted to see the families. Of his team. Like he had to explain what happened or something. Like he needed to shoulder the blame and let them take it out on him. Even though he already took it out on himself plenty."

Her heart contracted for her brother, made it hard for her to remember her other questions.

"I'm sure we can find the names," Matt stepped in to say. "But if you remember any of them, that would be a huge help."

"Sure, I remember. Gideon used to say their names like he was praying over their souls. Ralph Esterhausen. He had a wife and a couple of kids. Then there was Jonny Danzi and Hank Garrett." He pressed his lips together, drawing in a deep breath. "And Karmen Sanchez."

"Karmen?" Ari asked. "That's four. I thought there were three."

"Yeah. He had a thing for her. I could see it. She was on base with us, but she wasn't actually part of his team. She was a combat medic. We always had a medic with us when we were outside the wire." He glanced at Ari. "On a mission, I mean. Sniper got her when she ran to help the guys." He drummed his fingers on his knees for a couple of seconds, then finally said, "I told him not to go see the families. I knew it'd be bad. But he wouldn't listen to me." After another great sigh, he added, "I wouldn't say we fought about it, but he didn't like what I had to say. I just didn't think he should do that to himself. Let sleeping dogs lie and all." He leaned back in the chair. "That's all, kiddo. I wish I could tell you more, but I hope you find him. He'd wanna know you forgive him for leaving you with your mom."

"Forgive him?" Ari shook her head. "I never needed to forgive him for that."

"That's just the kinda guy he is. Always responsible for everyone else. That's why he pulled all those pranks. 'Cause he didn't want people to think too hard about where they were and what their families were doing without them."

★ ★ ★

They left Zach Smith when his wife got home. Matt had found him to be a really good guy. It was obviously difficult to revisit his painful past, but he'd given them everything he could, even if it wasn't nearly enough.

After they'd said their thanks, Zach had wrapped Ari in a bear hug on the sidewalk, telling her it was from Gideon. She'd cried, but her tears hadn't all been sad this time. In addition to soaking up Zach's stories about her brother, she glowed with renewed hope.

"We'll find the families of the servicemen and see if they know anything more. I'm sorry we didn't learn where your brother is."

"Don't be sorry," she said softly. "It was so good to hear about him after so many years of knowing nothing at all. Hopefully, one of the people Zach told us about will know where Gideon is." She curled into her corner of the car as they headed out to the freeway and to the Regent Hotel, clearly exhausted by the day's revelations.

When they checked in to their adjoining—but separate—rooms a short while later, they found a huge fruit platter loaded with chocolate and champagne, along with sweet-smelling bath products in a gift basket. The digs were sumptuous, as was everything in any of Walter Braedon's hotels. The manager had tripped all over himself to make sure they were comfortable, and Matt had reserved the best table in the restaurant for dinner.

Ari looked as though she hadn't been sleeping well, and Matt wanted to pull her into his arms and tell her everything would be okay. That he'd make absolutely sure of it.

Instead, he said, "It's been a tiring day. You must be overwhelmed." Gideon wasn't even his brother, and Matt had still been swept into the high emotions between Ari and Zach as they spoke of him. "Maybe you should relax in the tub before dinner," he said, pointing to the basket of bath salts.

She blinked up at him, but he couldn't quite read her expression. Finally, she nodded. "A few minutes to decompress is a good plan."

The little smile she gave him made his heart flip over. She had a way of turning him inside out with the smallest, sweetest things.

"This might help too." Picking up the champagne bottle, he poured her a glass. Then she swiped a couple of strawberries and headed to the door of her adjoining room.

"Thank you," she said before closing him out.

He'd never felt so close to happiness—and yet so far. She was getting naked right on the other side of that door. He imagined steam rolling out, begging him to follow like a trail of breadcrumbs. It drove him crazy knowing how much she loved soaking in the tub, the sweet-smelling steam, her soft skin...

But damn it, making love to her was not why he'd brought her on this trip. Nor had he asked for adjoining rooms. The hotel staff had simply assigned them, without realizing it would drive him absolutely bonkers.

Burying himself in work was the only remedy. Not on his company or the new product launch, but on tackling the next lead that could help locate Ari's brother. Picking up his cell, he called his PI again and put Rafe to work on the next of kin for the slain soldiers on Gideon's team.

Ari had told him more today about the friends she

made in foster care, her band of sisters, just like the Mavericks were his brothers. Being a foster kid wasn't war, but bad things happened. It didn't have to be physical abuse—the verbal kind was just as bad. His father had proved that time and again. And Matt saw how Evan's wife, Whitney, could slice his friend to the bone with a few well-aimed words. At least, that seemed to be her goal, whether her aim hit the mark with Evan or not. But where Matt couldn't find a way to help his friend with his bad marriage, at least he could help Ari.

She'd not only dealt with losing her family and ending up in the foster system, but she'd survived with a joy for life he could never have imagined from someone in her circumstances. Finding her brother would make her life complete.

If he failed her...

Damn it, he wouldn't let himself think that way.

When his phone rang a moment later, he picked up, saying, "Hey, Will, I was just about to call and check on Noah."

"Noah's great. He and Harper and Jeremy are playing Chutes and Ladders right now. She's as crazy about your kid as the rest of us. And Jeremy never wants him to leave."

Harper was the mothering type. It wouldn't be too long after the wedding before he'd be buying baby booties for them. Will's childhood had been as bad as Matt's—but he'd come a long way since then. Matt knew his friend and fellow Maverick was going to be a hell of a dad.

"Thanks for taking such good care of him."

"Always. How are things going down your way?"

Matt had explained the situation when he'd asked Will to take Noah. "Not as much luck as I'd like. Zach Smith was a great guy and filled Ari in on some of the past years, but he hasn't seen Gideon since they got back."

"Anything you need from me, just let me know." Will didn't know Ari well, but from the tone of his voice, Matt could tell he wished there'd been better news. "How's Ari taking it?"

"She's putting up a good front. We've got a couple of leads on where he intended to go after he got out, so hopefully those will turn up something positive. Can you keep Noah another night or two?"

"No problem. Mrs. Taylor made a huge batch of chocolate-chip cookies to keep him going. Here's the little guy now."

After Will handed Noah the phone, Matt said, "Hey, buddy, I hear you're having lots of fun with everyone. I miss you so much."

"I miss you too, Daddy. And Ari. She would have so much fun playing our game."

"I know she would. She's taking a bath, otherwise she'd be here to say hi too. She misses you—she told me that lots of times today."

"Can you give her a good-night kiss for me?"

Matt swallowed past a lump in his throat. "Of course I can. She'll love that."

"Love you, Daddy! I gotta go, it's my turn now."

"A good-night kiss for your nanny, huh?" Will said when he picked up the phone.

Matt laughed as if Will was crazy for insinuating that he'd made anything sexual out of his kid's sweet request. But even to his ears, that laughter sounded hollow.

Because he wanted nothing more than to give Ari a good-night kiss.

One that lasted all night long.

Chapter Eighteen

"What would you like to eat?" Matt asked over champagne. Their corner of the restaurant was out of the way, the lights low, candlelight flickering.

Ari fluttered the menu in front of her, setting off a breeze of the floral salts she'd bathed in. When he'd knocked on her door, the room had been awash in fragrance. And his mind had been awash in her.

Her lilac jacket made her cheeks bloom, and beneath her white T-shirt, the matching lilac bra was a tinge of color that shouldn't have gotten his motor going. Yet the evidence of her lingerie revved him up, reminding him of the night he'd undressed her, the craziness of his need. Even now, he could remember how good—how sweet—she'd tasted.

"There are so many great choices, but the chicken Marsala looks good for tonight."

"Are you ordering that because you really want it? Or because it's the cheapest thing on the menu?" It was a five-star hotel with a five-star restaurant, white tablecloths, bone china, crystal glasses, and prices to match. "You can have anything you want, Ari."

The heated look in her eyes sent electricity shooting through him. He wouldn't pretend he didn't know what she wanted. The same thing he wanted—and it had nothing to do with dinner. It was all he could do not to throw down his menu and drag her upstairs.

But he had to walk the straight and narrow, because nothing had changed since that steamy kiss in the pantry. She was still the best nanny Noah had ever had. Matt was still her boss. And blurring those lines could screw everything up. She'd had enough darkness in her life. He wouldn't add to it by saddling her with his past or his failures.

Tamping down his desire with a Herculean effort, he asked, "Is there anything you haven't tried?" Damn if that question didn't make it worse when he thought of all the untried pleasures he could bring her.

Ari rescued him by saying, "Rack of lamb."

He grabbed the conversational straw she offered. "You've never had lamb?"

"I had lamb chops once. My third foster family. There were six kids, and we each got a teeny-tiny one." She demonstrated the size with her thumb and forefinger. "It wasn't enough to decide if I liked them."

"Then rack of lamb it is." He wanted to give her all the things she'd never had enough of.

As soon as they'd ordered, he said, "I know how hard it was not getting the news you needed from Zach. I'm really sorry about that."

"Why do you keep apologizing?" The waiter chose

that moment to bring their salads. "Let me rephrase," she said once the man walked away. "Please stop apologizing. I learned more about my brother today than I've heard in sixteen years. Alias Smith and Jones." She smiled. "And a prankster. I loved learning that about him." She twirled her fork in her fingers, clearly lost in her thoughts. "Gideon was always looking out for everyone. When I was a kid and things were bad, he always tried to make me smile. He must have done the same thing over there. That's what you did for me today," she said, a soft shimmer in her eyes. "You gave me pieces of my brother I wouldn't have had otherwise. I don't know how to thank you for that."

"You don't need to thank me."

He didn't point out that while they'd been able to find Zach Smith, finding her brother was still a very difficult proposition. He didn't want to destroy her hope or her joy in the things she'd learned today. Matt loved how she always saw the bright side. Living with a mother who'd abandoned her for her next fix and then to foster care, Ari was a remarkably glass-half-full kind of woman.

She pushed the spring greens around on her plate. "I searched for three *years*," she emphasized, leaning forward, dropping her voice to a near whisper that was raw with emotion. "I got nothing. But you make things happen just like *that*." She snapped her fingers in the air. "You found Gideon's friend. Someone who made him come alive in his words. So yes, I need to thank you."

She made Matt feel like a hero, when really it was a matter of money and having contacts in the right places. But he wanted to be her hero. And he wouldn't rest until he found her brother.

"I *will* find him for you."

"I know." She was so sweet in her faith in him. In the next moment, as their meals were laid in front of them, she burst out with, "Oh my God, will you look at that rack?"

Matt let go of a laugh that came straight from his belly, and the waiter dipped his head to hide his smile. If Ari had any idea of the double meaning, she didn't give a hint.

She ate the way she did everything, with enthusiasm, moaning around a mouthful. The erotic sound kicked his pulse even higher.

"You've got to try some." She held out a forkful she'd just cut.

He wanted nothing more than for her to feed him, so he cupped her hand to pull her closer as he let himself take what she was offering.

"To die for, right?"

Jesus, she didn't know the half of it. Had no idea what was happening to him under the tablecloth or that his heart had powered up into heavy metal drumming mode.

"Try mine." He dredged a hunk of lobster tail in butter.

She put her hand under the fork to catch a drop as her mouth closed around the tines. She slowly drew away, driving him a little mad. A *lot* mad. Eyes closed, her lashes long and lush, she moaned her appreciation. Then she licked the drop of butter from her palm.

When she opened her eyes, they shone with the knowledge of what she was doing to him. Sweet *and* seductive was one hell of a combination. One he wasn't sure he'd be able to resist forever—even though he gave self-control his damned level best.

"Ever had lobster before?"

She shook her head, her smile half-cocked. "Like I said, SpaghettiOs were gourmet in my house."

"Canned stew in mine." He wanted her to know he'd been there too. They shared common beginnings, making them alike in so many ways, yet different in how they'd each reacted. "Watered down so it would stretch further." Although his dad's portion never got the extra water.

"Sometimes we'd fry just bread because there was no cheese for grilled cheese sandwiches." She made another *mmm* sound that tightened every muscle in his body. "Isn't it amazing how you can invent really good stuff when you don't have enough?"

He had never thought of the deprivation of his youth that way, yet he remembered how Susan and Bob had always brought joy into their house without much of anything. "At Christmas with the Mavericks and Susan and Bob, we had hot chocolate and made garlands out of paper and popcorn and hung it all on a fake ficus tree Bob rescued from the dump. Nobody cared it was made out of plastic. It was about being together." Matt's own home had been bare of decoration because his dad wouldn't waste the money. With Bob and Susan, it had only been about the joy. The way Ari was all about hope.

"Gideon always found the perfect gift," she told him. "It never cost a lot of money, but he never let us forget it was Christmas."

"And after your brother left?"

Anyone else with her rough childhood would have gone down the rabbit hole at his question. Ari simply shrugged. "I was never as good at finding stuff. Gideon had a knack. He just cared so much."

She was resilient, pulling the love she'd felt for her brother around herself like a warm coat, even after all these years apart. A lot of people would have been permanently beaten down by now. Not Ari. She'd triumphed.

No doubt about it, she was definitely Maverick material.

⋆ ⋆ ⋆

Matt refilled her champagne glass. Ari didn't know how much she'd had, but she felt light and airy rather than drunk. Exchanging the lamb for lobster had been almost sexual, and the attraction between them sizzled barely beneath the surface. But the night was about so much more than just attraction.

They'd talked for hours, and it turned out that they shared so many common experiences from childhood. Of course, they also talked about all the things Noah did and said that cracked them both up. She adored hearing about the other Mavericks and Matt's foster parents. She didn't want dinner to end.

Just when they were about to get up from the table, his phone buzzed. Reading the screen, his expression grew serious. "Rafe just texted to let me know that Karmen Sanchez's mother lives the closest, in Bakersfield. He also found her phone number."

She wanted to rip the cell out of Matt's hands to call the woman. But this wasn't just about Ari, was it? She wasn't the only person who had lost someone they loved. "Do you think it will open up old wounds for Karmen's mom?"

Matt curled his fingers around hers, and her heart turned over as though she were doing somersaults on the trampoline.

"I don't know." His voice was so soft, his touch so gentle. "Maybe no one's mentioned her daughter in years, and you'll give her a chance to talk about her. To remember her."

He astounded her with his insight. It was exactly what she'd been trying to say about Gideon—that the memories Zach Smith had given her were precious.

She thought of her mother, and how no one had talked about her after she'd died. Yes, she was a drug addict who had dragged her daughter from filthy apartment to dirty dive, one after the other. But Ari had loved her. "When my mom died and they took me away, it was like she didn't exist anymore, as if talking about her would remind me of some terrible time."

Matt's hand tightened around hers, giving her his strength, his heat, his power. "But you wanted to remember, didn't you?"

"I needed to. Not everything was totally bad. She loved me, and sometimes she'd hug me so hard I could feel that love deep inside." She'd only been able to talk about this to Rosie and Chi. And now, after all these years, she was telling Matt. "How do you remember your parents?" In all the things they'd spoken of so far, they hadn't shared this.

His hand flexed over hers, and she thought he might not answer until finally he said in a quiet voice, "I prefer to remember what it was like in Susan and Bob's house."

She melted for him, for the little boy who'd never found what he needed in his own home. Knowing that made her feel even closer to him. "Everyone's different." She offered him comfort with the rhythmic stroke of her thumb.

For a long moment, he watched her thumb go round and round on his hand, and the heat of his skin penetrated deep inside her. Finally, he raised his gaze from their linked hands. "Karmen's mom could be like you, wanting to remember. Let's call her now. It's not too late." Without letting go of her hand, he picked up his phone again and tapped the number his investigator had texted.

Her heart choking her throat, she listened to his gentle voice, his careful explanation, and finally his thank-you.

"Tomorrow," he said. "She'd like to talk to us. We can be down there before noon."

Ari wanted to throw herself at him, cover him with kisses, and show him how much what he'd done for her really meant. How much *he* meant.

Because in her heart, there was no going back.

Chapter Nineteen

"Thank you," she said at her hotel room door. "Not just for dinner." She put her hand on his arm, his tendons flexing beneath her fingertips. "For everything."

The way he gazed at her had the breath catching in her throat. But instead of kissing her the way she so badly hoped he would, he said, "Breakfast at eight sound okay? And then we'll get on the road."

Of course she nodded. "It sounds great." It seemed a crime to sleep alone after all they'd shared today, but unfortunately this wasn't a decision she could make alone.

In her room, she wandered past the huge bed to the sitting area with its small sofa and two chairs surrounding a fireplace. Turning in a circle without sitting down, she finally realized the connecting door was still open. Crossing to close it, she saw Matt standing just beyond the door, his gaze on her as if he hadn't looked away since she'd entered her room.

He'd given her such joy—the things she'd learned about Gideon today, the potential for what she might discover tomorrow. All of it encircled Matt, his generosity, his caring.

"I almost forgot to tell you." His voice was raw with emotion and desire. "Noah wanted me to give you a good-night kiss."

That was all it took. She didn't think rationally, didn't want to remind herself that this relationship could never work unless they were both fully on board.

Her body cared only about what she wanted, needed.

Craved.

She threw herself at him, almost launching into the air, and he caught her, hauling her high against him until she wrapped her legs tightly around his waist and curled her arms around his neck. He slammed the connecting door shut and shoved her up against it, his mouth on hers, kissing her until her breath mingled with his as though they were one.

He was so hard between her legs, and she was miles beyond hot, wet, and ready. She kissed him with ferocity, hugged him tighter, moaned her need into his mouth.

Pinning her body to the door, he held her face in his hands, dropping kisses over her cheeks, her mouth, her ear, tipping her head to get at her throat. He bit her neck lightly, then trailed back to her ear, kissing her until she trembled with desire.

"What do you want?" he whispered.

"Everything." She wasn't afraid to admit it. But she

didn't want to go there alone. She needed him to be as fearless as she was. "What do *you* want?"

"You." Something rough and potent in his voice took that single word far beyond the physical. "I want to strip you down, bare you one gorgeous inch at a time, and love you the way you deserve to be loved."

Everything inside her turned to liquid fire under the heat of his gaze. He let her slide to the floor, stepping back to look down at her. His fingers traced her curves with barely a touch, making it all the more intoxicating.

Then he skimmed beneath the lapels of her jacket. "I looked at you across the table tonight, the lilac jacket…" He pushed it off her shoulders, let it drop to the carpet, and rested his hands at her waist. "The white shirt…" He tugged it from her jeans, began drawing it up, the backs of his fingers hot against her skin.

She couldn't breathe, couldn't speak, couldn't even say his name to beg for more.

When he pulled the cotton over her head, he stared down at her with such heat in his eyes that she felt spotlighted by his desire. As if she were the only woman he wanted, the only one he'd ever want.

"There it is," he whispered. "All that pretty purple lingerie. I saw the hint of it beneath your shirt, and you have no idea what that did to me." He slid one finger beneath the strap of her bra, brushing down, coming perilously close to her nipple as he dipped into the cup.

Then he pulled the straps off her shoulders, letting them hang a moment down her arms. Decadent. Sexy.

Unbearably erotic.

He toyed with her, his hands at the zipper of her jeans, driving her crazy. Finally, he slipped the top button loose. "I wonder if your panties match that lovely lilac." He drew on the zipper, hissed out a breath as he saw the fabric of her panties. "Hell, yes. You can make a man wild with imagining what's beneath all these clothes." Then he hooked his fingers inside her waistband and stripped off her jeans. All the way down, going on his haunches before her. "God, you're beautiful."

He pulled everything off, including her shoes, as she braced herself on his shoulder. His skin burned even through his shirt. Then he looked up at her, his gaze following the length of her body, his eyes as hot as a wildfire. Rising slowly, he let his fingers take the path his gaze had moments before. She trembled for him.

"I need to touch you." He seduced her with his words, his heat, the way he snapped open her bra in the front and moved to circle her nipple with one possessive stroke. She was naked except for the tiny bikini panties.

And she was all his for the taking.

"I need to have you, skin on skin. *Now.*" With that, he stripped away the final wisp of fabric covering her. "You steal my breath. My sanity." His admissions were raw with heat—and emotion.

"You steal my sanity too," she whispered. "And I want to strip you down the same way."

"You took the words right out of my mouth," he said in that low, commanding voice that always made her come apart at the seams. "It's your turn now, Ari."

Her hands on his belt, she didn't fumble. The hot flare of passion burned in his eyes as she undid his zipper with an achingly slow glide. And her mouth watered for his taste.

Finding the hard jut of him with her hand, she knew taking him that way wasn't something she could do badly, even as inexperienced as she was. He was so special, and she wanted it so much. She stroked him with the tiny pearl of moisture on his tip.

"Everything," he said. "Take it all off."

She stripped off his shirt, caught for one moment by a dusky nipple. She licked him, sucked the nub into her mouth. Then bit him lightly. His body surged in her hand.

"So you want to play dirty, huh?" he whispered. Then he gently steered her to her knees...and she swore every last part of her liquefied.

She tugged off the rest of his clothes until he was gloriously naked, and she was eye level with all that beautiful flesh—thick, full, hard, and long. Up close and personal, she was able to appreciate his magnificence in a way she hadn't that one special night.

Then she took him, just the tip, circling with her tongue, and his body arched, his hands tangling in her hair. "I've imagined this. I've dreamed about you, Ari. Over and over."

Knowing he'd dreamed of her the way she had of him, the moment overwhelmed her, and she took him deeper.

"*Jesus*," he whispered through a sizzle of breath.

The sound made her feel beautiful and wanted and powerful. Power was something a girl like her had never found before. It wasn't even something she'd known she wanted until the moment he gave it to her.

Then he hauled her to her feet, kissing her open-mouthed, his taste still on her tongue. "You feel so damned good," he murmured. "But it's too soon. This night needs to go on forever. And I can't control myself around you."

She didn't hold back her smile. Refused to hold back anything. "Then don't."

He lifted her high and gently tossed her on her stomach in the middle of the bed. He climbed after her, stalking her, pulling her up on her hands and knees and moving in behind her, his thighs taut against hers.

"Are you sure you mean that?" His words were harsh with need as he ran his hands down her back to her hips, resting them on her bottom. The things he said and the way he touched her made her feel raw and needy, her skin sensitized all over.

She'd never expected to find a man she could be so totally open with, so completely available to, giving him anything he wanted, and yet trusting that she'd be okay. Not just okay—*amazing*. She wouldn't let herself be afraid to ask for everything. To ask for *him*.

"Yes." She wriggled back against him, loving the way his muscles tightened against her. "Take me, Matt."

"I will." He pressed a hot kiss to her shoulder. "But I want you to close your eyes and *feel* first. Feel what you do to me, Ari."

Nudging her legs farther apart, he slipped his rock-hard erection between them, stopping just short of entering her.

He was hard and pulsing against her sex, and with her eyes closed, her senses came totally alive. She was lightning ready to strike at any moment. When he slid a hand under her belly and found the center of her arousal, it was the ultimate—and the very best—shock to her system. She felt him everywhere, his fingers slip-sliding over her until she throbbed madly, his big muscular body blanketing her, his mouth on her neck, his kisses in her hair, his breath at her ear. There was delicious friction everywhere, beautiful sensation all over.

"*Matt*." Everything he did made her body surge and crest. It was so good. Too good. Scary good. She wanted to be fearless, but she was in so deep now that it frightened her a little. "I don't… I can't…"

"You can. For me, Ari. Only for me."

With his words, she shattered, his deep voice wrapping around her, his arms tight and possessive.

She shuddered with a pleasure so intense that she lost all thought—there was only his heat surrounding her, taking her higher.

"I love how ready you are for anything," he murmured. "For *everything*."

She trembled with the sensuality of his touch. "Don't stop."

"I already told you," he whispered as he hauled her back against his hard chest, her legs splayed open over his. "I can't stop. Not when I'm with you."

She couldn't see his face, could only feel his heat between her legs, his breath in her hair. Instead of pushing into her, he simply held her against him as he ran his big, strong hands over her belly, her breasts, up to her throat. He nudged her head aside to give him access to her neck and caressed her with his tongue, licking in tantalizing paths.

"Put me inside you, Ari. Make us both feel good. So damned good."

She loved that he knew so many different ways they could be together. Even slightly kinky ways. Especially those.

"You brought condoms," she said as she reached back and realized he already wore protection.

"I didn't plan this," he whispered against her hair. "But I'm a man who's learned to be ready for anything. And still, I wasn't ready for you." He buried his face against her neck. "You were standing in sunlight the first time I saw you…and you were perfect. I've been trying so hard to fight what's between us."

"The first time I looked at you—" She felt overfull with emotion, but it no longer frightened her. "I knew you were special. When we finally spoke, once I learned what a wonderful father you are, what an incredible man…" She covered his hands with hers and held them over her heart. "I started falling. And I can't stop."

"Ari—" She heard the groan of conflict in his voice. "I'm not a hero."

"You are, and you don't even know it." She tipped her head back against his shoulder to look at him. "I'm not fighting what's between us anymore. And I don't want you to fight either."

"How can I?" The words came out on a growl as he cupped her chin and kissed her. "How can I keep fighting when I see how good you are with my son? When having you in my arms is hotter than I'd ever thought possible. When I think about you all day—all night."

His exquisite words pulled her closer, became a part of her, and now, finally, she needed to do what he'd commanded in that sexy voice. Shifting her hips back toward his, she slid onto his beautiful erection, one glorious inch at a time. They both held their breath until the moment of complete connection, his chest to her back. She felt stretched to her very limits. And filled all the way to her heart.

As he moved inside her, his hands roamed down

her body, leaving fire in their wake. And when he slipped his fingers between her legs, stroking her most sensitive spot, she hovered right on the edge of total bliss.

"I can feel you everywhere."

"I feel *you*, Ari." Holding her tightly, he continued that intoxicatingly slow rock-and-roll of their bodies. "You're so soft. And so strong at the same time. So sweet. So perfect." Shifting his hips, he reached a spot inside that made her tremble and quake, and when her body involuntarily rose to a faster pace, he held her hips, forcing her to match his slow, erotic, mind-altering rhythm. "Slow, baby. Slow and *wild*."

She moaned deep in her throat, the sound so rough she couldn't believe it came from her.

"I know." His voice was harsh, overwhelmed. By pleasure. By need. By *her*. "I'm right there with you."

Her legs shook, her breath quavered, her mouth falling open with small cries she couldn't contain. Then everything shot down to the point where their bodies met, where he filled her, joined with her, where they'd become one.

And she exploded over him.

GodYesAri

The words he said—*groaned*—blurred together as he never stopped moving, never stopped touching. Hands everywhere, their skin sweaty and slick against each other.

When she couldn't remember her own name, let

alone his, he withdrew and rolled swiftly to his back, lifting her onto him so they were chest to chest, face to face, heart to heart. "Again. Like this."

As she took him deep inside once more, she closed her eyes, relishing that he was her perfect fit as sensation began to build all over again, slow and heated.

"Put your hands here." He brought her palms to his chest.

She leaned over him, the angle changed, and she gasped. He grinned, the sexiest smile on the planet. "Yes. Right there. That's where I want you. Hot and wet and trembling over me. All around me."

And then he found her with his hand again and everything inside her burst into flame one more time.

When she finally resurfaced, she was on her back, with him tall above her, her legs draped over his hips. He pulled them high, holding her at the ankles, her feet bracketing his ears.

He'd turned her into a wild thing tonight. But this—having him in so many incredible ways—ways she hadn't even known existed.

She clutched the comforter in her hands, threw her head back, and cried out, wordless sounds, his name, *God*. The pleasure was relentless. Never-ending, so that she was barely able to tell where one climax ended and another began.

Finally, he came down over her, falling with her into ecstasy, clutching her so tightly that she could barely breathe. She could only pray he wouldn't fight what he felt for her anymore.

And she wished with everything in her that it would never end.

* * *

After long minutes in his arms, Ari laughed softly. "Oh my God." Her breath was warm against his ear. "I didn't know it could be like that."

He cradled her close, moving slightly to the side so he didn't crush her frame. "It's never been like that before." Only that one beautiful, perfect night with her had come anywhere close.

Tonight, he'd wanted to experience every ounce of pleasure he could wring from her. Through her climaxes, he'd barely been able to hold himself back, the effort tensing all his muscles—until the moment hit him when he had no choice but to take her hard and fast, losing himself in her. *Finding* himself in her. Until there was nothing but sensation, her taste on his lips, her soft skin, her scent dragging him deeper. Until there was no real world outside, no thought, just the silkiness of her limbs around him and the pulse of her body—liquid heat, molten desire in his arms.

Even now, he was so crazy with need for her that tension coiled through his body, heated him, hardened him again, making his blood crackle in his veins and his skin hum with electricity. She'd hit every pleasure point, and yet he still had to squeeze his eyes shut in an effort to try to regain his control.

But he'd never had any control with Ari. Not when his need for her had always won out over what he believed to be right.

He'd wasted so much time thinking about right and wrong. Yet he was wrong about one *huge* thing he hadn't considered. While he'd told himself how young she was, how innocent, he'd discovered that not only was she strong and resilient, but she'd also managed to hold on to her hope and joy against all odds.

He'd never known a woman like her. She was utterly *fearless*.

The one night they'd shared—he hadn't wanted to acknowledge how special it had been. But there was no denying it now.

"Stay," he murmured.

He wanted her in his arms all night. Wanted to wake up in the morning with her. Wanted her to be the first one he saw when he opened his eyes, the first one he touched. Wanted to make her smile. Wanted to give her pleasure.

He wanted *her*.

* * *

Ari's dream was pure pleasure, her body cresting a great wave. A wall of heat at her back turned her insides red-hot, and then Matt was filling her, their bodies moving together as though they were floating on the ocean, its waves rocking them.

She wasn't exactly aware of when the dream ended

and reality began—only that the pleasure climbed higher and higher, tingling in her belly, spreading out to her limbs.

His chest was plastered to her back, her leg pulled high on his hip, opening her to his possession as he stroked her intimately. Instinctively, she braced her hand on the bed and pushed back on him. She wanted to wake every day just this way, to his hands on her, his breath flirting with her hair, his body buried deep.

He groaned and flexed inside her, his erection a throb that made her ache for more. Her breath came faster, matching the rhythm of his body inside her and the swirl of his fingers between her thighs.

How could her body keep burning hotter? How could these sensations keep intensifying?

There was no one like Matt. No one who'd ever made her feel the things he did. No one who'd made her matter with his words, his body, his kiss, his touch.

"Please, baby," he begged her. "Take me with you."

In the darkness, his hands and his kisses taking her higher, it was his words that released her—knowing that, just like her, he needed to beg, to plead to be taken in and held tight.

And when she plummeted over the edge, crying out her pleasure, the ultimate pleasure was taking him into that crazy, wild plunge right along with her.

Chapter Twenty

The next morning, the touch of Matt's hands over hers made Ari feel that everything would be all right—even as they turned onto Mrs. Sanchez's street and faced the unknown.

She hadn't expected this neighborhood. She'd always thought of Bakersfield as a cow town, with farms and stockyards and fields. But the houses in this neighborhood were mansions. Not in Matt's class, but certainly way above Ari's or Zach Smith's. The lawns were green even after a thirsty summer, and tall, stately trees flanked long driveways.

Mrs. Sanchez lived in a two-story home with dormer windows and a circular drive. Matt parked beneath the portico and took Ari's hand as they climbed the steps to the double-wide front door. The knocker was as shiny as gold.

"I wonder how Gideon felt walking up these stairs." Probably as out of place as she felt the first time she'd set foot inside Matt's mansion.

She wouldn't have been surprised if a butler had opened the door, but they were greeted by an elegant woman, her gray hair piled stylishly and her olive complexion made up tastefully. Her blue pantsuit fit her graceful curves as though it had been hand designed.

"Miss Jones?"

"Yes." Ari stuck out her hand. "And this is my friend, Matt Tremont."

They shook, then Mrs. Sanchez flourished her hand, stepping aside for them to enter. "Please," she said with a smile. "Come in. I'm so glad you called."

In the spacious tiled foyer, fresh flowers adorned a table, potted plants stood in the corners, and a wide, carpeted stairway led to the second floor. She ushered them through double doors into a large, sunny lounge already set with a coffee service. The atmosphere was completely different from Zach Smith's home, and yet, it was just as welcoming. Matt sat beside Ari on the couch while Mrs. Sanchez poured.

"Gideon was such a nice man. It was so thoughtful of him to come see us. My husband was still alive at the time, and I can't tell you how much your brother's visit meant."

"We're very sorry for your loss," Ari said, her throat tight. She knew the trauma of losing someone you loved. Especially family. And this woman had lost both husband and daughter.

"Thank you, dear. Now, why don't you tell me how I can help?"

Ari held her coffee cup but didn't drink from it.

"I've been looking for Gideon since he got out of the Army."

"Goodness, you haven't seen him since then?"

Mrs. Sanchez put a hand to the pearls at her throat. Ari guessed her to be in her mid-sixties, with the same Latina coloring as Rosie. Her voice was cultured, and she wore a gold band of diamonds on her left hand.

"No, ma'am. In fact, I haven't seen him since he joined up when I was eight."

"That's far too long," she said sympathetically. "I wish I could lead you to him, but though he used to call me every year or so, I haven't heard from him in…oh, at least two years." Her eyes deepened with sadness.

Matt took Ari's hand as if he knew exactly how hard it was not to let the disappointment creep over her. As she'd told him last night, she was thrilled to have learned so much about Gideon. And she wasn't about to give up.

"Did he ever say where he was when he called?"

"He didn't, I'm afraid. I collected these pictures for you, though." Mrs. Sanchez leaned forward, pulling a manila envelope from beneath the coffee tray. "Your brother was such a good man. He brought some photos of Karmen that he thought we'd like to have." She held the envelope on her lap a moment. "We were so proud of her. After 9/11 she wanted to do something for her country. We lost a nephew when the towers went down. She was in high school then, and she'd always wanted to be a nurse. We got her to agree to go to college first." She fingered her pearls again. "Perhaps I was hoping she would change her mind along the way, but she signed up before she graduated." Her sigh was deep and filled with sorrow. "I was afraid from the moment she was deployed. But you have to let your children follow their path, no matter how much you fear for them."

"She was so lucky to have you as her mother," Ari said as Mrs. Sanchez slid the collection from the envelope and passed over the small bundle.

"You are just as sweet as your brother." She leaned close, pointing to the first photograph. "That's my daughter."

It had been taken on a military base with Army vehicles in the background. "She was beautiful." The woman wore fatigues but no helmet, her dark hair short and thick.

Mrs. Sanchez smiled fondly. "She was such a pretty child, with lovely long, curly hair she inherited from her father. She loved seeing foreign places. My husband and I weren't big travelers, so I'm not sure where Karmen got that bug from."

The next photo was of a group of ten soldiers in desert fatigues, helmets, and guns, all the paraphernalia making them almost indistinguishable.

"There's Karmen." Mrs. Sanchez pointed.

"I thought she was a medic."

"She still had to carry a gun when she went out in

the field with the men." Mrs. Sanchez blinked rapidly, until finally she smiled again. "Those men depended on her, and she wanted to be right out there giving them aid."

Ari picked out Zach Smith in the photo next. And then, she finally recognized Gideon standing next to Karmen. She'd remembered him as the boy he'd been, the older brother. But this was a man, broader in the chest, with hard life experience in his eyes.

She held out the photo for Matt to see. "That's my brother." Her eyes stung with tears.

Mrs. Sanchez touched her hand. "My daughter sent us photos, of course, but there was something extra special about hearing about her from a comrade who knew her over there. Your brother told us how many lives she saved and said she was a brave soldier. It's exactly what Karmen would have wanted the men and women she served with to say about her."

"I'm sure she was one of the best," Ari said softly.

She shifted to the next picture, this one of five soldiers in full gear. Ari picked out Karmen and Gideon immediately. Her heart stilled all over again.

"Your brother said that was his team, even if Karmen wasn't actually under his command, and sometimes they were assigned other medics."

God. His team—they were all gone except Gideon. One of the men looked a little older—probably the married one with children. And the other two, despite their gear, didn't look much older than Gideon had been when he left. All of them gone.

The packet of photos trembled in Ari's hand as she moved to the next one. The group was larger this time, maybe fifteen or so, and the backdrop was unidentifiable—the inside of a tent perhaps, she couldn't be sure. Dressed in fatigues minus the gear and helmets, they all wore big smiles, laughing, arms thrown across each other's shoulders. Once again, Karmen stood next to Gideon, his arm around her just as it was around the man next to him.

But he was turned slightly toward Karmen, looking down at her. Ari felt a hitch below her ribs, knowing without a doubt that Gideon had been in love with her. And when she'd died along with the rest of his team, he would have believed it was his fault.

It wasn't true, of course. It was war.

But the woman he'd loved was still dead.

Ari gripped Matt's hand more tightly, and when she looked into his eyes, she knew he'd seen the same thing in the picture. Thank God he was here with her and she didn't have to do this alone.

More than ever, she needed to find her brother, to show him he wasn't alone either.

Though Mrs. Sanchez obviously missed her daughter with all her heart, she managed to keep herself together where a lesser woman would have fallen apart. She showed them the wall of pictures along the upper hallway—Karmen as a baby, a young girl, a teenager, a prom queen, a soldier. She was obviously an only child, though in many of the photos she was surrounded by cousins, aunts, uncles, and grandparents. There were pictures of her in dress uniform with her parents. She had her mother's face and her father's smile. She'd been a beautiful young woman full of promise, and she had given all that promise for her country.

"She never complained about the dust and dirt." Mrs. Sanchez smiled, her eyes far away with memory. "She'd been such a girly-girl. Always the perfect party dress, the perfect hair, the perfect makeup. But Gideon said she was perfectly happy to be one of the guys."

"I'm so glad he was able to share his stories with you."

Ari barely held back tears. Only by reminding herself that she was on the same path her brother had walked, and that she might find him around the next corner, was she able to keep herself together.

When they'd finished the pot of coffee and the plate of pastries, Ari said, "Thank you—we've taken so much time."

"You haven't. You've helped me remember Karmen all over again. In the rush of the day, we sometimes forget to just sit and remember."

"And you've helped me remember my brother." Ari gave Mrs. Sanchez an impulsive hug.

"I hope you find him, dear. If he should ever call again, I'll tell him how to reach you."

"Thank you. For everything."

After they'd said their good-byes and Matt had walked Ari down the steps to his car, she turned suddenly, went up on her toes, and threw her arms around him.

"Thank you," she whispered against his neck as he rubbed his hands up and down her back. "He was just a boy when he left. Now I know the man he turned into." She pulled back and looked into Matt's eyes. "He's out there." Determination fueled her. "And we're going to find him."

"I'll do everything in my power." But he frowned slightly. "I'm concerned that he hasn't called Mrs. Sanchez in two years, though."

She understood his unease, but she couldn't give in to it. "I was just a little girl the last time I saw my brother, but I know how deeply he would take the responsibility for his team—even when he couldn't have saved them. If he's gone into hiding, it's because he hasn't come out of the dark place he fell into when his friends died. He needs me to show him that it wasn't his fault. That there's someone out there who loves him unconditionally." And she needed her brother too. "Look at Mrs. Sanchez. She's lost so much, and yet what Gideon brought her has meaning for her to this day. I can show him that people still love him."

"Any way I can help you, Ari, I will."

She smiled up into Matt's beautiful eyes. "You already have, more than you'll ever know."

* * *

After dinner at a local Italian restaurant, they'd just finished wishing Noah good night over the phone, when Rafe Sullivan texted again to say he'd had luck with another name on Zach Smith's list. Ralph Esterhausen's wife lived in Lancaster, about an hour and a half south. Ari's stomach was jumpy with anticipation—and hope—that Mrs. Esterhausen might have heard from Gideon more recently than Karmen's mother had.

Matt immediately called, leaving a message when no one answered. "If I don't get a callback tonight," he told Ari, "we'll head down tomorrow morning and call again on the way."

The hotel Matt found for them wasn't a five-star Regent, but it was far better than the kind of roadside motel Ari could afford. And when he asked if she wanted separate rooms before they checked in, she answered him with a kiss that made words completely moot.

The past two days hadn't been all sunshine and rainbows, but even the hard parts were bearable with Matt beside her. Seeing all those photographs, running her fingers over Gideon's image, and knowing he'd called Mrs. Sanchez for years, made Ari believe more strongly than ever that they'd find him.

Just as she knew deep in her heart that Matt was so much more than a one-night stand.

His touch, his gaze—and especially his kisses—told her that she mattered to him. She loved the way he'd held her hand as they talked with Mrs. Sanchez, as if she belonged to him. As if he understood how badly she needed his solid presence beside her.

After seeing the pictures today, Ari was certain her brother had lost a woman he'd cared about deeply—and that it had devastated him. If Gideon had known how it all would end, would he have kept his heart safe? Or would he have fallen for Karmen anyway?

But Ari already knew the answer. Her brother would have risked his heart no matter what.

Just the way she was risking hers for Matt.

If it one day turned out that she'd misjudged Matt's feelings...well, she'd deal with it when she had to. But right now, all she wanted was to confirm the beauty of life by making love to him over and over, then falling asleep in his arms.

Their room had a king-size bed, a small sofa under a bay window, and a big bathtub. "I made sure they gave us the room with the largest tub available." He cupped her cheek, his lips so close to hers, his body warm, enticing. "Why don't you take a bath while I run a few errands?"

"Errands?" Instead of getting naked with her right this second?

He was planning something, and judging by the burn in his eyes, it had to be good. And he knew her well—a few minutes to decompress from the high emotions of their day would be nice.

"Yes." He kissed her for long, sweet moments, their breaths almost one. "Errands."

"And after your errands?" She let her heated question hang between them.

He gave her one more wicked smile—and a kiss so hot it started a fire inside of her—then left.

Slipping into lavender bathwater a few minutes later, she closed her eyes and went over everything she'd learned about her brother. When sorrow threatened, she pushed it away.

Close. She was so close. Not only to finding Gideon—but so much closer to Matt too.

Being with him like this was her dream come true, as well as everything Rosie and Chi had warned her she couldn't have. But they were wrong. She had it right now.

And she wasn't letting go.

Chapter Twenty-One

Ari had just climbed out of the bath when Matt returned. By the time she walked into the bedroom, wrapped only in a thin bathrobe, she found him sitting on the small sofa, a bottle of champagne in an ice bucket and a plate covered with a cloth napkin on the coffee table in front of him.

He didn't say anything, just gazed at her with such heat she actually lost her breath. "Should I put on some clothes?"

"No."

Oh God, just one little two-letter word was enough to make her whole body tingle. She bit her lip, wishing she were experienced enough to know the next move to make. But then she remembered his hand engulfing hers as he sat beside her today, sharing her emotions, soothing her, simply being there, as if nothing else was more important than that moment—and everything eased.

"Come here." His deep voice was full of so much sinfully hot promise that her legs trembled as she crossed the room, the robe still tied tightly around her waist.

"Have some champagne."

He poured one glass for her, one for him. The burn in his gaze scorched her as she sipped, the bubbles going straight to her head.

His eyes followed her every move, lingering on her lips while she drank and tracking her when she set down the glass. "Good?"

She nodded, licking the sweetness from her lips.

"And about to get so much better," he murmured. "I'm going to make you feel so good you won't think of anything but my touch. My kiss. My body inside you. I want to help you to forget everything bad. Tonight there will be only this, us, together." He dropped his voice even lower. "Now take off your robe. Slowly."

As he leaned back, stretching his arms along the sofa, Ari's heart beat so hard she could feel the pulse in her fingertips. No one but Matt had looked at her as though she was the sexiest thing he'd ever seen and he wanted to devour every inch of her.

Instead of untying the robe's sash, she slowly slid the fabric off one shoulder, revealing the swell of one breast as well.

"Perfect."

God, his voice, that word, his eyes on her. She pushed the robe off her other shoulder, letting the thin terrycloth fall to the upper curves of her breasts. Turning her back to him, she glanced over her shoulder, then shrugged and the robe fell to her hips, leaving her naked to the waist.

"So pretty." His words were raw with need.

His voice turned her liquid inside. Under his gaze, she reached for the sash, only to have him stop her with another of his delicious commands. "My turn now."

Rising from the couch, he stalked her, stopping so close behind her that her body tingled with static electricity. He palmed her breasts, and she gasped at the intimate sensation of his big, warm hands over her, his hard body behind her. He thumbed her nipples, turning them diamond tipped.

"Do you have any idea what you do to me? You make me *burn*."

She was hypnotized by the harsh need in his voice, and by his touch as he leisurely, tantalizingly slid his hands down her rib cage and stomach to the fabric sash. Blood rushed so fast in her ears that she was dizzy with desire as he slowly undid the bow she'd tied.

Finally, the robe gaped open. A beat later, with fabric pooling at her feet, she was completely bared to him. Everything, from her body, to her heart.

To her soul.

He pressed one hot kiss to her shoulder, then followed it up with the sexiest of orders. "On the bed."

She was naked. He was completely dressed. He was naturally dominant in bed—which she loved, so very much. But in their two precious nights together, he'd taught her how to take a little power for herself.

Bending over, her back to him, she stretched, slowly, deliberately, to grab the top of the bedspread. He groaned.

And she smiled.

After pulling the covers back all the way to the sheets, she crawled onto the bed until she was on all fours. Then she slipped down onto her haunches and looked over her shoulder.

His nostrils flared as though he was scenting her the way a lion tracks his mate. "On your back." His words were barely a whisper on the air. "Then close your eyes and put your arms over your head."

She turned, lay back, and closed her eyes, her body buzzing with desire as she lifted her arms to the pillow.

"Are you ready, baby?" His voice seemed to stroke her, the sheets beneath her heating slowly as she lay there.

"Yes."

The bed dipped, and he slipped something over her eyes. Cool and smelling like lavender—she realized it was a gel eye mask. As good as a blindfold.

With a caress of soft cloth, he bound her right wrist, pulling her arm higher until she was restrained. He did the same with her left wrist, then put his hands on her ankles. "Do you trust me?"

She couldn't speak, could only nod. But that was good enough for him as he gently spread her legs and tied her ankles down too.

★ ★ ★

She was so damned gorgeous, her limbs spread, her skin creamy and flushed with arousal. He wanted to dive on her, take his fill, drown in her, make her scream. Yet he wanted it slow too, wanted to build her to a climax that would rock her world and his. He wanted to worship her body for hours.

And more than anything, he wanted to erase the sorrows of today. Yes, she'd learned a great deal about her brother, but even being the most positive and hopeful person he'd ever met, the dead ends racking up one after the other had to be a killer.

The champagne, the blindfold—and everything else he'd bought—were a temporary escape. As much as he could possibly give her.

"Is this okay?" He didn't want to frighten her, but he'd found that when sight was taken away and movement was impossible, all the other senses kicked in, intensifying every sensation.

"I'm a million times better than okay."

Did she have any idea what her eagerness did to him? Especially when it was so perfectly matched to his. "Tell me the moment you're not. And I'll stop."

"Don't stop." Her lips were luscious, begging him to taste them. "Please don't stop."

He leaned in for a kiss, realizing too late that it was a huge miscalculation. Because one kiss was more than enough to drag him all the way under, rather than allowing him to continue to tease and tempt her until all thoughts but pleasure were driven from her mind. So when his cell phone rang just then, he realized answering it just might be the perfect way to drive her absolutely crazy.

"I've got to take this."

For a moment, she was completely silent, her head turned slightly toward his voice. Then she said, "What?" with total disbelief. "While I'm lying here spread-eagled?"

"It won't take long." He grinned. "And while I'm on the call, I want you to lie there thinking about what I'm going to do to you."

"But—"

He laid his hand gently over her mouth as he picked up the call. "Bruce, thanks for calling me back. I take it you've had a look at the spreadsheet I sent over?"

She didn't make a sound, simply licked his palm—and the shock was so great, so hot, that he almost forgot about Bruce altogether. He simply *wanted*, his body hard and raging.

Barely listening to his accountant's response, Matt dragged his fingers down to her knee, only to slide up once more, this time gently slipping his palm over her hot, wet center. She stifled a moan, her body shifting restlessly.

"Sounds good, Bruce," Matt said, trailing fingers over her abdomen, her skin jumping beneath his touch.

"Thanks for taking a look at it so fast."

By the time he hung up the phone, Ari was writhing on the bed. And it was so damned good, exactly what he'd wanted—to give her long minutes, even hours, where there were no bad things and no sorrow.

Just all the pleasure he had to offer.

* * *

Everything was sharper like this—the sound of Matt's voice, the feel of his hands. She couldn't see, could barely move. But she could feel him with every sense. And that made it all the more powerful.

His touch on her while he talked to his business associate had been so hot—and so unlike the calm, intelligent businessman and loving father. She loved how, on the road, his outer mask was falling away to reveal the sexy, predatory male he was at his core.

Hearing the sound of his clothes being tossed across the room, one piece after the other, she couldn't wait for the taste of him, for the feel of his skin against hers as she dragged him inside her. But when the bed dipped a moment later, rather than his hands and mouth on her, the touch was as light and airy as…a feather.

"Tell me how it feels," he urged as he stroked her nipples, swirling around them.

"Sexy." Especially when she felt the downy caresses on her breasts. "So soft it makes me crazy."

He played along her arms, her belly, her thighs, her

knees, and down to the soles of her feet, making her tremble as though her entire body was an erogenous zone. Then he ran the feather between her thighs, the fleeting touch sparking off minor explosions along the surface of her skin.

Finally, he swooped in, sucking her nipple deep into his mouth, and her body arched involuntarily with a pure shaft of pleasure. Then he nipped her…and everything that had coiled so tightly inside her burst wide open.

"*Matt*," she cried out. He laid his hand between her legs, barely stroking her at all, making her come simply from the heat of his touch.

She was still floating, hazy and deep in pleasure, when the bed moved, and he padded softly across the carpet, then back again. He scuffed the side table, and the mattress dipped beside her once more.

Cupping her head, he tilted her until a glass touched her lips. "Drink."

The champagne was cool, fizzy, delicious, and she swallowed thirstily.

"Now this. Open your mouth." He touched something to her lips, and she tasted chocolate. "Bite."

Sweet, succulent fruit spiked with dark chocolate detonated on her taste buds. Chocolate-covered strawberries. She ate greedily, then Matt licked her lips clean, setting her insides completely ablaze. It was almost more than she could bear when he caressed her nipples with the cool fruit, trailing from one to the other.

"Look at that sticky mess I made." His deep, sexy voice rumbled over her. Through her. "I have to clean you up."

Oh God, she could come again from nothing but the raw need in his voice. And as his tongue followed the path of the berry, licking, sucking, tantalizing, she twisted her hands, grabbing hold of the silky scarves binding her wrists, stretching them as taut as her body felt.

Tapping another strawberry against her lips, she took another bite, and then he smeared the other half over her breasts, her stomach, her thighs. Straddling her body, he licked her clean. The pleasure was almost more than she could bear, especially when he drizzled champagne onto the mix and licked that too.

When he'd used his tongue over every inch of the strawberry's path, he kissed her. He tasted like champagne and chocolate and the salt of her skin. He sizzled in her mouth, taking her luxuriously, sucking her lips, her tongue, then going deep.

Finally, he peeled himself off her. But he wasn't done. The bed shifted again, followed by a pop, more sounds, rustles. With a *pfft* of air, something cool and creamy shocked her skin.

"This is why I suggested we skip dessert at the restaurant." He dragged the smooth, chocolatey flesh of another strawberry through all the creaminess on her body and fed it to her. "I wanted to eat it off you instead."

Everything was erogenous when he was doing *this* to her. She moaned and arched her body to meet his mouth. Without sight, she was reduced to sensation. A slave to his lips, his tongue, his hands, her body an instrument he was expert at playing. Until he picked up the can again and she almost bucked off the bed as the cold cream covered her sex.

The sweet treat melted beneath his tongue, and so did she, crying out. The pleasure he gave her was so intense it was almost painful. So good it was exactly the right kind of bad. So close and yet so far.

Because she needed more. She was about to beg, but he knew what she needed even before she opened her mouth. He entered her with two fingers, and she went mindless, out of control. She rode the edge of climax as if it were a tsunami on the horizon, ready to roll in, consume her, and drag her under until she was drowning in pleasure.

Then Matt put his hand under her hips, lifted her against his mouth, and the tsunami crashed over her, a huge wave of bliss—and of wonderful, amazing *Matt*—tumbling through her.

* * *

Ari was still tied down, her moans and cries of pleasure a symphony in his ears. Beyond control, beyond mere need and desire, Matt reared up, grabbed her hips, and slammed home deep inside her. He'd put protection on when he retrieved the whipped cream, knowing he'd need to be ready, anticipating the total collapse of his willpower.

She was covered in streaks of cream and chocolate, her skin deliciously sticky as they slipped and slid together, her body clenching him hard, amplifying the heat between them to dangerous levels.

He covered her mouth with his, kissing her hard and deep. She tasted sweet and was so damned hot as she came again like rockets going off, the explosion far greater than the excitement of having scarves around her wrists and a blindfold covering her eyes. More vast than the taste of her on his lips and tongue, even as delectable as she was.

It was how she felt around him—like he was meant to be here with her.

Only her. Only him.

He lost himself in the connection, loving how she kept pace with him, crying out as she rolled from one peak to another without stopping, both of them wild. Crazy with need. Overwhelmed by pleasure.

Long after they both finally drifted down, she was still blindfolded and tied, their bodies fused, his sprawled across hers. "Oh my God," she whispered.

"I believe you said that last time." He kissed her ear, her cheek, her lips, her neck. She tasted like whipped cream, chocolate strawberries, and all woman.

"But after what just happened in this bed," she said,

a smile in her voice, "it needs to be repeated."

How could he have thought of her as too young, too innocent? She was so unabashed, unashamed. No restrictions, no mind games, just honesty.

"I love that you let me tie you up."

"You'd never hurt me," she said so simply that his heart turned in his chest, beating hard against his rib cage. "I trust you."

He was floored all over again that she believed in him not only to find her brother, but to treat her right. Beneath the weight of her trust, he crumbled. Slipping off her mask, he said, "But you don't know me very well."

She tipped her head up and looked him in the eye, her gaze fierce. "Yes, I do. You're a great father. A great friend. A great son." She smiled a soft, sensual smile. "And a wicked lover."

She might not understand just how deep his scars ran from his childhood, but she was right that he'd already let her in more deeply than he'd ever intended. How could he not when she was so kind, so sweet, so caring, so loyal? Her trust was monumental, and he wanted to earn every ounce of it. He just wasn't sure he could in the long run—not when behind his mask of success and wealth, his darkness still lingered. The fact that he could even be this close to her now was such a gift. One he would appreciate forever, no matter what happened between them in the future. And since tonight was about taking her beyond her pain, he ruthlessly shoved away his fears as he slipped the scarves from her wrists and ankles.

She pushed herself up on her elbows and looked down her body. "I'm a mess."

He licked her breast, her abdomen, her thigh, then headed down to the ties at her ankles. "You're gorgeous." She blushed, as she always did at his compliments, her skin heating against his, her cheeks turning pink. "Hasn't anyone ever told you how perfect you are?"

She wrapped her arms around his neck as he carried her to the bathroom for a shower. "My friends think I'm great."

"I mean men, boyfriends, admirers." In the bathroom, he let her slide down until her feet touched the floor and their bodies were flush.

She was quiet for a long moment before she finally said, "It was always better to downplay myself. So I wouldn't be noticed."

Knowing she had to be talking about some of the foster fathers she'd lived with—and the ways they must have tried to hurt her—he barely bit back a curse.

"You don't have to worry about anything now, Ari." He kissed her with everything in him, deeply, sweetly. For now he refused to think about tomorrow or the next day. Too soon, they'd have to return to life as it had been before this trip, when she would become his son's nanny again and he would worry about the consequences of touching her, of wanting her, of hurting her.

But as long as they were on the road together, away from real life, she was his.

Chapter Twenty-Two

Matt hit the End Call button on the steering wheel the following morning. "Mrs. Esterhausen still isn't answering."

"Maybe we should postpone," Ari suggested.

"We're almost there. If she's not home, we'll have lunch and try again. If she is, we'll be polite and go away if she doesn't want to talk." Determination was clear on his face. "You need to know if she's seen Gideon."

Feeling as though he knew her inside and out, she said, "You're right, I do need to know." They'd brought joy to Mrs. Sanchez. She'd welcomed the chance to go through her daughter's things, to remember her all over again. Ari prayed they could do the same for Mrs. Esterhausen.

"Have I mentioned today how brave you are?" Matt kissed her fingers. "Brave and beautiful."

Her heart swelled at his sweet words. *How could she have been so lucky as to find him?*

Last night, he'd made love to her a second time in the shower with the water beating down on them, washing every inch of her the way he'd kissed every inch earlier in the bed. In the middle of the night, he'd woken her again, pleasuring her until she was a puddle of need. And again, with the morning sun falling across them, his hands on her hips guiding her as she'd ridden them both into oblivion.

I love you.

The words inside her screamed to get out. But though her heart felt close to bursting, the time wasn't right. She didn't want him to think she'd blurted it out simply because she was grateful for his help in finding her brother—or that it was all the hot sex. When she finally told him how deep her feelings ran, she wanted him to know the words came straight from her heart to his.

So she kept the emotion close, savoring it the way she did the feel of his skin on hers and his body inside her.

The miles rushed by until they were on the street where Mrs. Esterhausen lived. There were no boarded-up windows, no trash blowing in the breeze, yet the neighborhood looked exhausted. Most of the houses were in need of paint and new roofs, and the sidewalks were cracked by overgrown tree roots. In front of the Esterhausen place, the lawn had given way to scrubby tufts of grass and weeds. The white picket fence had grayed and was missing some of its pickets, like an old woman who'd lost her teeth. A rusting Chevy sat on blocks on the far side of the driveway. The shades were pulled, and there was no other car in sight.

He leaned over for a quick kiss meant to bolster her bravery before they both got out of the car. The gate to the front path hung open on a broken hinge, and her chest felt tight knowing that it was probably due to the loss of husband and father. Just as Ari's life had changed when her dad died.

Matt's fingers closed around hers as they walked up the path. The doorbell didn't ring when they pressed the button, so she knocked. For the count of ten, they heard nothing. Then a thump of a door closing came from inside the house, and she knocked one more time.

At long last, the door opened to reveal a dark-haired woman, her face as drawn and exhausted as the neighborhood. "Yeah?" she asked, holding the door with one hand. Her gaze flicked between Ari and Matt. "I'm not interested in whatever you're selling."

"We're not selling anything, Mrs. Esterhausen," Ari told her.

The woman narrowed her eyes warily. "How do you know my name?" She might have been pretty a long time ago, but now her body was too thin, her face cut with deep lines that aged her by ten years.

"My brother, Gideon, served with your husband and—"

"What could you possibly want now?" Her voice turned hard and harsh, almost like a slap across Ari's face. "After all this goddamned time?"

"Ma'am—" Matt began.

Mrs. Esterhausen stabbed a finger at him. "I'm asking her, so you just shut up."

Matt's fingers tightened around hers, and Ari knew he was about to jump in to protect her. But she couldn't let him go off on this poor woman.

Squeezing his hand to show him she was okay, she said, "Please, I'm sorry if we're bothering you. But I've been looking for my brother, and I came here today to ask you if you've ever seen him."

"I saw him. He let my husband die out there. Then he came here expecting me to forgive him."

Ari felt her body tingle, like a foot that had gone to sleep. First there was numbness, then pins and needles, then knives as the woman said, "My husband is dead and your brother still gets to live? No." She glared at Ari. "*No*."

"Ari," Matt said softly, never taking his eyes off Mrs. Esterhausen.

She knew he was trying to warn her that they should leave before things got any worse. But though her heart was beating so hard it felt as if it might pound right out of her chest, Ari couldn't leave.

The widow had to get it out. Ari knew what grief did, the terrible things people were capable of, the awful words they said. This woman's children would be in their teens now. She'd had to raise them alone.

"The Army giveth and the Army taketh away," the woman spat. "They left me with nothing. And what does your brother do? He brings me goddamned pictures." She cursed in disgust. "I threw them back at him. I don't forgive him. I don't forgive the Army."

"I'm sorry," Ari said. "I didn't mean to hurt you like this. I won't bother you again."

"You better not. Now get off my property. And if you do find your brother, tell him to go to hell."

Ari backed away, pulling Matt with her. She almost tripped off the concrete porch, and once they were outside the broken gate, Matt bundled her into the car, then quickly climbed in behind the wheel and drove them away.

After a few blocks, he pulled to the curb, shut off the engine, then gathered her into his arms. "I'm so sorry. That wasn't right. It doesn't matter what happened, she didn't have the right to do that to you." He stroked the tears from her cheeks. "Don't cry, sweetheart."

"They're not for me." Some were, but mostly, "I'm crying for Gideon." For the things the woman must have said to him, the rage she must have taken out on him. "No wonder he disappeared. It would have been horrible." She buried her face against Matt's chest. The ache of Gideon's trauma was almost too much to bear.

"I should never have brought you here. I'm so sorry I insisted."

He held her tightly, his warmth flowing into her. And God, she needed him, his arms around her, his breath in her hair, his heart beating against her ear. "It's not your fault. I needed to come here today so that I'd know why Gideon disappeared." She inhaled a shaky breath. "I bet he never made it to the families of the other soldiers. Not after she ripped him apart."

Matt gently wiped away another trickle of tears, first with his fingertips, then with his lips. Soft kisses meant to heal. "I've never met your brother, but something tells me he *did* make it. Because if he's anything like you, he wouldn't have stopped until his mission was complete."

Matt was right about both her and her brother. Gideon wasn't a quitter, which meant there were two more families she needed to talk to. But she was suddenly tired of fighting the fear she'd always worked so hard to hold at bay where her brother was concerned. She sighed as heavily as if a plank of rocks were squeezing out all her breath. She'd never felt this close to hopelessness before.

"I know we should keep going, but I'm not ready to look for the rest of them yet."

"Taking a break can help you see everything more clearly. You've more than earned it, Ari. It's a long drive home, and there's a place in the mountains between here and the Grapevine where we can stay before we get home to my rambunctious five-year-old."

And then he closed his arms around her again and held her close to his beating heart.

* * *

Ari was so emotionally wrung out that as soon as they checked in to the hotel, Matt tucked her into bed for a nap and wouldn't let himself join her so she would actually get the sleep she needed.

Out on the grounds, his hands balled into fists as he thought of Esterhausen's widow. The woman's grief had leaked from her pores, permeating the air, making everything tense and achy. Her anger had been agonizing, and allowing her to take it out on Ari had gone against every one of his protective instincts.

But he hadn't stepped up to protect her, because Ari clearly hadn't wanted him to. Controlling himself from ripping into the widow the same way she'd ripped into Ari had taken a monumental effort. Despite his fury, he couldn't slam someone who'd already been beaten by life and loss.

Knowing that Esterhausen had left behind two boys who would now be fourteen and seventeen, he'd already set the wheels in motion to make an anonymous donation to their college funds.

But that still left Gideon Jones, who was as lost to Ari now as he'd been before their road trip.

Matt looked up at the blue sky above, knowing better than to think a silent wish could come true. He made it anyway, praying he could give Ari her heart's desire and hand over her brother.

The depth of his emotion left him shell-shocked.

The last two nights with Ari in his arms had been just this side of heaven. But watching her allow the widow to abuse her today…

He cursed low and long, outside, where only the trees and the wind could hear. He'd wanted so badly to help her, protect her, comfort her. But he'd been helpless in the face of her anguish.

Once upon a time, he'd thought he needed to make it through alone. But the Mavericks had proved they'd be there for him dozens of times over the past decades, just as he was there for them if they ever needed his help.

Plunking down on a bench beside a gorgeous cluster of blue hydrangeas, he pulled out his phone and made a call to Will. Not to check on Noah this time—but because he needed to talk to one of his closest friends. Needed to lay out the whole debacle, from the moment the widow had opened the door, to Ari's tears, to once again not being able to step up to find her brother.

"Man, that's tough," Will sympathized a few minutes later when Matt finally fell silent.

"I wanted to strangle the woman for her cruelty, but I had to remember what she's been through and that I couldn't lash out to keep Ari safe."

"You're a better man than I am," Will said. "I would have lashed out first, thought second." He paused a beat before asking, "How's Ari doing?"

"She's getting some rest. She's wrung out." It

wrung him out too, her pain, the horror and loss, but telling Will helped ease the tension. The Mavericks neither wore their hearts on their sleeves nor talked about women like drunks at a bar, but they were always there for each other. "She's indomitable. And still convinced I can find her brother, even after this."

"You guys need a break, man."

"Agreed." If Matt could rewind time and live today over, he would have taken Ari home instead of meeting the bitter woman. But even as he thought that, he knew Ari would willingly take any chance to find her brother, no matter how difficult. "I don't want to tackle the other soldiers' families until Ari's over this one."

"Hell, I'm real sorry about all of it. But I'm glad you'll be home for Halloween. Noah's been frantic that you won't make it to the party."

"We won't miss it. And thanks for taking such good care of him."

"Anytime, you know that. Everything else okay?" Will left a pause as pregnant as a woman screaming her way into the hospital.

"Business is fine." If he ignored the question Will hadn't actually asked, maybe it would fade away.

Will let out a low laugh that told Matt things wouldn't go his way. "I meant with you and Ari."

"I... We..." Damn it, even to himself, he sounded like a lovesick fool. One who no longer knew which way was up and which was down.

"Look, Matt, don't worry. I know that whatever happens between you two, you're the kind of guy who'll always do the right thing."

That just made it worse.

When Will hung up, Matt stared unseeing at the phone for a few long moments. His friend had said "you and Ari" as if their getting together was a given. As if it was okay.

But was it?

Could he actually have his beautiful nanny for more than just a few secret days on the road?

All his life, Matt had been careful. He'd learned to control himself, because his father had made him pay whenever he did or said the wrong thing. Only during those early months with Irene had Matt forgotten all his caution. If not for Noah, he never would have forgiven himself for letting down his guard with anyone who wasn't a Maverick. Once he had a child of his own, he'd needed to be hypervigilant with the precious gift he'd been given. And he'd beaten himself up every time he'd blown it.

But with Ari, he forgot those hard-won lessons again and again. He could never have imagined needing a woman the way he was terrified he needed her.

If it did all go wrong, it wouldn't be just his son who paid the price by losing his beloved nanny. Matt would lose too.

He'd lose the brightest light he'd ever known.

Chapter Twenty-Three

When Matt returned to their room, he found Ari still sleeping. She'd been as low as he'd ever seen her when they checked in, and even as she slept, uncharacteristic frown lines marked her brow.

He'd give absolutely anything to return her joy to her. Will had said Matt was the better man. But wouldn't the better man put some space between them until he was certain they could make things work in the real world, not just in secret?

He cursed silently as he watched over Ari. While he couldn't stand the thought of leading her on, there was no way he could leave her alone either. Not today when he needed to find the light as desperately as she did.

Stripping off his clothes, he forced away thoughts of anything but making her happy right here in this moment as he slid between the sheets. He pulled her close, and without waking, she snuggled, sighing sweetly, her arm across his chest.

He lay quietly, relishing the feel of her, soft and warm in his arms. Had any woman's skin ever been so smooth? Had any lover ever been so trusting?

He trailed his hand along her arm, twirling a lock of her hair around his finger. As he listened to her gentle breathing, he couldn't keep his hands off her. Couldn't keep from kissing her cheek, her hair. Under the covers, he nestled her more deeply against him, her fragrance filling his head.

She made a light sound, beginning to wake as her leg slid up his calf, and he tucked his hand under her thigh to press her hips tightly into his. Her fingers flexed on his chest as he moved his lips over her soft skin.

"You're so beautiful. So sweet." He took her mouth, kissing lightly. "So giving. So kind." Her arm curved around him. "I love how you are with Noah." His fingers rambled over her bare back to the waistband of her panties. "I love the sound of your laughter." He buried his face in her hair, then moved to her ear, tracing his tongue along the shell so that she shivered in his arms. "You're strong and smart and funny." He gently bit the curve of her shoulder, and she rewarded him with a soft laugh. "I love that you take Noah to see mummies and monkeys."

"Gorillas," she corrected, a smile in her voice as she came fully awake.

His heart expanded as he pulled back to see her smile. "I love how open you are with me. That you trust me to love you the way you deserve to be loved."

She cupped his face in her palm. "Love me, Matt.

Please just love me."

Their mouths melded in a long, drugging kiss that sent his heart soaring. Rolling her onto her back, he braced himself over her, kissing her cheeks, her eyes, and finally her lips. They had until tomorrow morning, and he wanted to love her long enough to make her forget the unbearable scene at the Esterhausen place.

* * *

Their coming together had always been about pleasure, about how many times he could make her come, how crazy she could get, how hard and fast he could take her.

But tonight, Ari wanted the precious intimacy of Matt inside her. Just that. As if it weren't merely sex, but a total union. She wanted to relish the feel of him without being blinded by her own climax. Not yet. First, she wanted to savor him.

After he stripped away her bra and panties, she trailed her fingers along the arrow of hair stretching down into his boxers. "You're so beautiful," she said, the same words he'd said to her. "So sweet." She cupped him inside the cotton. Hard, hot, ready. "So giving." He'd treated her so tenderly, soothing the hurt of that horrible visit. She couldn't remember all the things he'd whispered to her, only that they'd wrapped around her heart and drawn her to him. "I love how you stood up for me."

He closed his eyes and breathed harshly. "I should

have done more." His voice broke softly with his anguish.

"You already do so much. More than anyone else ever has." More than she'd ever expected anyone would.

He was a protector, always looking out for her, physically, emotionally. And as he slid on latex, she let him protect her again, though she wanted nothing more than to feel his bare skin against hers.

She was already slick with desire, and part of her wanted the bliss, the mindless pleasure that would come if he took her fast, hard, out of control. But he filled her slowly, as if he were pouring himself into her, seeping into all the cracks and fissures that had been inside her for years. She swore he was healing them all, even the fracture she'd suffered today. When their bodies were finally tight together, she let out a sigh of soul-deep pleasure.

Then he kissed her.

They kissed forever, with only the sound of their breath and their mouths sliding together. It was sweetness, it was beauty, it was beyond pleasure.

She felt alive and beautiful and totally possessed.

Slowly, she raised her legs to his waist, and he moved deeper still, so high inside her that she could almost feel him touch her heart. His stillness let her feel everything fully—the pulse of his blood, the way her body tightened and rippled over him of its own accord. She curled her arms around his neck and kissed him with everything in her heart, until he was all she could taste and smell and feel. Until he was simply everything.

The other nights they'd shared had been bliss, but this was pure heaven.

She locked her feet at his back, and he moved to accommodate her. Then, suddenly, she needed more—and yet again, he read her mind, moving slow and sweet, so utterly tantalizing, her nerve endings coming completely alive.

All the while, he kissed her, angling his head to take another long sip of her. When he groaned, she felt the vibration in her mouth, her throat, against her chest.

She gasped, finally breaking free of his lips as he slid over her most sensitive spot inside, setting her on fire. "*More*," she begged, and he gave it to her, his muscles gathering for speed, friction, and crazy wild sensation. She clung to him, rocking, letting him take her higher, until they were flying.

Then everything splintered, and she crashed through, holding him tight, hauling him with her, shuddering, quaking, losing herself in him, just as he lost himself in her.

Ari came to her senses slowly, drinking in the salty-sweet smell of their sex, the tightness of her muscles, his body on hers, his throb deep, his breath still wild in her hair, his skin stuck to hers. She didn't want him to move, craving his weight on her and his pulse inside her. As if they were one.

"That was just what I needed. *You* are just what I needed."

"I needed you too, Ari." Finally, he moved, and her arms slipped away, only her hands remaining on his shoulders as he levered himself above her. "I wanted to be there for you with that woman today. I wanted to protect you. I wanted to avenge you."

She held him still, his face now in her palms. "You're the most beautiful, kind, caring man I've ever known." She could no longer keep the words inside. Or how true they were. "I love you."

* * *

She loved him.

Matt reeled as her words played over and over inside his head. It was pure instinct to claim her mouth again as emotion grew bigger, stronger inside of him. Though he hadn't said he loved her too, she didn't hold anything back, just kissed him as fearlessly as she'd declared her love.

A week ago, he would have tried again to tell himself she was too young, that she didn't have enough experience to know the real thing. After all, he'd once been young and naive enough to think he loved Noah's mother.

But the past days on the road had proved Ari's age had nothing whatsoever to do with how strong she was. How brave. How fearless.

All he wanted was to make her happy, and hearing

those same words from his lips would bring her the joy he sought to give her. But Matt never made promises he couldn't keep.

Ari was beautiful and special and unique, but he still didn't know if he was capable of giving her what she truly needed. She deserved real love, which meant you never, ever let a person down. Yet he'd let her down today, hadn't he?

Because no matter how much Ari thought she could take, he should have gotten her out of there the moment the widow Esterhausen started to spew her vitriol. It was exactly like that day the little bully had slapped the book out of Noah's hand. Matt had watched, waiting for the right moment to step up, only to be too late.

That was why he couldn't say those words back to her yet. Not until he knew for sure that he could be a better man who would never, ever let her down. Which meant, at the very least, keeping his promise of finding her brother.

Still, he needed to give her something right now. Needed her to know how much she meant to him, even if he couldn't give her the words he knew she wanted to hear.

He drew back from her beautiful mouth. "Ari—"

She put a finger over his lips. "I love you. I need you to know that. But that doesn't mean you have to say it back tonight."

Her smile was as sweet and gentle as her touch,

and he was amazed that she could bare her heart to him so fearlessly. He'd brought her into his life so that she could teach his son, but Matt was the one who was learning the most from her.

Learning how to trust again.

Learning how to find joy in the little things, like a sunny afternoon on a backyard trampoline.

Learning how to have hope even when the odds all seemed stacked against you.

"Ari—" he began again, but before he could fumble his words, she kissed him, taking all the things he felt but didn't know how to say and transforming them into sweet, boundless pleasure.

Chapter Twenty-Four

They headed home the next day, stopping briefly at Matt's house to pick up the Halloween costumes before going to Will Franconi's place in Portola Valley.

Matt hadn't said he loved her, and Ari wouldn't lie to herself and say it didn't hurt. But there was something different and special in the way he looked at her now, in the gentleness of his touch, the sweetness of his kisses.

Ari had stopped fighting the depth of her feelings days ago, weeks even, but she knew that Matt needed more time, especially given how things had gone with his ex. Who wouldn't need extra time to heal after that train wreck?

But letting herself fall headlong in love didn't mean she'd completely lost control. There was no way she could look at Daniel, talk to Susan and Bob Spencer, mingle with Matt's friends, or pick up Noah in her arms, if they were all thinking she was some dumb hick who'd tumbled foolishly into bed with the rich guy she worked for. Or worse, that she was a schemer who was only after his money.

A powerful instinct told her that the only way what they'd shared could work outside of these few private days on the road was if they were both equal partners in love—not if she was the only one with hearts in her eyes. Which was why she didn't want to claim Matt publicly until he was ready to claim her too.

That was the last thing they'd talked about before they'd gotten out of the car in Will and Harper's driveway. Matt had looked slightly uncomfortable as he'd said, "While we're here, I don't know if we—" He'd broken off with a low curse.

"I agree." She'd been trying to figure out how to say the same thing and was glad he'd brought it up first. "What happened…it would be best to keep it just between us for now." Though he'd started the discussion, he didn't look relieved about keeping them a secret. She'd tucked the evidence away inside her heart as yet more proof that he truly cared about her even if he hadn't said the words she so wanted to hear. "I'm not ashamed of what we're doing, but it's just all so new." *And you need more time.* "For now, it seems like enough for the two of us to keep figuring things out without everyone else weighing in."

He'd been silent for several beats before finally nodding. "You're right. My friends and family are great, but they can be a hell of a peanut gallery." He reached for her hand and held on tight. "This road trip was great, Ari. I loved being with you."

I loved being with you wasn't *I love you*, but she'd refused to ruin things because he wasn't as far along the emotional track as she was. Nor had she kissed him in broad daylight in his friends' driveway, even if she'd been desperate to feel the strength of their connection one more time before the party began.

Her answer had been simple. "I loved it too. Thank you for taking so much time off to help me." Then she'd made herself pull her hand from his and get out of the car. As Will and Harper had greeted them and shown them to their separate bedrooms, she'd made herself act like the nanny again, rather than a lover.

Just as in Matt's home, she was put up in a magnificent guest suite in order to dress for the Halloween party. And now, Noah was there with her as she helped him into his costume.

"You're adorable," she told him, squatting down to his level.

"Don't want to be adorable." He screwed up his face. "I'm scary."

She hugged him close, her heart overflowing. "I'm certainly scared. Give me a roar."

He roared, and though she had to admit it sounded more like a squawk, she pretended to be terrified, making him giggle.

"All right, let's go." She took his hand to lead him out.

The house was starting to rumble with all the guests arriving. Will had invited his employees in the local area and their families. A bartender manned the open bar near the fire pit, while at the front door, Cinderella greeted the guests. The special hooped metal skirt over her fancy ball gown held champagne flutes and rolled on wheels, allowing her to move. The glasses on one side were filled with bubbly and the other half contained punch for the kids. Everyone was fascinated as they plucked drinks right out of metal holders on her skirt.

Left of the entry hall, the dining room table was stacked with trays of food that attracted as many people as Cinderella did.

Near the bottom of the stairs, Susan Spencer turned to them. "It's so good to see you again, Ariana." She'd been very sweet to Ari when they'd volunteered at the youth home in San Jose. "Oh my goodness, look at my big boy." Susan bent down, holding out both Noah's arms encased in the green satiny suit. When Bob Spencer, Will, Harper, and Jeremy had gathered round, he roared for his audience.

"Noah's Godzilla," Jeremy crowed, dressed in a Frankenstein monster costume.

Ari gasped with laughter at Will beside him, dressed as Jeremy's Bride of Frankenstein, complete with the freaky wig. These men might all be billionaires, but there was certainly nothing stereotypical about any of them. Especially Matt. Her heart beat faster just thinking of how close they'd become this week.

Noah shook his head at Jeremy. "I'm T-Rex from

Jurassic World."

Ari had come up with the idea that, since he was afraid of the movie dinosaur, becoming one might help him get over his fear. It appeared to be working when he roared again, sounding much better than the squawk he'd produced upstairs.

Susan shuddered dramatically. "I'm very scared."

"You should be, Grandma." Noah flexed his hands in his green clawlike gloves. His tail swayed, its spine stiffened so that it curled at the end. Then he threw himself at his grandpa Bob.

Together, Bob and Susan were dressed like *The Addams Family*, Morticia and...Ari couldn't remember the husband's name. Susan looked fabulous in the slim-fitting black skirt. And Bob was regal in his tailored suit.

He hauled Noah up and swung him around, the dinosaur tail narrowly missing Jeremy. "Grandpa, put me down. I'm supposed to bite your legs."

"Oh yeah, sorry."

They all laughed as Noah growled and roared again while wrapping his arms around Bob's legs.

"You look so lovely," Harper Newman said, her hand on Ari's arm. She was radiant even in Dr. Frankenstein's white doctor's coat, white face paint and black lipstick. "I love your Esmerelda gypsy girl costume."

Ari twirled and the little fake coins on the skirt tinkled. Then she waved her hand at Will. "I'm surprised at who chose to be what character in the Frankenstein story."

Jeremy thumped his hand to his chest and smiled wide. "I chose. I wanted to be the monster. And if I'm the monster and Harper's my sister, then she couldn't be the bride." He pointed at Will. "So we made Will the bride."

Will gathered Dr. Frankenstein close and whispered something in her ear that made her laugh.

Ari loved the team they made, Will, Harper, and Jeremy, in the hall greeting guests, laughing and talking with everyone. It was great that they'd costumed themselves as a unit, with a very alpha Will dressing in drag just to make Harper's brother happy.

They were joined a moment later by Daniel, who held champagne for her and punch for Noah. He wore his usual khakis and sports jacket.

"Thank you," she said, taking the champagne after a quick hug. "I can't believe you're such a party pooper that you didn't dress up. You could have been Uncle Fester from *The Addams Family*."

"Do you hear that, Mom? She called me Uncle Fester."

Susan rolled her eyes teenage-style. "You'd make a better Thing."

"Isn't Thing the weird hairy creature?"

Susan laughed and ruffled her son's hair. "No, dear, but that's apt since you need a haircut. Thing is the severed hand."

Daniel held up his arm, pulling back the sleeve of

his jacket. "See, I came in costume. I'm Thing. I just haven't been severed yet."

They all laughed, and it was so good to feel like one of them even if she wasn't. Not yet. Not until Matt was ready to let himself love her the way she was sure he wanted to. But she understood how past experiences made you scared to trust or to risk. So she'd be patient, no matter how badly she wanted to hear him say *I love you*.

"Where's Sebastian, dear?" Susan asked, her hand on Will's arm.

"He and Charlie are up at the haunted house putting on the last-minute touches."

Harper looped her arm through Will's. "Charlie was wonderful in lending her artistic talents for the haunted house. Did you see it up on the hill?" She waved in the general direction. "Jeremy wanted to do something fun, and they've gone all out for him with scary creatures. She made a lot of them, in papier-mâché instead of metal. And there's—"

Jeremy pulled on her arm. "*Har-purr*," he said with huge exaggeration. "Don't spoil the surprise."

Harper put her hand over her mouth. "Oops."

"Oh my." Susan gasped. "Will you look at that dashing figure?"

Everyone in their group looked up the stairs. Matt descended dressed in an immaculate tux that fit him so closely it defined every one of his magnificent muscles. He'd slicked his hair back, and he sauntered down the steps like he owned the world. Which he undoubtedly did.

Ari's mouth went dry just watching him. He held out his hand to her when he reached the bottom, saying, "Bond. James Bond. At your service."

She shook his hand in a daze, feeling heat all the way to her toes. He was so polished and perfect. She wished she'd dressed as a Bond girl to match him.

Then, realizing too late that everyone's eyes were on them, she withdrew her hand, sliding it behind her back to hide how his touch affected her.

"Daddy, guess who I am?" Noah was bouncing, his T-Rex tail hitting the floor.

"Oh no, it's T-Rex!" Matt cowered, throwing his arms out in fear. Noah roared, a loud, perfect rumble that shut down all conversation for three seconds while everyone in the hall stared.

"It's going to get me," Matt cried and ran in small steps so Noah could catch him.

"Really," Daniel drawled. "James Bond should have more dignity."

"At least I dressed up," Matt said, pulling on Noah's tail.

"You're just wearing your tux."

Matt suddenly crouched in a Bond shooting stance, reaching quick as lightning behind his back to draw out a gun, and shooting Daniel with a stream of water. "Bull's-eye."

Just like that, Ari fell in love with him all over

again.

It was his laughter, the water pistol, the way he'd played the terrified victim with Noah. And how beautiful he was in that tux. You could love a friend. You could lust after a man. But with both lust and love coming together, it was enough to make a girl swoon.

Noah grabbed Matt's hand. "Daddy, take a picture and send it to Mommy. I want her to see T-Rex."

Matt shot a quick glance at Ari, and the look said so much. Irene was the ghost in Noah's funhouse—and if he didn't hear back from his mother, he'd be hurt all over again.

Quickly hiding his reaction, Matt said, "Sure, buddy." He caught a shot of Noah roaring, then texted it. "It'll scare her to death."

Thankfully, two seconds later, his phone pinged. Irene had sent back a terrified smiley face followed by lots of heart emoticons, which made Noah laugh.

For one long moment, Ari felt as if she were alone in the hall with Matt, everyone watching Noah, only Matt's gaze on her, communicating silently. He could have refused to take the picture. But he'd done the right thing, giving Noah the contact with his mother that made him so happy.

She wanted to reach out to touch Matt even if the time wasn't right. And she might have if Jeremy hadn't started to chant, "Haun-ted house. Haun-ted house." Noah joined in, then Susan and Bob, and finally the downstairs filled with the cry.

Will climbed two stairs and clinked his glass. "Silence!" he called out. "Let me see if the ghosts are haunting." Reaching into his Bride of Frankenstein pocket for his phone, he pushed his wig slightly out of the way so he could put the cell to his ear. A few seconds later, he held up the phone and yelled, "The haunt is on!"

The cheers were deafening.

"You've all got your tickets." Cinderella had handed them out along with the drinks. "Rob the bartender will call the numbers every fifteen minutes. We've got a shuttle bus in front to take you to the haunted house when your number is up."

A shuttle bus. A real haunted house. So *this* was how billionaires did Halloween.

"I didn't get a ticket," Noah pouted.

Will leaned down, almost toppling his wig. "That's because you get to go on the first bus. You're special."

"Wow," Noah said with a huge smile. "I'm special."

Will said to the adults, "Privileges of being a Maverick—we all get to go first."

"But Evan and Whitney and Paige aren't here yet," Susan said.

"We can't keep this crowd waiting," Will replied. "They might attack with pitchforks."

The Bride of Frankenstein gathered up his monster and his doctor and led the way to the first shuttle bus. Ari slid into a seat and Matt followed, pulling Noah onto his lap, the dinosaur tail sticking into the aisle.

Like a brand, she felt Matt's heat through the thin material of her gypsy skirt. And she wished she hadn't made that promise—to them both—not to touch him while they were here.

* * *

Ari was beyond gorgeous as a gypsy girl, her midriff bared, her calves laced with gladiator-style sandals. The cleavage in the deep vee of her tight, sparkly top made all of Matt's pistons fire.

He'd stood at the top of the stairs watching her for long moments before coming down. She was so natural, so easy and real as she'd laughed and joked with the Mavericks, with Noah, with Susan and Bob. She fit so well with everyone he cared about, the way Harper and Jeremy did, the way Charlie and her mother, Francine, did.

He'd wanted to claim Ari in front of everyone. But how could he when he was still unable to shake the feeling that, ultimately, he wouldn't be able to be there for her when she needed him most?

Can't stick up for nothing and nobody.

His father's voice still plagued him. And it was true that he hadn't yet found her brother. Hell, he hadn't even been able to tell her how he felt.

But God help him, he still couldn't stop touching her.

Noah grabbed the seat in front to shout with glee at

Susan, and Matt leaned close to whisper against Ari's ear. "I don't know how I'm supposed to keep my hands off you when you're dressed like that."

"As a matter of fact, you aren't," she whispered back as she shook his wandering hand off her thigh.

"Oh. Yeah. Sorry. It just happened."

"Liar," she whispered. But she couldn't hide her smile—or the glimmer in her eyes that said she loved the fact that he was driven to touch her. And while guilt simmered low in his gut and knowing he hadn't yet declared his feelings for her, he simply couldn't put any distance between them. Not when they'd been so close over the past three days. He craved that closeness now.

The bus zigged and zagged up the winding drive to Will's workshop, where he and Jeremy had built the Cobra. Next to it, workmen had toiled for the last month constructing a haunted house right out of *Psycho*, complete with a long set of stairs leading to it. For safety, Will had installed lighting on the steps and in the spooky graveyard alongside it. But inside it would be dark and scary. And intimate.

Dark enough, he hoped, to get his hands on Ari for a moment or two.

Clambering out of the shuttle, Noah pulled at his hand, surging ahead as scary calliope music played like at the Haunted Mansion at Disneyland. "Daddy, Daddy, we gotta be first."

Matt would have preferred to be last, so no one

would see him grab Ari. But Noah couldn't be held back.

Hands pushed Matt forward. "Come on. Little kids gotta see." That was Bob, maybe Daniel too.

Noah grabbed Ari's hand as the doors opened automatically into near pitch darkness. Red laser lights flashed on, splashing the front hall as if it were covered in blood. A man laughed from an overhead chandelier, and the red lights caught his dangling feet.

The laser lights led them along a hallway, where a door opened suddenly and a mummy grabbed for Noah. He squealed and jumped and wrapped an arm around Ari's leg. "It's the mummy from the museum," he whispered with awe.

The mummy retreated, and the door slammed. It had been so lifelike that Matt thought a real person might be under all those bandages.

The house was filled with eerie sounds, doors slamming, and things that went bump in the night. The laser lights herded everyone along the designated path of mummies, ghosts, vampires, shapeshifters, fire-breathing dragons, headless bodies, or sometimes just dozens of eyes staring out, blinking, coming closer, closer. The long zigzag hall ended, and they were forced up a set of steps. Hands reached out to grab, and Noah was constantly shrieking with delight and terror.

Upstairs, they were handed blindfolds by a woman dripping blood, and they entered an old-fashioned gag room with bowls of fake eyeballs and beating hearts and entrails that you stuck your hands into. Noah laughed and screamed and *ewwed*. Ari shrieked right along with him, especially when Matt put his cold, wet hand on the sliver of bare back between her skirt and top.

She slapped at him and pulled her blindfold down far enough to playfully glare at him. Of course, he wasn't wearing his blindfold. How else was he supposed to find her?

They toured bedrooms that turned cold and beds that rose off the floor while ghostly sounds surrounded them. The old attic rattled with chains, and bones rolled across the floor. And everywhere, gory, scary creatures jumped out unexpectedly.

Noah was thrilled, shouting and giggling all the while. Clawed hands grabbed his dinosaur tail, pretending to drag him away, until Ari rescued him from the beast.

At last, they exited out a side door that led them through the graveyard filled with eerie sounds and ghostly clankings, finally making it down to the drive just as another busload of partygoers was climbing up the front steps.

"That was so fun." Jeremy bounced as excitedly as Noah.

"Daddy." Noah tugged hard on Matt's hand. "I wanna go again."

"Me too," Jeremy cried with equal enthusiasm.

"Aren't you hungry, buddy?" Matt asked. "I'm

starving so bad it hurts."

Will elbowed him. "You always are."

"We'll take him back through." Susan leaned down to Noah. "I was so scared I want to do it all over again."

They were about to part, half of them heading to the bus to go down, the other half following the group who'd just entered, when Charlie appeared out of nowhere. Sebastian was right behind her, his hands on her.

Sebastian always had his hands on Charlie, and for the first time, Matt understood why. He felt the same way about Ari, and with a light tug on her skirt, he signaled her to come with him rather than following the others back into the house.

"That was brilliant, Charlie." Daniel grabbed her up in one of his bear hugs.

"I've never had so much fun building anything," she said, laughing. Wearing overalls after obviously putting the final touches on her magnificent creation, she hadn't dressed in her costume yet. Neither had Sebastian. "Will had all the workmen out here, and I just figured out the stunts. He hired a troupe of actors from the high school to play the monsters grabbing people."

"You all outdid yourselves," Susan said. "Charlie, dear, where's your mother? I was so hoping to have a nice chat with her."

"The party is too much for her to handle," Charlie

explained, curling her fingers around Sebastian's. "But we'd love for you and Bob to come for lunch at Magnolia Gardens tomorrow. Mom wants to show the place off to you. They have a marvelous Sunday brunch."

"That would be wonderful."

That was all the chitchat Noah could handle, tugging on Susan's hand. "We'll talk later," Susan said, then let herself be led away. "Don't worry, Matt," she called. "I've got him until we find you again."

"We're holding up the next busload." Will clapped Matt's shoulder. "And we'd better get this guy some food before he wastes away to nothing."

Yes, he was starving. For Ari. On the bus, he slid into the seat beside her and worked like hell to keep his hands to himself on the short drive. Back at the house, he walked toward the food since it was expected of him, but instead of piling a plate high, he circled the table and headed for the other door.

"If you don't want me to grab you right here," he murmured to Ari, "you'd better follow. Or I'll be forced to drag you off."

"You're incorrigible," she said, a pleased lilt in her voice.

They waded through the crowd toward the back hall and down the spiral staircase to Will's media and game rooms. At the far end, the basement gave way to the pool deck, and Matt led Ari around the corner to the changing rooms Will had built for his pool guests.

Opening a door, he nudged her inside.

"Are you crazy?" she whispered.

He locked the door, then gathered her into his arms, nuzzling her neck. "Crazy for you."

Chapter Twenty-Five

Matt kissed her long and hard, pushing her up against the wall, holding her there. Giving herself over to him completely, she wrapped her arms around his neck, kissing him until she couldn't breathe, until her body was melting against his. The small changing room turned into a sauna from the heat they generated, and the little coins on her skirt jingled against him.

"We should get back to the party before anyone realizes we're missing," she said. But she clung to him because, God help her, she didn't want to go back.

"I need to love you first, or I'll go crazy. I'm barely keeping it together as it is."

He raised the material of her skirt, the coins tinkling harder and faster—like the beating of her heart at the word *love* falling from his lips. Sliding his hands up her thighs, he palmed her sex.

"God." He closed his eyes as he slipped his fingers into her panties and touched her the way she was dying for. "You're so ready for me. Always so hot and slick."

She knew she should care that the party was going on all around them, that Noah was out there somewhere and Matt's family was nearby—but she simply couldn't. When Matt touched her, everything else ceased to matter.

"Your skin is so soft." He dragged down her panties, letting them fall to the floor so Ari could step out of them.

"This is crazy." Yet she nipped at his mouth, his chin, every hot, sexy, beautiful part of him she could reach.

He stole her breath with another kiss, backing off only to say, "Tell me you want me as bad as I want you."

"*Please*, I need you. So bad." Not just his touch, his kiss.

She needed *all* of him.

He trailed his hands over her body, going down on his knees as he bunched the material of her skirt into her hands. "Don't let go," he commanded in a super sexy tone that made everything inside her sizzle. Then he breathed on her, warm air that sent sensation spiraling down to her center. "I can't get enough of you. I can never get enough."

He pressed kisses to her warm flesh, and her body blossomed for him. He teased her with those kisses, then opened her to his mouth, tonguing her very center. A wild madness took her over. Moaning, she put her hand to the back of his head as he suckled her and sensation rocketed through her. She whimpered, clutching the skirt tightly in one hand, holding him close with the other. Her legs shook with a rush of pleasure. Her skin heated, and she tipped her head back against the wall, eyes closed, savoring without sight, just as she had the night he'd blindfolded her.

As he worshipped her with his mouth, she sucked in a breath, feeling the weight of it in her chest before letting it tremble out. And when he entered her with his fingers, finding that sensitive spot inside, the words spilled out.

"Matt."

"Please."

"I love you."

He held fast to her as her body quaked. He took her higher until she was on the edge, where there was only touch and sensation and the feelings inside her as she came apart, her legs buckling beneath her as she tumbled down into his arms, the little coins jangling.

He pulled her onto his lap. "God, I need you. Now. I don't care where we are. I need *you*."

She wrapped her fists in his lapels, drugged with desire for him. With all her love shining for him. "Yes. Please. Hurry." She couldn't wait.

Thank God, he had a condom ready, and when it was on, he held her tightly at the waist. "Take me, Ari, all of me."

She would take *everything*. Sliding down, the feel of him filling her all the way to her soul, she moaned, digging her fingers into his arms. "Matt," she whispered. And then she well and truly took him, moving fast and crazy, wanting it so badly, feeling his answering need in the pulse of his sex inside her. He held her face, brought her mouth to his and drank down her moans. They moved like one body, one soul, one never-ending kiss.

Until the world exploded around them, like fireworks, like rockets, like a solar flare. They held on, drained every ounce of pleasure, their bodies fused, an indelible part of each other.

In a heap on the floor, he held her as her body shuddered with the last tremors of pleasure coursing through her. She lay against him, clutching his tux, keeping him tight against her.

"You're perfect," he whispered into her hair. "I love the way you come, like you're lost to everything but me."

"I am lost," she whispered. She had been since the first time she'd seen him with his son. So loving. So sweet.

"I never meant for this to happen." His words were thick with guilt, and his emotions speared her, sinking even deeper than the first time he'd apologized for taking advantage of her. "The way I felt about you from the moment I saw you. How badly I want you. But I can't stop myself, Ari."

"*No.*" The one word was harsh on her lips. "Don't tell me you regret anything. That you feel guilty." She looked him straight in the eyes. "Not now. Not after all we've done."

And not after you know that I love you.

"Ari—"

But she wasn't finished. "The first time I saw you, I was attracted to you." She licked her lips, tasting their loving all over again. And not regretting one single second of it. "Just because I didn't know this would happen, that we would become so close, doesn't mean I'm not glad that we have."

"You need to be with someone hopeful. Someone with a good, clean past who'll never let you down." His anguish made her whole body ache.

"Matt." How could she make him understand? "You came out of a bad childhood and had a bad relationship, but you're still perfect just the way you are. You've never let anyone down, not Noah, not me. And you deserve happiness."

He deserved *her*.

"More than anything," he said, "I want you to be happy. But I can't leave you alone. I had to touch you tonight."

"I love that. It makes me feel special. *You* make me feel special." She couldn't stand to hear him explain again why he shouldn't love her. No one could touch her the way he did without huge feelings. Without love. "And I'm happier than I've ever been."

"But I haven't found your brother for you."

"I—" She stopped. She'd been about to say that she knew he would. Because she believed in him with all her heart. But suddenly she saw that her faith in him was just one more screw tightening the pressure on him to always make things right. And if he couldn't, he felt as if he'd let down the people he cared about. "I don't expect you to solve my problems, Matt. You're doing your best, and that's all I could ever ask for." He opened his mouth—likely to refute what she'd said—and she put her fingers over his lips. "My brother will come home. Someday, somehow. I feel it in here." She put her hand to her heart. "I'm not expecting you to work miracles. But you've already done more for me than any other person on earth."

He pulled her close, holding her tightly for a long moment. She could only hope her words had seeped in, but all he said was, "I shouldn't keep you in here any longer, or someone will find us. I know you don't want that."

Maybe she did want everyone to know. Because it might be the only way Matt would admit his feelings.

No. She sighed, knowing she couldn't force him. He had to figure it out on his own.

And she needed to be fearless enough to give him the time and space to get there.

"I wish we could stay like this all night," she said into the warm crook of his neck. "But we should leave."

Pulling her to her feet, he left her for a moment to step into the small bathroom. His tux was straight when he came back, and he helped her smooth the layers of her skirt and the tinkling coins. Then he ran his fingers through her hair, gently pulling out the tangles he'd made.

"Do I look okay?"

He held her gaze. "Absolutely beautiful."

"I'll go first." She didn't want to go at all, but the idea of hiding inside the changing room was worse. Her hand on the knob, she was about to dash out the door when he hauled her close for another kiss.

It was only when she was rushing out onto the pool deck that she remembered her panties were still on the floor.

* * *

Running a hand through his hair, Matt spied the lacy scrap on the floor. He hadn't even taken care to make sure she got them back on.

I love you.

She'd said it again.

And the words haunted him.

How could she be so sure? She'd said it didn't matter that he hadn't found her brother. But how could he prove himself to her—how could he prove that he was worthy of her—without keeping that promise?

He scooped up the panties and shoved them deep into his pocket. He would give them back to her tonight. After Noah was asleep and the house was quiet, Matt would ravish her all over again. He couldn't stop, didn't *want* to stop, even if guilt ate him up from the inside out.

He walked out and closed the door behind him, turning to head back through the media room.

And he ran right into Daniel.

"*What the hell are you doing?*"

They'd been best friends since the age of eleven. They'd grown into manhood together. They'd made a pact to get the hell out of Chicago, to make it big, and to always be there for each other. The Maverick pact. Yet the look on Daniel's face was one he'd seen reserved only for outsiders. It was a look that said, *One wrong move and it's all over.*

Matt could have said he didn't know what the hell Daniel was talking about, but his friend had obviously seen Ari leave the changing room. He'd clearly been waiting for the man who followed her out, arms crossed over his chest, brows drawn together in a glare that would have made most men's knees crumble.

Damn it. This was exactly what Matt hadn't wanted to happen. "It isn't your business."

Daniel slowly unfolded his arms, his fists clenched. "I let her move into your house," he said in a low voice, fueled with rage. "I told her she didn't have to worry. I said you'd protect her the way I have." He moved closer to Matt, every step menacing. "Ari sure as hell *is* my business. Especially if you're screwing around with her."

Their voices were covered by the *ka-ching* of pinball machines, the laughter around the pool table, the clack of a foosball game and the shouts of its contestants. No one noticed them facing off.

At least, as long as they didn't start brawling.

"Are you going to deny it?" Daniel asked, his voice as menacing as his stance. "Are you going to make up some candy-assed excuse for why you were in there with Ariana?"

"Her name's Ari." Matt didn't know why it was so important to point that out. Maybe it was his way of showing Daniel that he knew her better than his friend did. "That's what she likes to be called."

"Well, I like respecting her by calling her Ariana. Because she's special."

"You think I don't know just how special she is?" Matt's hands fisted too.

"Then tell me what the hell you think you're doing with her."

Somehow, Matt stopped himself from cursing aloud. How could he answer Daniel when he was trying to figure out that very thing?

What the hell *was* he doing with her? Loving her? Showing her how special she was?

Or setting her up—setting both of them up—for heartbreak?

With some sort of internal Maverick radar, Sebastian appeared on the stairs, followed by Will and Evan. "Look who finally arrived," Will called out.

But Daniel was already headed through the door to the pool deck. Matt followed. So did the others. Since the Halloween chill had rolled in, the deck was deserted.

"What's up?" Sebastian asked, his gaze ping-ponging between them.

"He's making moves on his nanny." Daniel glared at Matt.

"Jesus, man," Sebastian said. "You're screwing around with Ariana?"

Evan stared at Matt as though he were a mutant bug, while Will, who'd already figured it all out, kept his mouth shut.

"She's more than my nanny." He couldn't keep lying to his friends. "And I swear I'm not just screwing around with her."

"What the hell does that mean?" Daniel growled.

Matt stared at his friends, his brothers in arms, his blood without being blood. "It means I care for her. That I don't want to hurt her." Hell, hurting Ari was the very last thing he wanted.

He waited for them to ask the obvious questions. What were his intentions toward her? How did he see her in his and Noah's future? Was he in love with her?

But, with the same Maverick radar that had pulled all five of them outside, none of them asked. He could guess why. They knew him well enough to understand that his head—that every part of him—was too twisted up right now to give them any straight answers.

After long, excruciating seconds, Daniel finally said, "If she gets hurt, I *will* beat the crap out of you."

Matt met his friend's gaze. "If I hurt her, you have

my full permission to tear me to pieces. But right now, this is something Ari and I have to work out ourselves."

They stared at each other, Daniel's gaze measuring, until finally the tension in his face eased fractionally. "All right," he said. Then he tipped his head like a shaggy dog. "I wouldn't mind if she became family. She's a good kid."

"She's not a kid, Daniel. She's a beautiful woman."

"I know that." Then he chucked Matt upside the head. "But you're an asshole for putting her in a compromising position."

"I am," Matt agreed. "Don't think I don't know how special she is, Daniel. Because I do. I've always known it."

Daniel slung his arm around his shoulders and herded him back inside. "Just keep treating her like she's special. That's what Ariana deserves. And if you don't"—he knuckled Matt's head—"I won't be the only one who beats the living daylights out of you."

The guys all *hoo-rah*ed their agreement.

Ari was sweet, giving, kind, caring—all the things he'd told her last night. Any rational man—a normal guy with a normal upbringing and normal past relationships—would see that loving her couldn't possibly be a mistake.

But Matt wasn't normal. And no matter how much empathy she had because they'd grown out of similar circumstances, it still didn't change his dark past, his parents, the mirror they'd held up to all his faults, his weaknesses. *You're puny and weak and you'll never be a man.* And now Matt felt like he was proving exactly that by not telling Ari how he felt about her—by keeping the words she wanted to hear locked up inside him. If only he could be absolutely certain that he wouldn't hurt her later on down the road.

Will grabbed his arm, jerking him out of his thoughts, holding him back while the others climbed the stairs. "I knew that trip wasn't all about finding Ari's brother."

"That's what it was supposed to be. I wanted to help her the way she's helped Noah." The truth hit Matt square in the chest. "But I found something else as well."

A connection to Ari. One so strong it left him reeling.

"Meeting Harper—" Will smiled with total adoration. "It was like a ton of bricks falling on me. Good thing she was patient, because it took me way too long to figure out I loved her." He looked at Matt. "I see the way you look at Ari. And the way she looks at you." He raised his eyebrows. "Makes me think the bricks might already have fallen." When Matt didn't know how to reply, Will added, "Here's hoping she's as patient with her Maverick as Harper and Charlie were."

Chapter Twenty-Six

After the haunted house tours ended, everyone crowded around the fire pit. Ari said a silent thank-you that the fire was covered by a grate so that they wouldn't risk Noah's dinosaur tail going up in flames. The Maverick men had disappeared, but the women they loved, plus Bob, remained.

And they treated Ari like she was one of their own.

The only thing unnerving her was that it felt a little hinky to be naked under the skirt, knowing that she and Matt had made love not far from where they all sat.

Yet she couldn't hold down a thrill at how magical Matt had made her world. She hoped it wouldn't remain a secret much longer. She was bursting with the need to claim him—and his son—as her own. They'd burrowed so deeply into her heart that she now knew she'd never be anywhere near as happy without them.

"Paige, you make a fabulous Cleopatra," Harper said. "I feel dowdy as Frankenstein." Seated on the end of the bench surrounding the fire pit, Harper held out her white lab coat, letting it balloon around her.

"At least you don't have to carry around your own asp," Paige said dryly, opening a small covered basket containing a plastic snake.

Everyone laughed. Paige Ryan was a pretty woman who had been transformed into a sexy siren by the exotic paint and gauzy dress of Cleopatra.

"Where's Whitney tonight, dear?" Susan asked as Noah climbed into her lap.

Balancing the basket on her knees, Paige spread her hands in the air. "You know Whit. She didn't feel up to coming tonight."

Bob, lounging next to Susan, said, "We certainly know her. Halloween parties are beneath her dignity."

"Now, Bob, stop," Susan chided him.

"Actually," Paige said in a soft voice, "she said I looked ridiculous as Cleopatra and refused to be seen with me."

"You look anything but ridiculous tonight, honey." Susan pursed her lips. "Perhaps," she said slowly, "your sister was jealous of how lovely you look."

Paige gave Susan an *are you crazy?* look, as if the idea of Whitney ever being jealous of her was preposterous. "She was just in one of her moods."

Ari had seen Whitney at Sebastian and Charlie's gala for *The Chariot Race*. Evan's wife was beautiful in an in-your-face kind of way. Whereas Paige was more like the all-American girl—though, in her Cleopatra costume she was certainly turning heads.

No wonder Whitney Collins was jealous. She wouldn't be used to having her sister steal the spotlight. And she definitely wouldn't like it.

Ari got up a few minutes later to get another drink, and on the way back to the fire pit, she stopped to watch Noah, bouncing between Susan and Bob, sometimes holding his tail, sometimes brandishing it like a weapon. She already loved him, and not just because of Matt. Noah was a special little boy all on his own.

"I'm so glad you love dinosaurs, Noah," Ari heard Charlie say, "because you're going to get a very special surprise soon." Sebastian's fiancée sat on the ledge surrounding the fire. Dressed all in black, she wore gloves shaped like claws that she snapped at Noah, who giggled and shrank back. "I'm a Zanti Misfit," she said in an ominous voice, snap-snap-snapping her gloves. Noah shrieked, loving every moment.

"Charlie fits perfectly with our weird Maverick sense of humor, doesn't she?" Daniel's voice was close beside Ari.

"She does. I like her a lot."

"We all do." He shoved his hands in his jacket pockets and grinned at her. "I'm kind of partial to you too."

She grinned back. "Thank you, Daniel. You're not so bad yourself."

He rocked back on his heels as they watched Noah try to catch Charlie's clipper-claw gloves. Then Daniel turned his gaze on Ari in a way that was more intense than usual. "I don't want to see you get hurt, Ariana."

Her heart plunged down to her toes. *Oh God…Daniel knew.*

"Matt's a great guy," he continued. Amid all the activity around them, his low voice kept them isolated. "He's one of my brothers even if we don't have the same parents. But you've got to know that he had a real bad time growing up. And then with Noah's mom."

Her throat clogged. Was Daniel warning her away from Matt, reminding her that she was just the nanny?

"I know," she finally managed past constricted vocal cords. "He told me what happened with them. All of them."

"He did?" Daniel looked surprised. "Well, that's good." But then he frowned again. "So now you know he has a hard time trusting."

"Yes," she whispered, her eyes stinging. She knew better than anyone, given that she'd said *I love you* and he hadn't. Though she suspected the person Matt didn't trust the most was himself.

"But you aren't afraid to trust him, are you?"

She blinked up at her former boss, a man who had always looked out for her, and had become her friend. He was second only to Matt in all he'd done for her. "Everyone says I should be, but I don't want to be afraid." She forced herself to hold his gaze. "I care about Matt. And Noah." She wasn't going to drop the word *love* on Daniel, but she had a feeling he could already hear it. "They both mean so much to me."

His gaze roamed her face before he finally nodded. "I won't be one of those people telling you to put up your guard." He paused, probably considering how to phrase what he felt she needed to hear. "But I also don't want you to get hurt. I sure as hell hope he'll realize how good you could be for him—and for Noah."

"You really think I'd be good for them?" It meant more than she could say that one of Matt's closet friends—one of his brothers, especially Daniel—believed in her.

"Of course I do." He smiled again, his gruffness fading beneath the upturning of his lips. "And if he hurts you, I'm going to beat the crap out of him. We all will."

She laughed, but it sounded a little soggy. "When you suggested me for the position as his nanny, I never meant for things to turn out this way."

Daniel pulled her in close, almost rocking her off her feet with his hug. "I know you didn't. You would never be one of those women who aims at a man's dollar signs or his big house. You took the job because you love kids and you could see how much Matt needed you. Everything else that happened..." He shook his head. "It's starting to seem like divine intervention. Like you were meant to come into their lives when they needed you most. But if he's not being as good to you as you are to him"—he shook his fist—"we'll smack some sense into him."

She wanted to laugh. She could actually have cried. Daniel was going to bat for her, even against one of his best friends, if it came to that. After all those years of feeling like she didn't have anyone, it was almost too much to believe.

"Now come back over to the fire."

He led her down to the fire pit and into the circle of his family.

The family she'd always wished for. Not just for one night.

But forever.

* * *

Matt hung back at the head of the stairs leading up from the game room. He'd searched downstairs and outside for Ari only to find her here, surrounded by his family. Laughing with them. Totally accepted by them.

The Frankensteins were once again a family, and Noah was poking the bolts at Jeremy's neck. Wearing a Dracula costume, Sebastian wrapped his cloak around Charlie and was playing with the strange gloves she wore. Bob was chatting with Daniel, while Susan was in a lively discussion with Ari.

Only Evan stood just outside the group, his gaze on his wife's sister, Paige. Steam practically wafted off the guy, and Matt wondered if he blamed Paige for Whitney's change of mind about coming to the party. Or maybe he was wishing that Whitney was more like her sister—not just that Paige was a sweet, good person, but in that she wanted to be one of the family.

Ari, Matt realized, had already become part of the family. As the party raged around them, the Mavericks were now their own group—and they'd automatically taken Ari into their midst, where she fit like another cog in their expanding wheel. Noah climbed onto her lap, and she cuddled him.

Downstairs, Matt's friends had gone to bat for her, threatening *him* if he didn't treat her right. And so they should—they knew better than anyone what a mess he was inside.

All he wanted was to treat Ari as well as she deserved. But what was best for her? To be with him—and Noah—including a whole bunch of baggage, not the least of which was Irene and the havoc she would cause from here to eternity? Or to find a man who was whole, dependable, and solid—a normal guy who would take care of her, one who would give her children all her own rather than asking her to raise another woman's son?

A muscle jumped in Matt's jaw as the difficult, conflicted questions spun around his usually logical mind. He was a man who always had an answer for everything—who'd built a billion-dollar business with those answers.

But tonight, he knew only one thing for sure: He couldn't let Ari go. Not yet, not even when he couldn't clearly see the answers to his future.

Not even if a better man would set her free.

* * *

Noah slept in the backseat all the way home, and after Matt carried him upstairs, he still slept while they wrestled him out of his T-Rex suit and tucked him in.

In the hallway, Matt took Ari's hand. "We need to talk."

She nodded, ready to burst since she'd talked with Daniel. "Daniel knows. How did he find out?"

Matt's sigh was loud in the hallway. "He saw us coming out of the changing room. And he was with Evan, Will, and Sebastian. I shouldn't have dragged you down there."

Her fingers went stiff in Matt's hand. She should have realized they'd *all* known after Daniel talked to her. But while she was embarrassed at being found out by the entire Maverick crew, she also couldn't forget that Daniel hadn't been angry. He'd actually welcomed her and given her hope.

"I wanted it as much as you did, so you didn't drag me anywhere." She shook her head. "But I don't want to cause trouble between you and your friends."

He frowned. "How could you possibly do that?"

"Daniel said he threatened to beat you up."

The last thing she expected was Matt's smile. "They *all* threatened me if I don't treat you right." He pulled her against him. "I told them how special you are and that I don't want to hurt you."

But he hadn't told them he loved her—just as he hadn't said it to her. She sucked a burning breath into her lungs.

Patience. She knew he needed time. But, God, it was hard. Especially now that everyone knew she was head over heels for him.

As if he could read her mind, he gently lifted her chin, forcing her to look at him. "Do you want to spend the night with me?"

"More than anything." She was in love with him, and he was her favorite place to be in the world. "But what about Noah?"

"I can be quiet. Can you?"

She loved to cry out for him when he took her to heaven. But not if she woke up his son. "I'll control myself." At least she would try. "I meant in the morning, though. How should we handle things if he sees us together?"

"You can just get him up as usual. He doesn't have to know anything."

If he wasn't ready to say he loved her, then of course he wouldn't tell Noah either. But with every word, the pain dug deeper, no matter how much patience—and the relentless hope—she always strove for.

Hiding her disappointment with a smile, she made herself nod. "All right."

"I know it's your day off tomorrow, but will you

spend it with us? We'll do something fun."

Her day off. It was a potent reminder that she was still the nanny, even if Matt hadn't meant it that way. "I'd like that."

He nuzzled her hair. "Good. Now come to my room, Ari. I'm dying to make love to you again."

Just like that, his sensual commands had her heart thumping and her skin heating. She felt raw on the inside, but heading back to her empty bed tonight wasn't even in the cards.

Inside his bedroom, Matt closed the door on the rest of the world. Mere seconds later her clothes were gone, his tux was off, and he'd lifted her into his arms, grabbing her up until she locked her ankles at his back. Walking her to the small sofa by the window, he settled her on his lap, and when she pulled up her knees to straddle him, he immediately entered her with his fingers, turning her into a wild animal. She didn't cry out, but when sounds began to bubble up her throat, she kissed him, spilling her cries into his mouth, knowing she was meant for this.

For *Matt*.

He miraculously produced protection, always looking out for her even in the heat of the moment, then drove deep, filling her, making her his.

When the earth-shattering climax took them both, they muted their moans of pleasure against each other's lips, kissing as if it were a vow.

For her, it was.

Chapter Twenty-Seven

The Sunday after Halloween, they went to Golden Gate Park. Ari had packed a picnic with Noah's help—he'd even cut the tomatoes himself. The day was so gorgeous they ate sitting on a blanket that Matt spread on the grass, watching a laughing, giggling Noah chase butterflies.

Matt's investigator was still searching for her brother, but Ari hadn't brought up the subject of visiting the families of Gideon's other fallen comrades. She still stung from their disaster with Mrs. Esterhausen, her stomach plunging with the memory of that day every time she thought of it.

She hadn't given up—but she needed to be a heck of a lot stronger for the next round. And she knew nothing would get her there faster than being with Matt and Noah.

During the next work week, she followed the usual routine, taking Noah to school, playing with him, teaching him, loving him as if he were her own little boy. They swam in the heated pool and worked on riding his bike. He was almost ready, and she couldn't wait to find the perfect moment to surprise Matt.

And then there were the nights—the long, delicious hours in Matt's bed, waking to his touch in the morning, his lips on her skin, his fingers tracing her curves.

Somewhere along the way, she'd stopped praying he would say he loved her. It would happen when he finally believed he didn't have to be Mr. Perfect in Absolutely Everything. For now, she simply treasured their moments together.

Well, except the early mornings, when she had to sneak out of Matt's room… She felt like his dirty little secret every time she took her short walk of shame. He would hate to hear her call it that, but in the early rays of light as she made her way back to her room, it seemed the sun through the windows illuminated a truth she didn't want to see.

* * *

The following Sunday, Charlie and Sebastian showed up from out of the blue in a big white pickup. Noah ran down the front steps and straight into Sebastian's arms. Matt's friend swung him round and round until the little boy was laughing and squealing with delight. Seeing Noah's closeness to the other Mavericks made Ari's eyes mist.

"We've got a surprise for you," Charlie said, bending down to give Noah a hug after Sebastian finally set him on his feet. She was outfitted in steel-toed boots, overalls, and a flannel shirt.

"What? What?" Noah jumped up, down, and around.

Matt looked on indulgently. With Noah's hand in hers, Charlie led him to the back of the truck and let down the tailgate. Then she picked him up, setting him in the truck bed to see.

Matt stepped forward, his hands out, as if he were afraid Noah might fall, but Charlie kept her hands steady on him.

Noah uttered a soft, reverent, "Wow." Then he tipped his head down to Charlie. "What are they?"

"That one is a Stegosaurus." She pointed to a spiny metal dinosaur with big plates behind its head. It was small enough for Noah to rest his hand on its back, the metal spines rounded so he wouldn't cut his fingers. "And that's a Brontosaurus." With its long neck, Noah would have to reach up to touch its head. "The flying one is a Pterodactyl. Uncle Sebastian brought a chain to hang it from the big oak out by your playground."

Noah turned to throw his arms around her neck. "Thank you, Aunt Charlie."

She beamed, and Sebastian slipped his hand beneath the fall of her hair. The gesture was loving, congratulatory, and possessive all at the same time.

It was the way Ari wanted Matt to touch her in front of everyone. As though she was *his*—and he was proud of it.

"After the costume you wore at the Halloween party, I'll have to make a mini T-Rex too." Charlie smiled, the sun lighting her face as she looked up at Noah. Then she scooped the boy from the truck bed and set him on the pavement.

"Charlie, thank you." Matt put his hand over his heart, as if thanking her from the bottom of it. "Making these must have taken so much time out of your schedule."

She shrugged beneath Sebastian's loving touch. "Whenever I needed a break from my other projects, the dinosaurs were a perfect filler." She beamed up at Sebastian. "A wise man once told me I have to take time out for things that I feel a passion for."

"Sage advice," Matt agreed.

"And since Charlie's also finished her monster T-Rex, we're having an unveiling at the barbecue this afternoon."

Sebastian's look encompassed Ari as well, and she felt the glow of being automatically included. Matt had done the same that morning when he'd assumed she'd join them at the barbecue Charlie and Sebastian were throwing. As though she was family.

As though she was *his*.

"Wouldn't miss it." Matt took a step closer to her, and her heart raced even though he hadn't touched her.

"All right, let's get these guys unloaded." Sebastian climbed into the truck bed.

Ari marveled with Noah while they set up the dinosaurs in the back garden. It was a perfect ending to a perfect week. A nearly perfect one, anyway. If only she could wait patiently for Matt to see clearly for himself that he loved her.

But she couldn't deny that every loving glance between Sebastian and Charlie filled her with a deeper longing—and more impatience—to share the very same emotions with Matt.

* * *

With his son's hand in his on the driveway as they waved good-bye to Charlie and Sebastian—and Ari only a touch away—for the first time in his life, Matt actually felt happy. Real happiness. It was more than the joy he always felt at being with Noah. For once, he felt content. Being with Ari was completely different from his time with Irene—not frantic and rushed, but sweet and miraculous.

These past weeks he'd been continually asking himself about love. Not just *was this love?* But could *he* love anyone right? Could he be there *always*, without mistakes?

In the end, it wasn't their incredible lovemaking that made him see the truth. It was how endlessly patient Ari was with his son—and how patient she'd been with him, never pressuring him to say *I love you.* And though Matt wasn't certain he'd do everything perfectly, he finally believed Ari wouldn't give up on him even if he took a few small missteps.

At long last, he could see things clearly rather than through a haze of fear.

He loved Ari.

Loved her in a way he hadn't known he was capable of after he'd lost his faith in the people who were supposed to care for him as a child.

Tonight. He'd tell her how he felt tonight after the barbecue, when she lay warm and soft in his arms.

The only thing marring his happiness was his total failure to give Ari her heart's desire. It killed him that he hadn't found her brother yet. But he would, damn it. He needed to make Ari as happy as she'd made him.

"Have I mentioned recently how happy you make me? How happy you make us?"

She beamed at him. "You make me deliriously happy too." She bit her lip before adding, "Noah and I have a special surprise for you." She held out her hand for Noah. He took it and skipped with her to the garage, where Ari punched in the code to open the door. "Stay right there," she called out to Matt as they disappeared inside.

Matt turned up his face to the sun, reveling in its warmth the way he reveled in the heat of Ari's smile.

"You can look now!" Ari's voice was accompanied by Noah's laughter.

Matt opened his eyes...and his heart choked his throat as he took in the near paralyzing sight of Noah hurtling toward the big slope of the driveway on his bike.

A two-wheeled bike that no longer had its training wheels.

"Remember to stay away from the hill, Noah," Ari called.

But Noah was too excited to listen, and the bike gained speed. Too much speed.

Matt's blood was like the roar of engines through his veins. Noah wore a helmet, but what if he barreled right out into the road?

"Noah!" Matt yelled, hit squarely by a vision of himself as a child, only a few years older than Noah, careening down a hill that was far steeper than he'd thought. "Stop!"

The gate was open to the street beyond it, and Noah was heading straight for it. Memories of agony and deep shame shrieked in Matt's head as he started to run. His gaze shot to the road for signs of a car, but no way could he get to his son in time. Even as he ran, he felt the remembered pain of all those years ago, heard the awful crack of his arm breaking, his father's voice calling him an idiot, a weenie, a good-for-nothing sissy.

"Noah!" His son's name screeched through the sunshine. A car, the road, the hill. *Jesus, God, please no.*

Just when he thought everything was lost, Ari was there, barring Noah's way, her fists on the handlebars. "Now, Noah, you know the rules. You need to stay up top," she said, chiding him softly. As if nothing cataclysmic or life-threatening had happened.

As if Matt hadn't just lost years off his life.

"Did you see that, Matt?" Somewhere through his haze of fear and fury, he vaguely noticed that Ari and Noah beamed at him with excitement shining in their eyes. "Noah can ride without training wheels. We've been practicing so he could surprise you." She didn't seem at all frightened by what had almost happened. "He did great, don't you think?"

It was hardly even a question. She simply expected Matt to agree, to congratulate Noah on his new skill—and to congratulate her for helping his son.

But Matt still couldn't see straight. Not when the only thing in his vision was what might have been.

Noah crushed beneath a car.

Noah with broken limbs.

Noah with brain damage like Jeremy.

And not when all he heard were the things his father had shouted at him on that day long ago, as his arm screamed in pain and tears streaked his cheeks. Insults and abuse that were seared into Matt's soul as deeply as his mother's refusal to step in and help had been.

"What the hell did you think you were doing?" His voice was so deadly cold, so brutally sharp, that Ari stopped short, her smile instantly disintegrating.

"In my classes I learned it's normal for a child Noah's age to begin riding without training wheels. Plus, I did some research on the Internet. And Jorge can do it," she added so softly that he had to read her lips over the rush in his ears.

"I don't give a damn about Jorge or your freaking classes or what the hell the Internet says."

He cursed, a four-letter word he'd never said in front of his son. But he threw it at her like a punch—then watched as Ari reeled from the blow.

"He isn't ready to lose his training wheels." Each word was a bullet. "Anything could have happened. Did you see how close he got to the road?"

"But I was there to hold on to him. To make sure he was safe." She paused, swallowing hard before adding, "I'll always be there for him."

"How the hell do you know you'll always be there?" he raged, his voice startling birds off their branches. She could never know what Noah might do in a split second. She could never protect him from everything, which was what Matt had vowed to do the moment his son was born.

Anguish tore her face, and she opened her mouth, closed it, then finally said, "I take care of him like he's my own child. You know that."

"He's *not* your child." Matt couldn't stop himself from shouting. "*I'll* say when he's ready to take off his training wheels or his water wings. *Not* you."

A cloud passed over the sun, over her face, over Noah. The silence that fell at the end of Matt's tirade was so sharp it sliced them all to ribbons.

"You're right," Ari finally said. "He's not my child. I'm just the nanny." Each word from her lips sounded more hollow. More bleak. She leaned down to Noah.

"It's time to get off the bike, sweetheart." Once Noah had, she gave him a kiss on the cheek, then, leaving them both, she headed back up to the hill to the garage.

* * *

Ari didn't cry as she brought the training wheels back from the garage along with a screwdriver. The horror of it all had dried up her tear ducts.

"I'm sorry. I made a mistake. You should put them back on."

"Daddy?" Noah whimpered.

But Matt didn't move to comfort his son, he simply screwed the wheels back into place, anchoring the bike.

How the hell do you know you'll always be there?

Ten words. But they were more than enough to put her in her place.

He's not your child.

God, how could she ever have forgotten? Just because she wanted Noah and Matt to be hers didn't mean they were. All the longing in the world didn't mean she'd ever truly belong with them. One night at a party with the Mavericks didn't mean she was part of the family.

"But Daddy, I was real good." Noah turned from his father to Ari. "Right, Ari?"

She couldn't answer him. Her vocal cords were swollen too tight. All she could do was nod.

Matt ratcheted down the last screw. "I saw how

well you did, but I still want the training wheels on."

"It's not fair!" Noah scrunched up his face and ran from both of them, tears streaming down his cheeks. "You're not nice, Daddy!"

"I'm so sorry," she said again, barely able to manage more than a whisper. Then she ran too, leaving Matt alone on the driveway.

As she climbed the stairs to her room, her knees seemed to creak like an old woman's, while her dreams crashed and burned, every single hope she'd ever had completely crushed. She'd been living in La-La Land. Rosie and Chi had warned her, but she hadn't wanted to hear them. Maybe Chi was right, maybe Matt had only searched for her brother out of guilt for sleeping with her that first time.

Oh God. Her legs wobbled, and she thought she might actually fall. She should have listened to her best friends, but she'd wanted to listen only to her heart, so she had deliberately forgotten her cardinal rule about remembering the difference between fantasy and reality.

How many times would she have to learn the lesson that she was temporary—disposable at the first sign of trouble? Just like with all her foster families. Even with her own mother, Ari hadn't been important enough to her to get clean.

In her room, she stuffed her laptop into her backpack and her belongings into her bag. She'd become so good at leaving over the years that she could pack up in less than five minutes. She supposed the reason she hadn't brought more things to Matt's home had been the deep-down belief that the dream wouldn't last. The fairy tale wouldn't actually come true.

Not for her.

She'd wanted to surprise Matt, and it *had* felt like the right time for Noah to learn. But in retrospect, there was no denying that she'd been wrong in not asking permission. Matt was Noah's father. He had the right to make the decisions, not her. And now, on top of it all, she'd turned him into the bad guy, just as Irene had done when she'd left for Paris without her son.

She'd seen the way Matt reacted the day Noah had fallen by the pool, had felt his anguish as if it were her own. He still wouldn't let Noah swim without the water wings, yet she'd removed those training wheels without a single thought. Partly because Matt hadn't specifically mentioned them. But mostly because she'd felt secure in the knowledge that he felt the same emotions that she did.

How could she have been so stupid as to step over his rock-solid boundary with his son?

The echo of their voices drifted up from downstairs—Noah's still upset, Matt's still tight with fear that his son might have been hurt.

Ari closed her eyes, trying to blot out the pain. "I'm so sorry," she whispered again, as if he could hear her.

Hands shaking, she wrote a note, agonizing over the words, then finally left it on her bed. He would find it.

And she knew he would be relieved that she was gone.

Chapter Twenty-Eight

Noah's feet pounded out of Ari's room a short while later, so heavily that the ceiling above Matt actually shook. He found Matt in the den where he was pretending to work. All he'd actually managed was brooding. Reeling. Trying to calm down so that he could think straight again.

"Daddy, Ari isn't in her room." Noah clutched a piece of paper. "Look."

Matt's heart was already in his throat, even before he took the note.

I'm sorry. I should have understood how you would feel. I wish you and Noah all the best. I hope you can forgive me.

He jumped up out of his chair and jogged down the hall, Noah on his heels, to check the garage. Her car was as gone as she was.

And the house suddenly felt completely empty with only him and Noah in it.

"Daddy, where'd she go?" Noah hung on his pants leg. "What'd she say in her letter?"

He hunkered down, running his hands along Noah's arms. "Ari had to—" Damn it, he could already see what this would do to his son. "She had to leave."

Noah's face fell, and tears welled in his eyes. "You yelled at her and made her leave."

He'd yelled. Just like his father. "Noah, you have to understand—"

"And I could ride the bike. I'm good!"

"I know you are, but—"

"You're not fair! You never let me do anything fun!" He swiped at the tear trickling down his cheek, his bottom lip trembling. "I love Ari and you made her leave!" He fisted his hands, and Matt saw himself in his son, so clearly. Too clearly. "I love her and now she's gone!" Then he ran upstairs. A moment later his door slammed.

Every word his son shouted pierced his heart. Especially when Noah repeated how much he loved Ari, forcing Matt to hear each word. He couldn't pretend it wasn't true.

How many times had Matt hid in his room while his father raged? On the day Noah was born, he swore he'd never put his child through that. As angry as he often became with Irene, Matt had never yelled at her in front of Noah.

Yet he'd done just that with Ari.

In one moment he'd snapped, and he hadn't just sounded like his father—he'd actually turned *into* him. As Noah had raced down the hill, Matt's brain had played out all the terrible things that might happen, and he'd slammed Ari with all his fear, his anger, his pain. He'd slammed his son as well, and stripped the joy from his accomplishment.

"But he's not ready," he whispered.

Only, no one heard.

Especially not Ari.

He should have been packing up a bag with Noah's swim stuff for the barbecue. But it was the last thing he wanted to do. Because without Ari, nothing seemed right. With her gone, all the sweetness that had filled his life for these few brief weeks was gone too. He wasn't even sure he could get Noah out of his room without dragging him.

If he and Noah went to the barbecue alone, the Mavericks would ask where Ari was, and he'd have to explain that she was gone. And he'd have to do it as he remembered every warm, wonderful thing she'd done since she'd come into their lives—how good she was with Noah, the games she played with him, the look of love on her face when she hugged him. And the look on her face as she and Matt made love, the scent of her skin, the taste of her lips...

No. He couldn't let himself remember. Not when it would only make him crazy.

He was a Maverick—which meant he was a master of self-control. He would force himself to forget. Just as he'd force himself to go to the barbecue. Because if he didn't, it would be akin to admitting his behavior hadn't been justified.

Noah wasn't ready. He just wasn't.

Yet somewhere deep inside, Matt could hear Ari's voice asking if maybe *Matt* was the one who wasn't ready. Who was he really protecting, his son…or himself?

Was that why he'd gone from ultimate happiness to inimitable rage in the space of five seconds? Why he'd been powerless to stop his reaction when the only thing he saw was Noah's crushed body? Because he didn't trust *himself* to keep his son safe?

Damn it. He shoved the questions away, telling himself for the millionth time that he knew what was best for his son.

Matt looked at his watch. It was time to go to the party. He was taking Noah. And they would have a good time whether they wanted to or not.

Ruthlessly, he tamped down the thought that nothing would ever be any good again without Ari.

* * *

As far as Matt was concerned, the day was too damn nice for early November, the sun bright, not a cloud floating anywhere. Noah put on his swim trunks and came out of his room without a fight, but he'd been uncharacteristically silent on the drive over. Who knew a kid could dish out the silent treatment so well?

Thankfully Noah came back to life as he ran to Charlie, chattering about dinosaurs. "I want to see the

T-Rex, Aunt Charlie."

Charlie was seated in a deck chair by the pool next to Harper, while Will relaxed beside them on a lounger, still fully clothed, his hands stacked behind his head. Jeremy, wearing a pair of orange trunks that were so neon you had to shade your eyes, sat on the pool's edge, dangling his feet in the water.

"Hold on, buddy," Sebastian called to Noah. "We'll all take a walk down to Charlie's studio after we eat. You'll see the T-Rex then." He was already firing up the barbecue.

"Where's your future mother-in-law?" Matt asked, a preemptive strike against any questions Sebastian might have about Ari.

"I sent my driver, so Francine will be here in half an hour or so. She gets a kick out of it, says the limo ride makes her feel like a queen." Sebastian didn't miss a beat before asking, "Where's Ariana?"

Silently cursing that his diversionary tactic hadn't worked, Matt said, "She couldn't make it."

Because I yelled and made her cry. Because she's gone and she isn't coming back.

"Too bad." Sebastian slid the barbecue lid down and surveyed his backyard pool. "She would have at least put on a swimsuit, unlike that weenie over there." He nodded at the group by the pool's edge.

The other Mavericks knew his dad had been an asshole, but Matt had never repeated ad nauseam the things his father had said. *Weenie* was just another word to Sebastian. But today, after hearing his father's voice in his head, after yelling at Ari, after making her leave, Matt felt his hackles rise and his hands clench.

"Don't call Noah a weenie." His voice was practically a snarl.

Sebastian turned, pulling his sunglasses down his nose. "I wasn't talking about Noah. He has his trunks on. I was talking about Will."

Matt closed his eyes and ratcheted down all the emotion threatening to come loose in his body. He was being an asshole. Again.

"What's up with you, man?" Sebastian asked, one eyebrow cocked. Matt was saved by Evan's arrival. "Where's Whitney? And Paige got the invite, didn't she?"

"Whitney is feeling sick, and Paige stayed to keep her company." Evan didn't remove his sunglasses, and Matt guessed it was so neither man would read the truth. But a moment later he yanked them off, saying, "Screw that, I'm sick of lying for her. The truth is, she pitched a fit that Paige was coming."

"But Paige always comes," Sebastian pointed out.

"That's what Whitney said." Evan shook his head. "So I told her to stay home if she was in such a nasty mood."

Whoa. Now, that was different.

Matt tried to tell himself that Evan had worse problems than he did. He was *married* to his problem. But Evan had always been loyal, never talking Whitney down even when the rest of them had had it up to their eyeballs with her. Yes, Evan had made her apologize in the past when she'd been downright rude, but he never badmouthed his wife to his friends. Unloading now was totally uncharacteristic.

Maybe Evan had finally reached his limit.

Which only made Matt think of his own limits—and Ari's too. Because she wouldn't have left if he hadn't acted like his father. Hell, if he hadn't *become* his father the moment Noah had careened toward the gate on his bike.

"Whitney's probably still pissed that Paige looked so good in that Cleopatra getup," Sebastian said. "Even I couldn't believe my eyes when I saw her."

Evan glanced at Charlie by the pool. "Don't let your fiancée hear you say that."

Sebastian smiled, and love seemed to ooze from his pores just looking at his woman. "Charlie was actually the one who first pointed out Paige's Halloween hotness, so I'm good here."

Running over, Jeremy interrupted in his loud, enthusiastic voice. "Can me and Noah go swimming?" The question was for the group at large, probably because Harper had sent him over to ask for permission.

Jeremy was the best big brother Matt could have asked for for Noah. He was extra careful, and he got down and played on Noah's level because he was a big, sweet kid himself.

Matt pulled the water wings from Noah's beach bag. "As long as Noah wears these."

Noah's bottom lip jutted out. "I don't want them." His voice was borderline mutinous. "Ari says they make it hard for me to swim. You never listen to her. That's why you sent her away—because she doesn't do everything you tell her to."

The pool deck fell inordinately quiet as Jeremy—missing the undertones of the conversation—grabbed the water wings, then sat down on the edge of the pool and began to secure the flotation devices to Noah's arms amid happy, exuberant talk.

Matt didn't wait for his friends to say anything. Not when he knew it would all come out now. "She's gone."

Chapter Twenty-Nine

Evan and Sebastian shot each other a look, then Evan asked, "You mean *gone* gone?"

"What other kind of gone is there?" Matt snapped.

"Well, there's gone and she's packed her bags never to be seen again. And then there's gone but she'll be back soon, and then you guys can work through whatever happened."

That was the *gone* Matt wanted. The one where Ari was there when they got home. The one where they could rewind to the way things were before this morning and none of it had happened at all.

He experienced a powerful urge to head home right now, just in case. But he knew she wouldn't be waiting. Who would, after what he'd said? After turning all her enthusiasm and excitement to tears?

Will rose and joined them. "So where *is* Ari?"

Naturally, Daniel suddenly appeared on the terrace. "Looks like I'm missing something. What's going on?"

"Ari's not here," Will explained.

Daniel glared at Matt, immediately jumping to

conclusions—the *right* conclusions. "What the hell did you do to her?"

"We had a disagreement about how to handle some situations that arose with Noah." He tried to keep his voice even and moderated. But he couldn't pull it off. "So we parted company."

He wondered if they could hear the translation: *I lost my cool and yelled at her. I'm head over freaking heels in love with her...and I still couldn't stop myself from turning into my father.*

"I don't get it," Sebastian said. "Everything seemed fine this morning when we dropped off the dinosaurs."

"And at the Halloween bash, you two were like this." Evan twined his fingers.

Meanwhile, Daniel was growling. "What kind of disagreement could have been big enough for you to *part company*?" He put the words in air quotes before he fisted his hands.

Harper and Charlie joined the fray, while over in the shallow end, an oblivious Jeremy whirled Noah around in the water. Matt wanted to shut out the world—so damn bleak without Ari—but he couldn't take his gaze off his son. Not for one minute.

If anything happened, he'd never forgive himself. Just the way he'd never forgive himself for what he'd said to Ari. For what he'd *yelled*.

"Noah's fine," Harper said, observing the direction of Matt's gaze. "Jeremy's a great swimmer and he loves Noah. He won't let anything bad happen in the pool."

It was just what Ari had promised. That she would always protect Noah. That she wouldn't leave.

Frustration—and the deep pain of loss—choked Matt as he forced himself to give them the basics of the story. Which didn't include him falling back into painful memories and losing his shit, damn it. He finished with, "Noah could have careened out of that gate right into a car."

Daniel didn't look at all appeased by Matt's explanation. "What the hell are you going to do when he's older and wants to know why he can't have a skateboard like all the other kids? You're going to stunt him."

"I'm not stunting him," Matt shot back. "I'm protecting him."

Throughout, Sebastian's hand idly stroked Charlie's hip. It was how Matt had wanted to be with Ari, touching her automatically, without conscious thought. Because he'd needed to. Because she'd wanted him there with her.

His heart ached watching them, just as it ached at the easy fit of Harper's hand in Will's. They were a unit that also included Jeremy.

Ari had fit too. Until he'd started yelling and driven her away.

In the water, Noah shrieked with laughter, then Jeremy shouted, "Come on, you can do it."

Noah dog-paddled to him, his face screwed up in concentration as he tried to do an overarm stroke. But with the water wings, he couldn't manage it. He wouldn't go under—but Matt finally saw that he couldn't actually swim properly with the wings in his way.

Ari had tried to tell him that. But he hadn't listened.

His father had never listened either.

"Did you fire her?" As softly spoken as Daniel's question was, it was still sharp enough to cut steel.

Matt had promised his friend he wouldn't hurt Ari. He hadn't just broken that promise, he'd shattered it.

"I didn't fire her. She packed her bags and left after I yelled at her for taking off the training wheels." A muscle jumped in his jaw as he forced himself to admit, "After I told her I didn't give a damn what she thought was the right thing to do for Noah."

He could feel the shock reverberate through every single person at the barbecue. They might be his friends, but it was clear they thought he'd lost his mind.

Evan spoke first. "You were a lucky SOB who could have had everything, and you let her walk away?" Anger—and a thick dose of bitterness—underpinned his words. "Are you crazy?"

Evan had never been a fighter. He'd kept his head in his numbers just like Matt had lived inside his books. Will, Daniel, and Sebastian had been the warriors, the ones who stood up for Evan and Matt, until they'd both learned to grab the world with both hands and twist it to their will. Evan was the contained one, the one who never showed his emotions, even though they all knew he had them. But today a dark fire lit his eyes, as if the emotion he'd banked his entire life was about to break free.

"You're afraid to grab what you really want because you don't think you have what it takes to hold on to it."

Matt's hackles rose, and even his fists bunched, as though he might actually fight his friend. He'd thought Daniel would be the one to come after him, not Evan. "Where the hell is that coming from?" No one else said a word, all of them equally taken aback by Evan's vitriol.

"The status quo, that's easy for you. It's going for it—it's falling for Ari and taking a risk by loving her—that terrifies you." Evan stabbed a finger at Matt. "You don't think we all see you're so scared that you're willing to throw away the best thing that's come your way since Noah was born? Just like an *idiot*?"

Matt heard his father's voice. Right there in his head. *You're a little weenie. Afraid of your own shadow. Be a man. Buck up.* In the yard, he heard his son's giggle, Jeremy's laughter, felt his friends' eyes on him. But inside him, his father's voice was roaring, *Freaking weenie. Scared all the time. Stand up for yourself, you idiot.*

Matt had Evan's shirt in his fists and his friend

shoved up hard against a tree before anyone could stop him. "I'm. Not. Scared."

Evan didn't look away, didn't even try to struggle out of his grip. He simply stared Matt down. "Prove it."

As if a bucket of ice water had been dumped over his head, Matt dropped his hold on Evan's shirt. Because he knew what his friend meant. He didn't have to prove his courage to the Mavericks.

He needed to prove it to Ari.

To Noah.

And, most of all, to himself.

For so long—way too long—he'd let his fears for Noah overshadow everything, even his common sense, so that he heard his father's voice in his own.

He'd seen only the worst and missed everything that was good.

Ari would *never* have let Noah reach the street. She'd stopped him, in fact. She had done everything in her power to protect him as well as Matt could himself.

Because she loved Noah.

And once upon a time, she'd loved Matt too.

His gaze on his son in the pool, he told his friends the complete truth. "She's the best thing that ever walked into my life. Noah loves her." Turning back to them all, he said what they already knew. Any fool could see it a mile away. "And I do too. I love her so much."

"Then what the hell are you waiting for?" Will asked.

"We'll take care of Noah." Harper leaned into Will as she said it.

Matt wanted the same kind of love she and Will shared, the love that had chased away all his friend's demons and set him free of the past. He craved the same kind of emotions that shone in Charlie's eyes when she looked at Sebastian, the adoration that overcame Sebastian when he held her hand.

Ari had given him all that. But he'd thrown it away because he was afraid that when push came to shove, he couldn't be there for her, that he'd let her down. When it turned out that the only surefire way he'd let her down was not telling her he loved her with every cell, every nerve, every muscle and organ in his body.

It was the only time in his life that he was truly the idiot his father had called him.

He and Ari could work out the rest of it—the water wings, the training wheels, the fact that she'd come to him as his nanny and had quickly become so much more.

If she was willing to give him another chance.

Moving to the edge of the pool, he hunkered down by the shallow end. "Hey, buddy." He touched the water wings. "Next time we swim at home, we're going to try it with the water wings off, okay?"

Noah's eyes went wide. "For real?"

"For real. But right now I've got to leave the party for a while."

Noah stopped, his wings bobbing on the surface as

he trod water, keeping himself up all on his own. "Where are you going, Daddy?"

"To bring Ari back."

Chapter Thirty

Sitting on the love seat in the window of her small apartment, Ari stared at the only place that was really hers. The Murphy bed was in its wall pocket, and used paperback books she'd bought at library sales lined the shelves on either side of it. She'd assembled inexpensive cupboards for her clothes, and the dishes she'd collected from thrift stores sat on shelves above the bar-size sink. She stored a few cans of food, some cereal, and a box of macaroni and cheese next to the dishes, which she'd hidden behind a pretty curtain because there were no doors. Her TV sat on a rolling cart she pulled into the middle of the room.

Her things were secondhand, but they were hers, and this was her home. But it no longer felt like home.

Not without Matt and Noah.

The heavy weight of despair crushed her heart as she remembered every word he'd shouted at her. Closing her eyes, she wrapped her arms around her stomach like a child with a belly ache. In those awful moments she'd actually reverted to the little girl she used to be. The one who would have done anything to be loved, to matter to the people who were supposed to love her, and who'd finally figured out that wasn't ever going to happen.

That little girl was always waiting for the next bad thing, always ready with her bags packed. Ready for the next time her mom got thrown out of their apartment. Ready when someone at the foster home didn't like her, didn't want her, said she ate too much, that she stole from the other kids, that she back-talked. Often she didn't even unpack, but lived out of her bag, just in case.

She'd been living with her bags packed all her life. And when Matt lost it over the training wheels, she'd had that bag ready to go. With a snap of her fingers, she could *poof* herself right out of there and run away. Leaving had always been the only way.

But today, unlike any other day when she'd grabbed her bag and run, a little voice inside her head wouldn't shut up. That voice kept reminding her that Matt had never once been cruel—not to Noah, not to Doreen or Cookie. Not even to Irene, who surely deserved his fury for the way she so thoughtlessly flitted in and out of her son's life. He'd never been anything but perfect, and sweet, and caring until he'd believed Noah was barreling out of control straight into traffic—and all his biggest fears looked like they were about to come true.

Had she been wrong to flee? What if, once his panic had receded, she'd explained why she believed Noah was ready for two wheels—and Matt had actually listened? Could they have worked things out if she'd stayed to talk with him? If she'd apologized for not informing him of her plans, would he have apologized for losing it with her?

She leaned her head against the window, staring out. Below, a woman walked hand in hand with her young child. They each carried a grocery bag in their free hand, and though the little girl clearly had trouble hefting her bag, Ari saw the pride in the child's face. She was helping, she was an important part of the family, and she'd been trusted with bringing home the food they'd eat that night for dinner.

Noah was the same, always wanting to help with making a picnic or cleaning up his toys, offering to work side by side with Matt on outdoor projects.

If Ari had stayed, could she have helped Matt understand that he didn't need to be so afraid for Noah? Could she have shown him that his little boy was capable of so much?

From the start, she'd seen that Matt needed a partner to help him figure things out, someone who could counter his fears for his son. She'd wanted to be that partner, to be his family…and Noah's mother.

After everything that had happened, even with her heart feeling like it had been run through a shredder, she couldn't escape the truth: She still wanted those things.

But she'd run away instead of fighting for the two

people she loved most in all the world.

She couldn't change her past—her mother's descent into drugs, her brother leaving, a string of bad foster homes. But she could change *this*.

She didn't have to run every time her feelings got hurt. And Ari refused to let her insecurities take over this time. Not when her heart was in deeper than she'd ever thought possible. Not when the most important thing in the world—her love for Matt and Noah—was at stake. Not unless Matt came right out and said he didn't want her and would never love her.

"I'm going back, and we're going to talk." Her voice was sure and strong, her words powerful as she picked up her bag and backpack.

She was going back, and Matt was going to hear her out. Even if putting her heart on the line again was terrifying—and the risk was huge that he wouldn't return her feelings—she wasn't running away.

Not ever again.

Their love was worth too much for that.

* * *

It hadn't taken Matt long to figure out where Ari would have gone. It still terrified him that she lived in this run-down neighborhood, but she'd taken care of herself long before he came along.

The lobby door wasn't locked, and he walked right in, hating that anyone could do the same. He scanned the names on the mailboxes. More than half had nothing but a number. The walls were covered with graffiti that stretched over the mailboxes as well. Finally, he found the name Jones written in small block letters, the apartment number below it.

The mixed scents of cooking followed him up the stairs. The aromas clashed instead of blending, as if they'd bled into the walls and started to rot. It was almost as bad as the old building in Chicago, and he expected to hear raised voices behind every door. But there was only the sound of footsteps above him. He turned on a landing, and his heart stopped.

Ari stood at the head of the stairs, one hand on the railing, a backpack over her shoulder and another bag clutched in her hand.

"What are you doing here?" It was obvious that seeing him on her stairs was the last thing she'd expected.

God, she was beautiful. Strong. Resilient.

Fearless.

Ari was everything he'd ever needed. *Everything.*

"I'm sorry." He couldn't wait for them to get behind closed doors before he apologized. "I shouldn't have lost it, and I'm so damned sorry. Please come back to me. To us. Let me make it up to you, Ari. We don't want to lose you. *I* don't want to lose you."

She stared at him so long he finally had to release the breath he'd been holding.

At last she said, "Come up and we'll talk."

His heart was pounding too hard, too fast, as he

followed along in the scuff marks on the ancient linoleum. After unlocking a door down the hall, she disappeared inside. When he came abreast of her, she stood there, holding the door open for him.

"It's not like your house," she said, but she didn't need to explain anything to him. He knew what it was like. And he respected the hell out of her for surviving all of it.

Yes, the carpet was threadbare, the sofa sagged in the middle, and the countertop was scratched, but the place was scrupulously clean and fresh smelling.

She set her bags by the door, then turned to look him in the eye. "I was coming back to talk to you." She took a deep breath. "I shouldn't have left that way."

He ached with the need to reach for her. His heart raced, and even his palms were sweating. But he had no rights until he'd groveled. Until he'd begged.

Until she'd decided whether or not to forgive him.

"I was an ass." His voice was raw. Tight. Desperate. "You had every right to leave after I went off half-cocked. You gave me your trust, and I threw it back in your face this morning. I should have never belittled your decisions, your education, your knowledge." His voice was hardly more than a harsh whisper as he said, "I didn't mean any of it, Ari. I promise you I didn't."

"Thank you for saying you're sorry—and I know you didn't mean it. But trust works both ways." Her voice was soft, but every word she spoke reverberated through him. "It didn't matter that I'd thoroughly thought it out, I was still wrong not to check with you first about Noah's training wheels. But even though you yelled and hurt me with what you said, that wasn't why I ran." He was destroyed by the pain on her face. "I always have my bag packed. At the first sign of trouble, I'm outta there. Because nothing has ever been permanent. No one has ever wanted me."

"No, Ari." His heart broke for her. "That's not true."

"It is. At least"—she swallowed hard—"it always has been. Which is why instead of talking things through with you like a rational human being, I ran away." She sucked in another breath, and it shook through her. "I should have been brave and stayed to face you. But I let my past take over again so that I immediately gave up all hope of a better future."

How could he ever have thought she was too young, too naive? Ari had the wisest soul of anyone he'd ever known. Except maybe Susan. That was the highest compliment.

And he'd let his past take him over too. "Ari—"

She reached for him, finally putting her hand on his arm, the warmth of her touch filling him. "I'm not done yet."

He shut his mouth.

"I made a mistake in not talking to you about taking off Noah's training wheels…but I don't want to be afraid you'll freak out the next time I let Noah do something I think is perfectly reasonable."

The next time? Did that mean she could forgive him?

Hope unfurled inside him. "I know how capable you are."

She shook her head. "You didn't today."

"That was a mistake." One he swore he'd never make again.

"What if I told you I think his water wings should come off too? And what if, the next time he wants to work with you at the stove or you get out your toolbox to fix something around the house, I say you should let him help?"

His gut reaction had always been to say no, and it was hard to bite the word back. "We can talk about all those things, and I promise that I'll consider your advice without freaking out." Wanting her to understand, he explained, "I can't forget how small he was when he came into the world and the nurse put him in my arms." It had been the best—and most overwhelming—moment of Matt's life. "I could practically hold him in one hand. I was terrified I'd drop him. I didn't know the first thing about babies, and when Irene took off because she didn't know how to take care of a kid, what she forgot was that I didn't know either. I never wanted to do the wrong thing."

"I know you don't," Ari said. "But what if I push up against another boundary that I don't know is there? I need to know more, Matt. I need you to let me in. *All* the way in."

He stilled. The only sound in the room was the

beating of his heart as she waited for him to actually figure out his shit. No one but the Mavericks knew how bad his past was, but Ari wasn't only in the inner circle.

She was the very heart of it.

"When I was eight, I fell off my bike and broke my arm. My father told me I was a whiner, a weenie. And he refused to take me to the doctor."

She gasped, as horrified for him as he'd been over her childhood. "How could he do that?"

"He was more afraid of having a sissy son than he was of my arm being broken—and my mother backed him up, like she always did."

She folded her hand around his, holding him. "I'm so sorry."

Her touch gave him the courage to tell her things he'd never revealed to another soul, not even Susan. But Ari needed to hear, so she could understand. So she could help him put the past behind him forever. "My father hated that I let other kids bully me."

She squeezed his hand, her eyes watery with her pain for him, and with her anger. "You don't *let* kids bully you. Sometimes you just can't stop them."

"He wanted to toughen me up so that I could fight them off. But even after my arm had healed, I still couldn't do that. I came home with a black eye, and he was pissed."

You effing weenie. When are you ever going to learn to stick up for yourself? How the hell did I get a son who's such a puny little weakling?

"He said he'd teach me to defend myself even if it killed us both." And it did kill something in Matt—not just his spirit, but his ability to trust. He spent years rebuilding himself, working hard to find faith in people again. He thought he had too, until today when he'd taken out all his fears on Ari just like his dad used to do. The only way he could make it up to her was with the whole truth. "He grabbed me by the hair, holding me up on my tiptoes. And he told me to punch him, to get myself loose." He closed his eyes because he couldn't get through the rest of his story if he looked at the horror in Ari's gaze. "I kicked and flailed, screaming at him. But I couldn't reach him. I didn't realize I'd started crying until I couldn't see him anymore through my tears."

I raised an effing little baby. You good-for-nothing piece of shit.

For a long, long time, he had believed his father—every single word, until this very moment.

"My scalp was screaming by the time he let me go. Without me landing a single punch. And he called me the usual names." The names were ingrained in his brain.

"Where was your mother this whole time? Didn't she stop him?" Ari's grip was tight with her distress.

He opened his eyes to the bleakness of hers. And it was all for him. Sympathy. Empathy. Her fierceness, all the things he'd wanted from the mother whose job it had been to protect him.

"She never stopped him. Not then, not ever. When he stormed out of the house, she handed me some tissues and told me to stop blubbering and clean myself up."

You're a mess. What would your friends think of you now?

Ari put a hand over her mouth. "Oh my God."

"She said I'd never grow up to be a man if I was whining all the time."

A tear trickled down Ari's cheek. "How could anyone say that to their own child?"

He reached out with the tip of his finger to wipe the tear away. "How could a mother turn to drugs instead of looking out for her kid?"

He'd never felt the bond of their childhoods as intensely as he did now. They'd both been abandoned. And somehow they'd found each other.

"When my mother was dying," he went on, "she said she was happy they'd made me who I was, that if they hadn't told me to buck up against the bullies at school, I would still be a worthless sissy."

Ari's nostrils flared with indignation. "*You* made yourself."

That was his Ari—always standing up for everyone else. And he prayed she'd be *his* again. His fearless warrior woman.

"I did remake myself. With the help of my friends, and Susan and Bob."

He wanted to press his mouth to hers and know that everything would be okay from this moment forward. But he still hadn't explained why he'd caged Noah in with his own fears.

"The only thing I've ever wanted to do is protect Noah. I never wanted him bullied or hurt. I never wanted to be like my dad."

Ari threw herself at him then, wrapping her arms around him, her warm breath at his ear. "You could never be like that."

He held her tightly, closed his eyes, and breathed her in for a few perfect moments before he made himself draw back enough to face her. "I've never done that to Noah, but I went off on you today. My words hurt you. Words I didn't mean, Ari. I wish I could take them back."

"I know you were frightened for Noah." Forgiveness shone in her pretty eyes. "It must have been like the day you fell off your bike. Maybe it even reminded you about what happened to Jeremy. You know that horrible things can happen, and you lashed out."

He slipped both hands beneath the fall of her hair. "I *never* want to lash out at the people I love. Not you. Not Noah. Not any of the Mavericks. Can't you see how wrong that is? How much like my father it is?"

She laid her hands over his. "I see a man who was pushed. You made a mistake. The same way I made a mistake. Can you forgive me?"

"There's nothing to forgive," he whispered. "I'm the one who needs your forgiveness, Ari."

"You have it, Matt."

He didn't think, didn't so much as pause before laying it out straight for her. "I love you. With all my heart."

Her answering smile was a beautiful thing, brighter than the most perfect sunrise, and so warm that the last patches of ice his parents had filled him with finally melted away.

"I love you too," she whispered.

"Remember that first night at dinner," he said, "when you showed me how Noah stood up for himself against that little bully's mom? I didn't see how right you were until now. He's stronger than I'd ever imagined." He ran his finger over her lips, wanting to kiss her so badly. "Keep teaching me how to let Noah fly, Ari."

"There's nothing I want to do more."

"Even if I climb the walls when he wants to do something truly crazy and terrifying, like getting his driver's permit when he's a teenager." For so long he'd carried on alone, but he saw them together years from now, still unable to keep their hands off each other—still supporting each other through thick and thin.

"Even then," she said with a smile. "It might not always be easy for you to listen to my opinions or take my suggestions. And sometimes I might be tempted to throttle your ex. But I want Noah and Irene to have the strongest relationship that she's capable of."

His ex was the only dark spot left. "I've always hated the pain Irene causes Noah when she leaves him." He looked deeply inside himself. "I think I hated her too, because she was like my mother." He'd wanted Irene to be everything to Noah that his own mother had never been for him. But Irene had no interest whatsoever in taking on that role.

"I believe she truly does love him, but she forgets she's a mother when she's out having fun." Ari's voice dipped low. "I also have a feeling Noah reacts to your unfulfilled expectations of her—and your anger—as much as he does to Irene herself. You'll never be able to change her, but I wonder if you could help Noah value the love she *is* able to give him, even if it's not everything you expect from her."

Ari was so wise. Just like Susan. Hadn't they both said virtually the same thing to him? His ex would never be a stable influence in Noah's life. But Ari could give Noah everything his mother couldn't. And he could shift *his* thinking enough to say, "She's usually up for short conversations over Skype."

"Thank you for proving that you're willing to change." Ari put her arms around his neck. "And thank you for coming to win me back. Just knowing that you love me, that I matter to you, makes me feel like I really am in a fairy tale."

"*I'm* the one living the fairy tale. You're the best thing that ever happened to me. And the best thing that ever happened to Noah. He wants you back as much as I do. Everyone does."

"Everyone?"

"At the barbecue, they were all over me to face what I'd done. They challenged me to be brave enough to go after you."

"They did?" Her lips trembled as if she wanted to cry and laugh at the same time. And judging by the heat in her eyes, she wanted to kiss him senseless too.

"They're all in your corner, Ari. They were pissed as hell I let you get away." He kissed her, sweet, hot, and fast. "I can't live without you. Noah can't live without you either. Be his mother. Be my partner in all the decisions we make for him. Be my lover." He stroked a finger down her cheek, then dropped to one knee and asked her the most important question of all. "Please, Ari, will you be my wife?"

Chapter Thirty-One

Ari felt as if her heart would burst as she gazed down at the beautiful man on one knee before her. *Her* beautiful man. The things his parents had done to him would have ruined a lesser man, but Matt had grown into a remarkable human being and an incredible father.

"I want to be your wife, Matt. I want to be part of your family." She pulled him back up to his feet and kissed him with all the love in her heart before adding, "I want to be a mother to Noah, a mother to all our babies."

It had been her ultimate dream. And now, her amazing new reality.

"I started falling for you that first day you let me play with Noah in the backyard of the youth home." She laughed, admitting the truth from the warmth of his arms around her. "I can't tell you how disappointed I was when you approached me at Charlie's grand opening just to ask me to be his nanny."

Matt chuckled with her, and she loved knowing he finally felt safe enough to let go of his fears and truly relax.

"I thought I had to fight my feelings for Noah's sake. I didn't want him to think you were going to be around forever when I expected that you'd eventually leave us. And I didn't want either of us to be crushed the way we've always been with Irene." He framed her face in his hands. "The real truth is that I never wanted to disappoint *you*. I wanted to step up, give you everything you need, find your brother, take care of you. But I let you down the way I've always been afraid I would."

How could he *ever* think that?

She opened her mouth, and he kissed her quiet, before saying, "My parents wanted to toughen me up, but deep down they saddled me with the belief that I wasn't good enough. They made me think I had to be perfect, to take care of everyone else, to make sure nothing bad *ever* happened, just to prove I was a man. You've helped me recognize how far overboard I went. I can't protect Noah from every bad thing in his life without stunting him or making him feel incapable. I can't force Irene to be the mother I think she should be. I can't even be sure I'll find your brother. I can only do my best." He brought her hand to his cheek. "I have scars, so deep that even Susan, Bob, and the Mavericks couldn't heal them. Only you can, Ari."

"You're healing my scars too." Her eyes were damp, and her voice shook slightly. "We've both got baggage, and I know it won't always be easy, but I'll never give up on us again. *Never*."

"No matter which of us makes a mistake in the future, I'll never give *you* up. And I will continue to do everything in my power to bring your brother home to you."

"I've never doubted that." She rested against him for a long, sweet moment, their arms tight around each other. "I just need to keep this place until we find Gideon." She gazed into his face, so beautiful that she lost her breath the same way she had the very first time. "Then I won't ever need it again."

"No, you won't." His deep voice resonated through her with a delicious thrill. "You'll be with me."

"Have I ever mentioned how much I love it when you get all possessive like this?"

"I wanted to possess you the first time I set eyes on you." His beard-rough cheek caressed hers. "Even when I told myself I could never have you, I wanted you so bad I couldn't see straight." He nipped her earlobe, making her shiver with need. "And a Maverick always gets what he wants."

Ari threw her arms around his neck, kissing him deeply. "Make love to me, Matt. I need you so badly, need you to—"

He cut off her words by shoving his warm hands under her shirt. Flipping her top over her head, he dipped down to kiss the swell of her breasts, his fingers slipping inside her bra.

"I know exactly what you need, baby."

He always had.

They both tore at her jeans, then his pants, throwing everything across the room until they were skin to skin on the couch.

"I love you," he whispered, rocking slowly against her, sensitizing every inch of her skin. "I love everything about you." He kissed her breasts until she moaned and writhed beneath him. "I want to do so many wicked things to you."

He worked his way down her body, proving over and over how much she mattered with every bite of skin, every erogenous zone. Finally, on his knees beside the couch, he licked the very center of her, sending her spiraling into sheer sensation. She shoved her fingers through his hair, so silky, so thick, as she reveled in the sweet, hot sensuality of his mouth on her.

Lifting his head, his thumb on the apex of her pleasure, he whispered, "I love you."

His voice wrapped around the words she'd longed to hear as he moved over her, giving himself to her with no reservations, no holding back. Just pure pleasure.

And more love than she'd ever known was possible.

She gasped out his name as he filled her up, her body, her heart, her very soul. The feel of him inside her was momentous, with spikes of pleasure shooting through her, setting every cell of her being on fire.

"I want this every day. Forever." His hand on her

hip, he pulled her even more tightly against him. His eyes were soft midnight, dark with desire, brimming with emotion as he made his vows to her. "I love you. I will always love you. You are my heart. You're my everything."

She came apart with starbursts before her eyes, the pulse and beat of his climax deep inside her…and the sweet certainty that every ounce of love she had to give would be returned a million times over for the rest of her life.

⋆ ⋆ ⋆

Giddy with happiness, Ari laced her fingers through Matt's as they stepped out of her apartment a short while later. Not even Gideon's absence marred the joy she felt, because she truly believed they would eventually bring her brother home.

Matt carried her bag, and she slung her backpack containing her laptop over her shoulder. She led them down the stairs, and as they turned at the landing, the light in the lower hall was blocked by a man studying the row of mailboxes.

"Can I help you find someone?" she asked.

He turned, and her heart stopped.

The man's hair was military short, and his muscles were as big as a weight lifter's. He was about Matt's age, his face tanned, with lines at his eyes as if he was used to squinting against the sun. An old, battered khaki rucksack lay at his feet.

"*Gideon,*" she whispered.

"Hey, kiddo." His voice cracked, as though he didn't use it a lot, and his eyes were no longer the startling blue she remembered. As though he'd seen things that had leeched the brightness from them.

Ari dropped her backpack on the stairs, and a beat later she was in his arms, hugging him for every one of the sixteen years he'd been gone.

"You're home," she whispered. "I've missed you."

"Missed you too, Ari."

When he finally let her go, Matt held out his hand. "Matt Tremont. I'm your sister's fiancé." Turning his head to look directly at her, he dropped every last wall. "You should know that I love Ari very, very much."

She gazed at the two most important men in her life, and a tear slid down her cheek. Matt smoothed it away before looking at her brother. "You weren't here to ask permission. But I hope you'll approve of our marriage."

Gideon looked at Matt as if he were measuring the man he was on the inside, and then back at her. Finally, he said, "I can see how she feels about you."

"Let's go have a cup of coffee and talk," Matt suggested.

"Yeah." Gideon nodded slowly. "We should talk."

They put his rucksack, along with Ari's bags, into the trunk of Matt's Jaguar. Gideon traveled as lightly as she did, and she wondered if he'd learned that with their mom too. Leaving the dingy neighborhood, they were soon sitting in a coffee shop with old-fashioned vinyl booths and freshly roasted coffee.

"How did you find me?"

Gideon reached into his pocket and pulled out a letter, stained, wrinkled, and smoothed flat again over and over. He slid the worn envelope across the table. The postmark was two years old. She didn't remember the address, but it was probably one she'd scratched off her list when she never heard back.

"I move around a lot." He stared at the letter. "Your letter finally caught up with me a year ago."

"A year ago?" She was thankful for Matt's warm grip and his big presence beside her. "Why didn't you call me?"

"I'm sorry, Ari."

Gideon watched her with those washed-out eyes. They weren't the eyes of the boy she remembered. He was bigger than her memory, and still handsome. But he was also...*distant* was the only word she could find for it. Like a shadow.

Instead of answering her question, he asked, "How did you two meet?"

"I hired Ari to take care of my son, Noah." Matt explained that she'd been his nanny without even the slightest hint of shame, then brought their linked hands to his lips and kissed her knuckles. "Your sister has grown into a wonderful woman while you were gone. I've been helping her look for you."

She forced herself to push away the ache of knowing Gideon had waited a year to come home. "What have you been doing? Where have you been?"

"I worked mostly construction since I got out." Gideon drank again, then set his cup back on the table. "Moving around a lot. I did a stint up in Alaska for a while." He laughed softly but not happily. "I'm a drifter."

"But you're home now." It suddenly hit her. "Are you staying? Or will you be moving on?"

"I'm not sure." Gideon wrapped both hands around his mug as if he needed the heat.

"You're welcome to stay with us," Matt said. And it was clear to Ari that he meant it.

When Gideon didn't respond—didn't give any hint of whether he'd take Matt up on his offer—the dam Ari had tried to build around her questions finally burst.

"*Why*? Tell me why you didn't come if you've known where I was for the past year?" Matt squeezed her hand, as she said, "I needed you, Gideon. You're my brother. The only family I have left."

He drew in a deep breath, looked toward the ceiling, then finally back to Ari. "I went into the military to help save you, but before I knew it, you were gone. I couldn't find either of you. Then I heard Mom was dead. When I still couldn't find you, I knew I'd failed you completely." Tentatively, he reached across the table. Ari immediately put her hand in his, swearing she felt the pain in his heart as he clasped it. "When I got your letter, I just couldn't face you. You deserve better than a brother like me."

A fist bunched around her heart, so tightly she felt tears rising to her eyes. She was holding on to both of them now, Matt and Gideon. Nothing else mattered.

"You didn't fail me. And you're here now. That's all that counts." The hope she'd held on to for so long had finally turned into reality. Still, she needed to know, "What changed?"

"The job I was working out in Colorado ended a couple of weeks ago. When I was packing up my bag, I found your letter tucked in a pocket." He shook his head. "I missed you so damned much, but I thought you'd be better off without me. So I called a lady I sometimes keep in touch with—someone I thought might understand. She told me you'd been there."

"Mrs. Sanchez," Ari guessed. "Karmen's mother."

"Yeah." He slipped inside himself for a moment, probably thinking about Karmen and remembering his guilt at losing someone else he'd cared for deeply. Feeling the pain all over again. "That was when I knew I needed to see you. Face to face, so that you could tell me to go if that's what you wanted."

It was exactly what Ari had said to herself about Matt. Face-to-face. Nothing else would do. She and her brother might have been born years apart, and lost to each other for far too long, but they were still so similar.

She squeezed his hand. "I'm so glad you came home. And I want you to stay." She turned to Matt.

"You swore you'd find my brother. If you hadn't taken me down to see Mrs. Sanchez, he might never have decided it was the right time." She pressed her lips to his. "I love you."

"I love you too," he said without hesitation, even in front of Gideon.

At long last, she had everything she'd ever wanted: her brother back home…and the most wonderful man in the world to love and be loved by.

★ ★ ★

The look on Ari's face when she saw her brother compared only to the moment Matt had first laid eyes on his son. Her happiness was his happiness.

They'd picked up Noah at Sebastian's without the fanfare of introducing Gideon or telling the Mavericks about their engagement. In Matt's mind, it was only fair to tell Noah first, preparing him for the changes without an audience.

"Ari's coming back for good." Matt held his son on his lap as he gave him the good news.

"Yay!" Noah threw his arms around Ari. "You're still going to be my nanny!"

"She's going to be more than your nanny," Matt clarified. "She's going to marry me and be my wife and your stepmother."

Noah's eyes grew so big they nearly popped out of his head as he looked between Matt and Ari. "Can I call you Mommy?"

Tears streamed down her face as she nodded. "Yes, sweetie, I'd love for you to call me Mommy."

After Noah was finally in bed, Matt, Ari, and Gideon talked long into the evening. They heard about Gideon's travels; he'd been to just about every state in the US. But he didn't discuss the war or his tours in the Middle East. And he didn't talk about Karmen Sanchez or Esterhausen or his dead comrades either.

Matt gave Gideon a guest suite on the opposite end of the hall, and when his door closed at last, it was finally Matt's turn to be alone with Ari. He climbed the stairs to their bedroom, carrying two glasses of champagne.

Their bedroom. He loved the sound of that.

When he opened the door, the room was redolent with the scent of her lavender bath salts. How many times had he dreamed of this, watching her in the tub, all her satiny skin naked beneath the bubbling waters?

She'd left the en suite door open. Kicking off his shoes, he walked across the carpet to the bathroom, drawn to her the way a moth has to fly into the light.

Ari was his light.

His breath caught and his mouth dried up as he stepped inside. Steam rose with the fragrance of lavender. She'd wound her gorgeous blond hair into a knot and secured it with a clip on top of her head.

"Your tub is so big I feel like I might float away." Water frothed all around her, the jets rumbling, heat rising.

"Champagne," he said, handing her a glass.

Her smile was as luscious as the curves hidden beneath the water. She sipped the champagne and made one of her delicious noises that tightened everything in his body.

She eyed him, sultry and sensuous. "Why don't you do more than watch? Get in here with me."

He shook his head. "I've been dreaming about what you do in that tub since the first night you moved in. This time," he said with a devilish smile, "I need to watch."

She wriggled down into the water, her body just an outline as the jets shot everything into a swirl around her. She gazed up at him with a wealth of wickedness that set him on fire. "Tell me what you want me to do." She draped one slick, bare arm out of the water. "And I'll do it." She gave him a look full of heat and boundless love. "Anything you want, Matt."

Despite his wealth, there were so many things he'd still wanted. Love. More happy children. The chance to wake every morning and fall asleep every night with the woman he adored in his arms.

Ari gave all of those things to him—and he would do everything in his power to give her just as much. Whatever she wanted, whatever she needed, he would always be there for her.

"I love you," he told her, his words reverent. Full of all the awe he felt whenever he realized she was truly his.

"You gave me my brother. You're letting me love your son as if he's my own. And you risked your heart for me. I love you so much."

He couldn't resist kissing her, and she reached up to grab his shirt, leaving wet fingerprints, as their mouths came together passionately.

"Now..." Her voice was breathless with need. "Tell me what would please you most."

He told her. And as she did exactly what he wanted, what he'd dreamed of watching her do all those long nights, he gave silent thanks that they'd have so many long—and beautiful—nights and days to come.

They had *forever.*

Epilogue

Laughter and voices rose to the high ceiling of Matt's living room. A piano player was tinkling away on the baby grand while a bartender refreshed Evan's glass.

He could hear Paige in an animated discussion with Charlie, asking how Sebastian's fiancée came by her inspiration for the incredible metal sculptures she built. Evan wasn't surprised by Paige's enthusiasm—she always wanted to know why people did what they did.

She hadn't wanted to attend the family Thanksgiving, not after the fight she'd had with Whitney over the Halloween party. But with Whitney in the south of France—she claimed it was to take the warm air and waters, but Evan knew it was mostly to get away from him—he refused to leave his wife's sister alone in her condo on Thanksgiving Day. So here she was, lovely in a blue dress that made her eyes sparkle.

Daniel and Matt were arguing about the appetizers. "What do you mean, there's nothing to nibble on?" Daniel said, disgust layering his voice.

"After slaving all morning, Cookie said she didn't want a bunch of appetizers to spoil the meal." Matt wore a tailored suit that made his muscles look huge. He'd come a long way from the scrawny kid the Mavericks had to rescue. They'd had to rescue Evan too.

"I bet you just forgot to ask Cookie to make any," Daniel drawled. He wore his usual khakis and jacket, as if he'd just driven down from the mountains. Which he probably had.

They usually celebrated the holidays in Chicago at Susan and Bob's house. But this year Susan claimed the house was in an uproar preparing for the wedding, and she didn't think she could pull off a Thanksgiving dinner too. So here they were at Matt's.

Ari settled the good-natured battle between Evan's food-obsessed friends by sliding her arm through Matt's. She was beautiful in a purple and white dress. Evan was happy that Matt had come to his senses and made the right move.

"I told Cookie there was enough to feed a herd of dinosaurs," Ari said, "and we were all going to be overstuffed if she cooked any more." She leaned into Daniel. "She's gone home to be with her family, but if you want me to sneak into the kitchen and grab you a drumstick or a wing, no one would be the wiser."

Daniel laughed as he threw an arm around her shoulders. "I'll go fish around for myself, thanks."

As Matt pulled Ari closer and kissed her, something inside Evan's chest tightened at the look of love and adoration on the big dope's face. He truly had his family now.

Evan had meant every word at the barbecue when he'd said that Matt was crazy to let her go. Matt had everything with Ari. And Evan was finally starting to accept that he had nothing at all with Whitney.

Just then, Lyssa walked into the room and wrapped him in a hug. "Why are you standing here all by yourself?"

Holding her away, he smiled. "You finally made it. Thank God they let you go for the holidays. We all thought that new job was going to be the death of you."

She rolled her eyes. "I'm toughing it out." Daniel's little sister had the same dark curly hair—though Lyssa's fell past her shoulders—and the same dark eyes the color of chocolate. She knuckled him. "The really nice thing is flying out on Daniel's jet. No waiting in long security lines or hanging around airports."

"There are advantages." He wrapped his arm around her waist. "How's my girl?"

She laughed, a pretty sound he'd loved since the first time he'd heard it all those years ago when Lyssa had been a happy, gurgling baby. "I'm not a girl anymore, *Uncle* Evan."

"Right. You're becoming a pain in the rear like all women," he quipped.

Lyssa gave him a look. He hadn't meant to sound bitter. It was supposed to be a joke. Yet something dark had entered his voice. The same darkness that was starting to leach into his heart.

"Well," she said brightly, trying to dispel the momentary blackness he'd dragged into the room. "Can you believe how much our group has grown in one year?" She waved a hand toward the assembly in the living room. Last year, there'd been only Mavericks, including Susan, Bob, and Lyssa.

"Now we've got Harper and Jeremy," Lyssa enthused.

Harper had dressed Jeremy in a tux, and he looked fantastic. And happy. Which was Jeremy's constant state as well as Will's these days. By the new year, Will would be married to the woman he utterly adored. The look on his face was both proprietary and humble, as if he knew how lucky he was and didn't take a moment for granted.

"Of course, there's Charlie and her mom too," Lyssa said, like a laundry list of the Mavericks Who's Who.

Francine Ballard, Charlie's mother, perched on the end of the couch. Charlie had given her a golden paper crown, calling her the queen for the day. Instead of tossing it away, Francine enjoyed every moment, popping it on her head and giving queenly waves every now and again. Evan felt a great admiration for her. Even with her gnarled fingers, she was always smiling, always with a sweet word to say, never mentioning her pain or the inability to do all the things she loved. She forced herself to walk a mile every day using her walker. How many people could say they tackled the hardest things in their lives—and beat them? Bob and Susan were tucked around her on a chair and the sofa, avidly detailing all the wedding preparations.

A loud squeal rose from the far end of the room where Noah was playing jets with Jorge and doing a damn good job of simulating the ear-piercing sound of engines. Evan thanked God that Whitney had flown the coop for this celebration. She'd definitely have made a scene.

"Ari's friends Rosie and Chi are a hoot, aren't they? It's so nice to have people my age to hang out with at these parties instead of all you old fogeys." All the Mavericks felt like they'd practically raised Lyssa, and she loved to tease them about the ten-year age difference. "Seriously," Lyssa said, "have you ever seen Matt so happy? Ari is so good for him. She told me she's teaching part time in the mornings at Noah's school now. Did you know she has a degree in child development?"

Ari truly was the best thing for Matt and Noah. And she would make a fantastic teacher. Gideon Jones, on the other hand…

"What do you think about her brother?" The man stood by himself, his gaze moving over the group, from one to the next, watching, always on alert.

"He's all broody and masculine," she said dreamily enough that Evan looked down at her in surprise. "I overheard him say to Ari that she'd tapped into the mother lode with Matt."

Evan's hackles rose, though he was shocked Ari would have agreed with something like that.

He must have tensed, because Lyssa whispered, "Down, boy. I might have been offended when Ari agreed. Except that she wasn't looking at the priceless paintings or the huge house. She was looking at Matt and Noah. And—" Lyssa sighed just like a woman dying to fall in love. "The look on her face was so adoring. She said she finally felt like she mattered to someone and that they meant absolutely everything to her. It kind of made me sad for what her life must have been like before."

"I never thought it was about the money for her."

"I'm sure it isn't for Gideon either," Lyssa went on. "Matt says he's been asking around about work. But seriously, Evan, how do you tell whether they want you for the money or for yourself? I mean, it was easy for you with Whitney because you didn't have any money back then. But now, it would be really hard to know for sure."

Eight years ago, he'd been twenty-six and Whitney barely twenty. His first million was still a couple of years off. His first billion further out still. But Whitney had wanted him even without the money.

At least, that's what he'd always wanted to believe.

But life with Whitney had become unbearable. They barely spoke—and when they did it was usually to argue about something. She did her own thing, and he did his. Even when they attended a party together, they were separate, she with her crowd, he with his.

He knew how badly the miscarriages had affected her. They'd affected him too, and those bad times had somehow become as huge between them as the Hoover Dam.

Whitney had never been what anyone would describe as sweet, but once upon a time she'd been fun and sexy. Until the aching loss of the children they hadn't yet been able to create turned her cruel and mean. Now she had her own bedroom, and they hadn't come together since that last miscarriage at the beginning of the year. He'd thought she needed time, but time had only made things worse.

The dam between them had burst the night of Will's Halloween party. When Paige arrived at the house, dressed in that sexy, mind-altering Cleopatra getup, Whitney had gone ballistic.

He could still hear her voice screeching in his memory. *Why does she have to go everywhere with us? When is she going to get her own life instead of living off mine?*

She'd stalked to her room and slammed the door. He'd planned to apologize to everyone at the party for her absence, but he was so damn sick of making excuses for her. He was terribly sorry for her pain—for the pain they both suffered over the babies they'd lost—but he was also tired of explaining away the horrible things she said and did in the name of her disappointment and grief.

Something had to give. Because Evan couldn't stand any more. At this point, he wasn't even sure he wanted to be married to her. Correct that—he was sure he didn't want to be married to the woman she'd become.

On Halloween night, he'd finally seen beneath Whitney's rage. And it was Paige herself who'd changed things, the sister who was always overshadowed, the sister who got the second look, never the first.

That night Paige had become a sultry seductress in her costume, bringing men to their knees.

And she'd made him look twice.

Not only because she'd been gorgeous, but because where Whitney had never fit in with the Mavericks, Paige made everyone laugh and listened when you needed to talk something through.

Paige.

Why couldn't he stop thinking about her?

Why couldn't he stop looking, even now that Halloween was long past?

As he glanced her way, the smile she gave him touched something deep inside. And he couldn't stop the unforgivable thought that he'd picked the wrong sister eight years ago.

★★★★★

For news on Bella Andre's upcoming books, sign up for Bella Andre's New Release Newsletter:

BellaAndre.com/Newsletter

For news on Jennifer Skully's upcoming books, sign up for Jennifer Skully's New Release Newsletter:

bit.ly/SkullyNews

ABOUT THE AUTHORS

Having sold more than 5 million books, *New York Times* and *USA Today* bestselling author Bella Andre's novels have been #1 bestsellers around the world. Known for "sensual, empowered stories enveloped in heady romance" (*Publishers Weekly*), her books have been *Cosmopolitan* magazine "Red Hot Reads" twice and have been translated into ten languages. Winner of the Award of Excellence, *The Washington Post* has called her "One of the top digital writers in America" and she has been featured by *Entertainment Weekly*, NPR, *USA Today*, *Forbes*, *The Wall Street Journal* and, most recently, in *Time* magazine. She has given keynote speeches at publishing conferences from Copenhagen to Berlin to San Francisco, including a standing-room-only keynote at Book Expo America, on her publishing success.

Sign up for Bella's newsletter:

BellaAndre.com/Newsletter

Visit Bella's website at:

www.BellaAndre.com

Follow Bella on Twitter at:

twitter.com/bellaandre

Join Bella on Facebook at:

facebook.com/bellaandrefans

New York Times and *USA Today* bestselling author Jennifer Skully is a lover of contemporary romance, bringing you poignant tales peopled with hilarious characters that will make you laugh and make you cry. Writing as Jasmine Haynes, she's authored over 35 classy, sensual romance tales about real issues like growing older, facing divorce, starting over. Her books have passion and heart and humor and happy endings, even if they aren't always traditional. She also writes gritty, paranormal mysteries in the Max Starr series. Having penned stories since the moment she learned to write, she now lives in the Redwoods of Northern California with her husband and their adorable nuisance of a cat who totally runs the household.

Newsletter signup:

http://bit.ly/SkullyNews

Jennifer's Website:

www.jenniferskully.com

Blog:

www.jasminehaynes.blogspot.com

Facebook:

facebook.com/jasminehaynesauthor

Twitter:

twitter.com/jasminehaynes1

Made in the USA
Middletown, DE
21 July 2016